whisper
of the
worms

whisper
of the
worms

MARCARDIAN

PARTRIDGE
A Penguin Random House Company

Cover design;- by Kamal Joseph

ISBN: Softcover   978-1-4828-3372-0
             eBook   978-1-4828-3371-3

To order additional copies of this book, contact
Partridge India
000 800 10062 62
orders.india@partridgepublishing.com

www.partridgepublishing.com/india

Acknowledgements

To

Jijo, for almost living with the manuscript, trimming and pruning it, till it went to the printer and Cynthia Rodrigues for the final touch.

Kurien and Tony, for painstakingly reading my first impressions. Also Kesavan Namboodiri, and Mathai. Your smiles gave me the confidence to complete this work.

My kids, for occasionally bringing me to sanity and my employer, for pushing me back!

Finally, my wife Jessy, for tolerating me and my obsessions.

Marcardian

To,

my sister Chinnamma, the angel born with a broken wing,
who lived unnoticed in her solitude, and
flew away early . . . .

1

"**O**NLY ONE YEAR?"

The doctor did not hear the question or maybe he was trying to evade it. He stretched his facial muscles, pursed his lips and looked at the lab reports through the bottom of his glasses and continued his silence, unmindful of the fierce anxiety writ large on the face of the Indian patient in Room No. 505 of Ville Platte Medical Centre.

The question hung in the air for some time without an answer. The patient was fully aware of the answer too. The question was just meant to elicit a better answer. He wished to hear that the disease was not serious and that nothing would happen to him in the near future. But the preferred answer did not come.

The face of the patient, Thobias Mathai, contracted further as if he had just gulped a heavy dose of bitter gourd decoction. He closed his eyes, threw off his bifocal glasses on to the bed, and covered his face with his palms.

Thobias had acted more or less the same way two days earlier, when the same doctor had sat by his side, gently putting his left hand over his shoulders, and informed him of the details of the diagnosis. The lung cancer had grown from the central region where the arteries and wind pipe join the lungs, and had advanced considerably in all directions, making surgery or chemotherapy out of the question. The doctor also drew a rough sketch of the lungs and marked the portion of the cells which had already lost their life. He did not conclude the discussion in a formal way by giving the future scenario of the disease. But it was clear that the patient had to live with it and go with it, may be within a year.

Thobias did not seek any clarifications at that time; he just covered his face as he did now, and then lay on the bed pressing his face against the soft pillow. The gentle vibrations of his body revealed that he was crying profusely and the pillow was effectively muffling the sound to the outside world.

The life of Thobias Mathai was not a great one; it had been a full-length struggle with a few short intervals in between. The fear of having to part from his dear ones too early, uncertainty about the next world, and the realisation that his contemporaries would live even as it was time for him to leave caused him to deviate from his normal nature of suffering without showing any emotion. He was aware that fate is predetermined and that he would have to leave planet earth before it had rotated a few hundred times on its axis.

Thobias did not disclose the diagnostic details to anybody; not even to his wife Theresa, or to darling daughter Annie, or to his sons Abi and Ashi. Why give them bad news and upset them for a whole year? Let them be happy for as long as they could. It would come as a shock at the end when they came to know about their Papa's ailment, but it would soon be over. Fortunately, memories are short and time resolves many earthly problems. Thobias took care to hide the more serious medical prescriptions and diagnostic reports under the bed, leaving behind a few minor reports and prescriptions for pain killers on the table to catch the eye of the unsuspecting visitor.

One careless act on his part, in asking Annie to bring the family photo and the Bible along when she visited him the following Sunday, caused the eyebrows of Theresa to shoot up. But nothing untoward happened, and in fact, Theresa was pleased with the increasing level of attachment shown by her dear husband towards God and the family. Thobias kept the laminated family photo on the side table, and spent considerable time looking at it.

It had been taken three years ago, on August 4, his 56th birthday. He had been sitting on a chair in the centre. He looked tall and fair, with innocent eyes, stiff well-combed hair and a friendly smile that could impress anybody. His head seemed to be a little smaller compared to his protruding stomach and long, muscle-free hands. The prominent and sharp nose gave him a handsome look. Even at 56, his hair was largely black with a few stray white streaks near the parting on the left side of his head. Theresa was standing behind to his right, her left hand draped over his shoulders quite authoritatively. Annie stood to her left, her chubby cheeks trying to prevent laughter from bursting out. Abi and Ashi were standing at the back like tall body guards, with serious looks, refusing to join their sister in her suppressed laughter.

The Bible was consigned to the second drawer of the table, unopened.

"Try to cheer up." That was the only reply from the doctor exiting the room. Obviously, he did not want to set a deadline, long or short, permitting Thobias Mathai to dream for better or worse.

His dreams did not go for better things. The family tomb at Parakad church came to his mind time and again. The concept of a family tomb had been introduced to the rural folk by Rev Fr Pullen. The enterprising vicar had started a school and constructed rooms that could be leased out, in order to ensure a permanent income for the church.

Thobias' family tomb was the third one in the second row. It was Thobias who had supervised its construction. Nearly nine feet deep, its bottom one foot was red soil, then two feet sand over it and the rest was left vacant at that time. Sides were made of black rocks and the top was covered by three concrete slabs which could be removed easily using the hooks fixed on them, so as to admit the guests without much labour. A small brick wall was built around the tomb so as to hold the neatly polished granite slab, with pictures of a Cross at the top and a flower and two candles at the bottom.

At the very bottom Thobias added one line, *"I am content. So thou wilt have it so."* While engraving the name, "Pappu born 1-5-1916 – died 30-6-1980," Thobias was simply calculating the possible order of entrants into that eternal home.

The tomb had not been there at the time of Pappu's death. There were no vacant tombs at that time, and it was difficult to construct one at short notice. Pappu was initially buried in the cemetery and the bones were later shifted to the newly constructed tomb, to lie together with his family in eternal rest.

Thobias did not attend the bone shifting ceremony, even though he was the most beloved son. The ceremony, like Pappu's death, was a lonely one. But that absence had been deliberate. Only brave people are expected to stand around while a dead body is being exhumed. Sometimes the body does not get decayed completely, making for an unpleasant sight. Thobias did not want to substitute the image of the smiling Pappu with the image of a few bones or something worse than that.

"Better go back to India," Thobias decided without much thinking. Thinking always required patience, which Thobias lacked.

"You want to get discharged?" the Indian nurse could not hide her surprise at the patient's immature decision.

"Yeah. I want it urgently." Thobias was firm.

"Why? Medication will be better here and it is fully financed. Do you think you can get better treatment in India?" The nurse still maintained a poor image about India.

"I want to be there during my last days. Please keep complete confidentiality about my disease and treatment," he said hastily.

"As you wish. Sign the undertakings. I will pass them to the doctor." The nurse seemed to have lost interest in the patient.

Thobias signed wherever they asked him to sign.

"Not reading them?" She expected more respect for the carefully worded undertakings.

"For what? All papers lead to the same thing." Thobias was aware that reading or not reading wouldn't make much difference to him.

Thobias kept the diagnostic report and discharge letter in a red file, inserted it into the top side partition of the suitcase and closed it with both number and key locks.

"You can get the exit pass at the third counter, ground floor. Wish you a speedy recovery," the nurse bid the customary farewell. Thobias did not understand why she was wishing him a speedy recovery, fully knowing that it was impossible.

"You have left a book in the room. I suggest you go back and collect it or wait for a few minutes while we will bring it here," the staff at the counter told him. Thobias remembered that he had forgotten the Bible in the drawer of the table. He did not wait for it. He also decided against one more trip to the room.

Back home, Thobias tried to remain as cool and as pleasant as possible.

"You did not inform me about the discharge?" Theresa always doubted things, and normally probed deep into the subject to clear her doubts. But this time she was busy assisting Annie as she prepared for her paper on Body Language for her final year psychology exam at La Deleolit.

"They say I am perfectly fine; all the tests showed negative results. The doctor advised me to take a rest from my hectic routine. Maybe age is catching up. Frankly, I would like to make a trip to Panamkara and be with Amma, maybe for slightly longer stay." Thobias summed up the hospital history and his future plans in short sentences, without looking into the eyes of his better half.

"I am happy about your going home. This is our twentieth year in the US and we haven't visited Amma even once." Theresa also called her *Amma* as there was nobody that she could call by that sweet name, having lost her mother in her early childhood.

"Amma called me many times, asking me to remind you about that. Even after thirty years, I am unable to read you fully," she said after taking a break from her work and coming closer to the bedroom door.

At the time of Pappu's burial, Thobias had taken a vow to visit him every year. The tomb had been made for that purpose, to keep the memory alive. But he had never returned again. Practical living overrode simple human emotions.

"I am reading something more in you," Theresa whispered while changing the sheets in the bedroom. "You are hiding something." She always had the sensitive instinct of a Doberman. For a moment, the room slipped into silence and Thobias felt that he was going to be cornered.

"There is nothing to hide. I am just getting emotional over the thought of our ancestral home." Thobias displayed innocence. He was happy that he could find a convincing answer. His ancestral home was an emotional point for him, and Theresa was well aware of it.

"I may be pushing off tomorrow itself. Can you take one day off?" Thobias knew that he could not keep a secret to himself for long, and it was better to leave at the earliest. He was not prepared to risk it as it could affect more people and spoil the mood and rhythm of their lives.

Surprised at the sudden decision, Theresa turned and asked, "So soon?" After a moment of silence she said, "Not tomorrow, the day after if you want." Thobias understood that she had already planned for the next day. She never disappoints her office boss too.

"I will pack your things for you before I go to office." She was duty conscious. Opening the sliding door of the wardrobe, she started pulling down a big suitcase.

"Select a smaller one." Thobias was sure that he couldn't lift or even pull such a big suitcase.

"But you said it is a lengthy stay." Theresa looked at him for a second.

"Not long enough to require such a big bag," he said, glancing at the suitcase.

"We will have dinner outside, on the rooftop of May Feathers." Thobias wanted to stop the discussion at home. *May Feathers* was their dine-out place on most Saturday nights.

"In a celebratory mood?" Theresa's doubtful look ended in a hearty smile. "Something special?" she asked again as it was not a weekend.

"I love you," he said, very softly, his eyes meeting hers. He seemed to be in a different world.

"That means you did not love me earlier? Thanks, anyhow. You are giving me a few good moments to remember." Her lips curved towards the left side, as always happened when she felt shy.

"I want to give you many moments to remember, but . . . ." Thobias did not finish the sentence and Theresa did not notice its soft ending as his voice was low and she was more absorbed in packing.

"Your suitcase is locked. I want to remove the old clothes," she said, asking for the key. She wanted to finish her job before going out.

"I will open it for you." Thobias did not want to give the key.

At the dinner, Thobias bought one bottle of Celebrity wine and raised a toast to each of them. "For the sweet memory of this happy evening. Share this in my name whenever you join together again."

"No, no," Annie protested. "This resembles the Last Supper. I don't like that mood."

"Okay, leave it. Cheer up." Thobias sipped the wine silently. There was no need to spoil the mood of others after paying through the nose.

Abi's mind was preoccupied with office affairs and with the deadline for finishing the new ERP module for Morleys. He did not talk at all. As the elder son, he was always responsible and serious.

"My vacation can be a bit long; take care of them," Thobias told Abi while walking back to the parked car. "I have given signed cheques to Mamma."

"Pardon?" Abi did not hear those words, as he was still immersed in his world of software solutions. Thobias repeated, and Abi nodded his head vigorously, this time in full agreement.

Sleep did not come easily to Thobias as he watched Theresa sleeping. It might be their last night together; thirty long years after the first night at the corner room of the *tharavadu* which was no more. Married life would complete its full circle, with the emotions and pain of parting replacing the thrill and curiosity of meeting. It was a long sojourn of thirty years; with love, without love, with acting, without acting, with deception, without deception, but always together as promised at the marriage ceremony at Muvattupuzha church. She had performed her role better than he had.

"You say you never got a kiss all your lifetime?" she had been very doubtful on the first night.

"No, dear," Thobias answered, feeling shy.

"Not even in your childhood?" She could not believe and probably avoided telling her own experiences.

"My parents were in the serious game of feeding the mouth, rather than kissing it." Thobias kissed that subject goodbye.

"You are an actor," she discovered later. "If there is an Oscar for real life actors, I am sure you won't miss it." Fortunately, the world was still far away from instituting such an award, allowing Thobias to go undetected. She was not aware that the acting of Thobias Mathai saved the marriage for years, till they became indispensable for each other at the fag end of life.

Today, Theresa was taken aback by the sudden spurt of love emanating from her otherwise inexpressive husband. She could detect the warmth in his words, and for a moment thought of staying back to see him off the next day. Still, she decided to stick to her office schedule.

"I will call you daily," she pretended casualness.

"You are coming with me to India?" Thobias made a spontaneous request and he immediately realised that he should not have asked that. Fortunately, she did not observe his wet eyes in her hurry.

"Are you serious? How can I, even if I wish to? Leaving Annie behind?" She stood still near the bedroom door. Her concern was genuine.

While leaving for office, Annie kissed him on his left cheek, wishing him a happy journey. Abi could not do it because he had left for office in the early morning, before Thobias had woken up. Ashi did not kiss his father before going to college. He waved bye with his left hand.

Thobias watched the pace of the eight-lane traffic through the window as he did when he landed here twenty years ego, but this time without any emotion. The pace of life and his growth were so tremendous that they never gave him time to think of the path of progress in this land of opportunities. It was not long before he moved from being an ice-cube packer at Well Mart to salesman, to cashier, to postman, to financial analyst, to project consultant, and finally to CEO of Ippy Mortgage.

Thobias walked once more within the villa. He sat on the feathery sofa at the central hall for a few minutes.

Before getting into the airport bound taxi, Thobias spent some time watching the villa in the background of the sloping lawn, bordered with daffodils. He also looked back more than twice at the villa from the taxi and waved at it, though there was no one to wave back. His eyes were wet.

2

LOOKING DOWN at the deep Atlantic from the window seat of the plane, Thobias did not feel any fear. There was nothing much to lose even if the plane made a nosedive. On his maiden journey to the US with Theresa and the children, nobody had been prepared to sit near the window seat. Thobias managed the courage to exchange seats with Annie and daringly looked at the Atlantic, concealing the fear within him. The blue ocean stretching all around was a magnificent sight for the brave.

His mind was blank for some time. He sat watching the small lights blinking in response to the pressing of the call buttons. The cabin crew were not enjoying the pace of the lights appearing from one end to the other, which forced them to walk faster.

Automatically, his mind began to plan; have to meet at least a few of those childhood pals, have to visit the family tomb, have to spend a few days exclusively with Amma and walk along with her in the courtyard, holding her hand, have to take a closer look at the waterfalls of Mulliri Mountain, have to walk through the paddy fields like in childhood, have to sit under the gooseberry tree for a few more hours and drink the sweet water from the stream lining the paddy field once more, and . . . and . . . The mind was still planning; planning too many things, ignoring the shadow of death.

Pappu's burial came to his mind vividly. It was the most touching scene in his life. Pappu had been his best friend. They were the only father-son duo at Panamkara who could sit in the toddy shop together, sipping coconut toddy.

After having three bottles of toddy, Pappu would become one of the best philosophers, leading Thobias to bigger subjects in the universe. At night, he was a teacher reading from Malayalam and English classics. Above all, he was his roommate for two decades.

Pappu was a thin man. Although the pointed moustache tended to create a more lasting impression of him, it was the innocent heart and the objective brain which were more visible to Thobias. Pappu's eyes were asking for something. Thobias could not study them closely. Even the black spot on the right side of his forehead and an inch-long scar on his chin caught the attention of Thobias only when Pappu was on his death bed at Saint Vincent Hospital.

Thobias still remembered the first stanza of the song sung by the nuns at the time of his funeral.

Everything is perishable,
This world and its bodily desires.
Everything fades and ends,
Like bubbles in water . . .

He could not recollect the remaining lines. Though he had heard them very often, the meaning had never struck him so clearly before.

It was sung when Thobias was about to kiss, for the last time, the stiff, cold face of Pappu, who had been dressed up in his best and lay in the neatly decorated coffin. Thobias had not been able to raise his head for a long time as he was weeping profusely, unmindful of the gathering around him.

Thobias had never kissed him when he was alive. It was not the fault of Thobias alone. During the day, Pappu would be in his farm, working under the scorching sun, covered in dirt and sweat. In the evening, his mood would be bad after having a bottle or two of toddy. He would be pondering over the unanswered issues of the universe. At the same time, he had to play the game of making both ends meet for a dozen or so onlookers at home. His entire life was sucked by it. Time was a luxury and kissing was a super-luxury for him. Pappu did not know about his son's kissing or crying. Had it been before his death, he would have definitely enjoyed it, and cried too.

Thobias could not hear those songs when Chinnu, his eldest sister, was buried in the same tomb. But, he could watch part of the ceremony through webcam, sitting at Ville Platte.

He imagined himself in the coffin for a moment, dressed in a spotless white *dhothi* and shirt, wearing newly purchased plastic shoes, with a rosary in his hand, along with a Cross, covered with fresh flowers. Then the natural kissing line, Theresa first, then Abi, then Annie, and then Ashi, like the seniority system in Smile Bank. Others would be watching the action from a distance, unsure about whether to go and kiss the stiff, cold body.

The crowd would disappear slowly. It would be a lonely rest thereafter in the family tomb, over the bones of Pappu and Chinnu, under a few layers of soil, in the deafening silence. Above the soil, memories would be alive for a few more days, before being confined to anniversaries and slowly fading to oblivion. After all, does it matter if anybody is remembered more?

Thobias allowed his mind to linger upon his sentimental period of life. Rajan was his best friend, maybe after Pappu, in those innocent childhood days. He was the icon of knowledge for Master Thobias on everything in the universe which was not written in the textbooks.

Their friendship became thicker in the fifth standard at Panamkara School. Rajan was there, sitting alone on the back bench near the western wall of the thatched school shed when Thobias entered it on promotion. It was Rajan's third year in the same class. It was Rajan who told him that Philo, Thobias' elder sister, had been his classmate in the fourth standard. But he did not tell him that Anna, the elder sister of Philo, was also his classmate in the second standard.

Thobias used to accompany Pappu in the early mornings, to help him in rubber tapping. Pappu would tap the trees and Thobias would clean the coconut shells and place them on the nails fixed on the trees. The coconut shells would become home to different types of worms and centipedes in the rainy season. Thobias never feared them. A black worm with yellow rings on it often emitted a nauseating smell of decayed onion. The worms were found in clusters, sometimes one above the other. They would disperse fast when the coconut shell was turned upside down, as if somebody had commanded them to escape. Thobias wondered how they communicated with each other so quickly.

"How do these black worms communicate?" Thobias asked Rajan one evening when both were sitting on the rocks on the banks of the River Kaliyar, waiting for the bathing crowd to disperse so that they could dive into the water with a splash.

"It whispers. We can hear it when we go under the soil. Don't you know our Pathrose? He once went under the soil in a big landslide at Mulliri Mountain in 1942. He was under the soil for three days. Luckily, he was saved after a strenuous rescue operation. When he regained consciousness two days after being rescued, he said he had heard many sounds inside the soil. Some souls who did not get entry into heaven talked to him. He heard the whispers of snakes and worms. He could understand them. But we can't believe him completely. He is a lunatic now." Rajan was not ready to illustrate any further.

"They were talking in Malayalam?" That was the only language Thobias knew at that time.

"I have to ask Pathrose," Rajan said seriously before diving into the water, making two somersaults. Thobias too followed him. But he could only make half a somersault and had to bear the pain akin to a severe beating as his body fell flat on the surface of the water. The pain made Thobias forget further doubts.

"Are you going to Mumbai?" the man on the right side asked Thobias. It was in a respectfully low voice but enough to wake Thobias up from his childhood reminiscing. The stranger seemed to have experienced a few more summers and springs than Thobias.

"No," Thobias' answer was brief. He did not even turn his head.

"Then you are a Keralite," the co-passenger arrived at a logical conclusion as the plane was scheduled to stop at Cochin after Mumbai. He looked at Thobias, expecting the welcome smile Keralites normally give when they are outside their state.

"Where are you in the US?" he enquired further.

"Ville Platte," Thobias was optimistic that the conversation would end this time.

"My children are in California. My wife and I came back to India two years ago and settled at Angamali."

"Okay."

"Old age is better spent in Kerala. But to live reasonably well, we should go out and earn first," he continued, in spite of the short responses. Thobias was unable to contribute anything towards the topic except smile at him.

"You did not tell me where your house is?" This time, he was determined to make Thobias speak.

"It is very close to Parakad church." The picture of the family tomb came to Thobias' mind.

"I've got a caretaker for my house and he makes food for me when I'm back," the co-passenger said proudly, indicating his living standard. It was necessary to have the protocols settled between the two strangers for future discussions.

"I too have one. The parish priest takes care of my home." Thobias smiled and looked at the ocean, avoiding his eyes.

The announcements from the cockpit about the speed of the plane and distance to Mumbai made both of them sit silently for some time.

"Parish priest?" the other man could not believe it. "But how do you pay him?"

"I have already paid for it," Thobias said.

"Would you like a drink?" a pretty airhostess interrupted the talk.

"Sure."

He pushed the side button of the seat to bring it to the vertical position.

Thobias went back to the deadline fixed for him. He was face to face with idea of life after the end of life. Will there be God? Will there be heaven? Normally these questions would not have come to his mind if it was a death after ageing, when the brain functioning would not be normal.

He had not gone through boredom free of wishes, hopes and desperation, nor had he been parked in the corner of the back room to watch the courtyard and count the falling leaves. Here, the hapless victim still carried an active brain and unnecessary common sense.

So many people talk and live for God. Hence He must exist. All good people who suffer here can go to heaven.

A smile crept to Thobias' lips when the picture of the Guardian Angel came to his mind. It was Sister Clara who had told him about the Guardian Angel, when he was in the second standard at Sunday School.

"Every kid has a guardian angel who takes care of the child in distress," Sister Clara had said, with an air of authority. "He will take care of each of us as long as we do not commit any sin," she said, explaining the technique of retaining the angel. Thobias tried to see the angel when he was alone, but it never came. Still he believed in the angel. But whenever he was with his earthly friends, he never bothered about the heavenly angel.

Childhood was not a great time in the life of Thobias. Still, he was happy as he saw life on earth as a recruitment trial for getting into heaven.

Thobias saw God's hand all around him. The creation of this beautiful earth, the moon hanging in the sky without support, the stars scattered in the sky, the timing of the day and night, the power of fierce thunder and the glitter of lightning in *thula varsham*, births and deaths, the lovely flowers in the convent garden and the big rocks of Mulliri Mountain, all were proof of God.

However, he was not sure why God had created cobras, which were often seen near the big *anjili* tree, and the centipedes that occupied the narrow path that led to Thayyil House, from where he had to collect milk daily. But Thobias' love for God was not a big force to prevent God's liking for cobras and millipedes.

What a contented and innocent life it was! God prevented bad dreams for Thobias, except when he forgot to mark crosses on all four sides of the sleeping mat. On those days, dirty millipedes were sure to enter the mat for a luxurious sleep. Habits seldom die. It was difficult for Thobias to mark crosses on the bed without Theresa noticing it on their first night.

Susy, the younger sister of Thobias, had died immediately after birth. He could only recollect the dark room where a kerosene lamp was kept and a bearded man inside the room chanting some prayers and blowing air on her face. Susy was in Amma's lap, a fair doll knowing nothing.

"She went to God," Amma whispered to Thobias the next morning. Amma's eyes were wet.

"Why did she go so fast?" Thobias could not understand the logic of going early to heaven. Amma did not say anything but only wept over the special love of God for the child, who was in her womb for ten months and in this world for another ten hours.

She must have been lucky. She cleared all the tests of God too fast.

"She will be in heaven only," Amma assured Thobias, when he started crying at the loss of his sister who was as cute as an angel.

In the evening, Thobias listened to a conversation in Amma's bedroom. "Had we taken Susy to hospital, maybe she would have survived," her voice choked in between. There was no answer from Pappu.

One had to walk 20 km to the nearest hospital, and there was no assurance she would have survived even after that. Still, there was a chance.

Pappu did not have a penny, even to pay the *tantri* who made the last ditch effort to retain her against God's wish by blowing air on her face.

"It was God's wish," both Pappu and Amma agreed later. Thobias also agreed and smiled. Those were happy days, in that abject poverty, thanks to the firm faith in God. Each setback was taken as God's testing. It was Rajan who spoiled that happy going.

It was a Sunday evening. Thobias was happy to move out of the home in the evening. The junction was nearly vacant except for the light from the hurricane lamps at the toddy shop. Rajan was sitting on the bench in front of Pareed's tea shop. An unfamiliar smell came from Rajan's mouth as Thobias came closer to him.

"Have you ever tasted arrack?" Rajan knew that Thobias was familiar with toddy.

"No." There was curiosity in Thobias' eyes.

"Would you like to taste it?" Thobias was not sure about the answer, but Rajan was. Both of them entered the arrack shop through the rear door and sat on two stools near the kitchen.

"Shivarama, bring a peg for my class topper," Rajan became the host and ordered. Thobias gulped the colourless liquid, and half of it came out from his mouth without his knowledge. It was very bitter. But the intoxication was worth the taste. There was no problem with further helpings. Thobias felt his body lose weight. He enjoyed the feeling of his legs losing their equilibrium and his hands refusing to obey the commands of the brain when they were asked to tie the *lungi* tightly. It brought a new meaning into his life. But there was also guilt in his heart.

"I think I committed a sin," Thobias confessed.

"What about me?" Rajan reduced the gravity of the sin by becoming an equal sinner. "You think Christians alone go to heaven?" He did not like the holier than thou attitude of the novice drinker.

"I have to ask Amma," Thobias took the question very seriously. Actually, he had never thought about this subject earlier.

"Don't ask Amma." There were many things Rajan had told him not to discuss with Amma.

"Let me ask you," Rajan continued. "What will happen to the vast number of Hindus in India? The Chinese are communists and do not believe in God. What about them?" He chuckled enthusiastically. "The white people practicing free sex also will not go to heaven. Finally, your God will be forced to give some moderation to fill the vacant places in heaven." Rajan was very familiar with moderation as he was moving from class to class entirely based on that.

With all the wisdom Thobias had, he could not answer these questions. A doubt started creeping into his so far heavily built up religious belief fort. It would have been a far happier life, had he not met Rajan that evening.

Rajan was a firm believer in rebirth. The sins of the previous life cause some people to take birth as handicapped, some as mentally retarded, some in abject poverty, some in great countries like America, and some in Panamkara without electricity, some as blacks in tropics and some as whites, some near toddy shops and some in cool hills away from the madding crowd.

Thobias' inherent confusion reached its highest pitch in a biology class when he was in the seventh standard. On the day of the inspection by the District School Superintendent, one Parameshwaran came as a substitute teacher to keep the noise pollution of the class to the minimum. He was a well-read man compared to his colleagues. He always talked authoritatively and Thobias never saw anybody in the school contradicting him.

"Life came to earth as a small minute organism, because of the availability of water, air and light. The fittest survived and evolved into more complex organisms over a period, ending in humans," Parameshwaran stated emphatically.

It was a new confusion for the already confused Thobias. He approached the best theology teacher, Amma, for details.

"Who told you all this? What rubbish they teach in school? I have to meet your teacher." She did not answer the question, and instead went to change her dress for a schoolward journey. But Pappu intervened in time to prevent a religious war. "Once in a while, let him hear the other side of the story," he pacified her.

Still, he loved reading the Bible; all words were nice and piercing. He continued it for many years.

"I will meet Rajan as soon as I reach there," Thobias said to himself. For the last twenty years, he missed his only attachment outside the family. He must be there, hale and hearty.

The airhostess came for another round, serving lunch and interrupting Thobias' thoughts. He looked at her faded red lipstick and the loss of glitter in the powder coat on her face. She was much prettier at the start of the flight. Maybe, there was no provision for a mid-air make up session in her profession. The smell of lunch made his mouth water. It also tasted watery, without salt and chilli.

Thobias wandered through the memories for some more time before slipping into a sleep. However, the landing announcement woke him up.

"Hey, we've reached Cochin," Thobias said enthusiastically. He was returning after twenty long years. He jumped with joy, forgetting about his dead lung cells for a moment.

3

THE PLANE GAVE A SMALL JERK when it touched the ground. "The outside temperature is 28 degree Celsius, and we shall be happy to fly you again," the sweet voice bid the customary farewell.

"I too shall be happy if you fly me again. But I am sure this is the last one," Thobias soliloquised while unloading his suitcase from the overhead luggage compartment.

"Only one bag?" the official at Customs Clearance was surprised. He did not know the amount of baggage that Thobias was carrying inside him. Thobias smiled and moved to the exit door, casually scanning the corridor lined with artificial flowers. The temperature outside was not high. A summer rain welcomed him, offering relief from the scorching heat. He always liked the smell that the first rain evoked. Thobias spent a few minutes embracing that feeling.

"You can enjoy summer rains better if you suffer the scorching summer," Pappu used to say. It was fun running around in the first rain, getting a bad cold, and lying down with fever. Those days were gone forever.

"Nobody to receive you?" the co-passenger joined him after Customs clearance, pushing half-a-dozen bags on a trolley.

"I am used to it; it has been a lonely journey always."

"I will drop you at the junction, and you can get cheaper taxis there," he said, waving to a person who was trying to locate him.

Thobias was about to follow him to his parked car, when he heard aggressive shouting from behind.

"Thobias Mathai, stop there please." It was a middle-aged police officer in his blue uniform coming running down the corridor at the extreme right end of the building.

"You are Thobias Mathai?" The police officer came close to them. He was panting heavily but was not bothered about it, and his expression indicated that he was prepared to run further if required. His hands were open and outstretched, probably to be ready to catch the targeted man if he tried to escape.

"Yes, I am." Thobias maintained his usual cool, but was upset at losing the lift offered by the fellow traveller, who was in a hurry to move to his car.

"Meet me sometime, if time permits," the latter extended his card.

"I will try. But time is my biggest constraint." Thobias bid him goodbye and gave his full attention to the official standing nearby.

"Can I see your passport?" The official had a facial expression akin to a smile to keep the situation normal. But the expression changed to an air of authority, as soon as the passport was handed over to him by the obedient Thobias.

"Follow me to the Protector," he pointed towards the immigration office situated on the first floor of the airport building, and Thobias followed him.

"You are coming after twenty years?" the middle-aged Protector offered a smile, suggesting that the situation was almost a routine.

"Yes." Thobias was happy to hear the very personal question from an unknown official.

"I have to impound your passport," he said softly, as if he were doing something bad to a man who was returning to his country after a long period.

"But why? I never broke any law," Thobias could not hide his surprise.

"It is an instruction lodged here," he pointed towards the computer monitor, indicating that he did not know the details. "There is something serious behind it. Impounding is done only in very serious offences," the Protector explained the general rule.

"Serious offence? There cannot be anything like that. Can you just cross-check the other details of the passport that is to be impounded?" Thobias suspected a noting error.

"The number E2489346, Thobias Mathai, son of Pappu, Panamkara. Isn't that you?" the Protector read out the details of the passport from the monitor and they matched those of the man now standing in front of him.

Losing the passport was not a big issue for Thobias Mathai, for he knew that it was of no use to him further. However, the manner in which he was losing it did not enthuse him.

"Are you giving me an acknowledgement?" Thobias thought it fit not to argue with the Protector.

"It will be acknowledged by the concerned department which ordered the impounding. It will be delivered at your residence in person. Just let us know if your address is different from what is recorded here." Thobias understood the system of tracking the offender.

"Can I leave?" It was a cool question from Thobias and both the officials were taken aback by the ability of the offender to lose things gracefully.

Thobias exited the airport building and entered a yellow coloured taxi.

"You want music, sir?" the driver extended hospitality.

"Yeah, old ones."

"Chandra kalabham charthiyurangum theeram,
Indra dhanusin thooval pozhyium theeram,
Eee manohara theerathu tharumo, iniyoru jenmam koodi?
Enikkiniyoru jenmam koodi?"

On this moon-lit sleepy shore, where the godly birds sheds it's golden feathers, will you give me one more birth, just one more birth?

There could not be a better song for that moment. It made him nostalgic and also posed a question to him.

"Do you want one more birth?" Thobias asked himself. "For what?" he searched his own mind for a truthful answer. His mind did not reply. Maybe, it expected a better life and kept silent.

"Sir, where exactly are we going?" the driver turned back and asked when the highway ended and the car reached the town of Muvattupuzha.

"Take the left turn. I will direct you." The winding country road and the greenery all around brought back many memories. The ancestral home at Panamkara no longer stood there. It had been pulled down after the property was given to his younger brother who built a new one in its place. Thobias had become an outsider at home and to all those loved ones long ago.

"Insiders have to become outsiders when new relations emerge," Thobias said to himself as the car stopped in front of a large gate, a few hundred metres away from Panamkara junction.

While gently opening the gate and entering the tile-paved courtyard, he noticed that the basement of the old ancestral home had been kept intact along with one wall. The calling bell let out a sober tune and a lean lady in her thirties glanced at him through the window.

"Who?" That was the question in her eyes, though she did not ask it. The visitor was silent. Still she opened the door, after carefully evaluating the visitor.

"Yes," she was irritated by the silence of the visitor and there was an air of authority in her first word. "Amma is sleeping." It indicated that there was no one else in the house and the visitor would have to wait till she woke up.

"I am Thobias, her second son," Thobias replied softly.

"Wow! The one in the USA? You behaved like an outsider. Amma talks about you and Theresa very often. I am Teena, caretaker here for the last two months." She offered a gentle smile. The smile was short and the lips regained their previous position immediately.

"Amma is sleeping under medication. She has not been sleeping well for the last two days and the doctor advised me not to disturb her."

Thobias slipped off his shoes and entered the hall. Things were arranged in an orderly and elegant fashion. Pappu's big photo was decorated with a single artificial rose on the wall facing the main entrance. Close to it, a touchingly beautiful family photo, taken fifty years ago, was affixed on a slender nail. Thobias looked at the photo. Master Thobias at ten was a lean, fair boy with short thorn-like hair resembling that of a porcupine, posing enthusiastically for the camera. It was taken immediately after the death of his grand-father whose large-sized picture was placed amid the group, making it an all inclusive family photo.

"Amma is in the bedroom towards the left," she was intelligent enough to understand Thobias' first priority. "It's a small room, but she likes to be there. She can look at the basement of the old house from there. She did not permit its dismantling."

"Your name?" Thobias asked, appreciating her in-depth knowledge of Amma's psyche.

"I told you already. I am Teena from All Saints Home Services, and I will be here for three more months."

Thobias stood near the bedside, watching Amma sleeping. She had become thinner, her fair skin was quite wrinkled, but the face still emanated some of that old radiance.

Thobias bent down and gently kissed her feet; the feet that had walked a long journey nearing a century, through all ups and downs, among thorns and flowers, through sorrows and pleasures, through love and hatred, through affection and quarrels, with Pappu and without Pappu, with Thobias and without Thobias.

A big picture of Mother Mary occupied considerable space on the wall on her left side. Rosaries of different colours were hanging on a nail. Two candlesticks with half burnt candles on them were kept near the picture. The same old Bible with a black cover decorated the side table along with a few medium sized bottles containing pink and white tablets.

"She is getting sleep after two days," Teena cautioned him against any attempt to express himself loudly.

Thobias placed himself on the wooden chair near her bed, and recalled the last conversation with her over the phone at the time of Pappu's death anniversary.

"When are you coming?" Amma had asked, as usual.

"Next year," Thobias gave his usual reply.

"Ha! Ha! When will be that next year?"

"Next year, Amma," he repeated.

"I know your problems. But I want to see you all before I go. I know my time has already come." It was silence thereafter.

Amma's prophecy is going to be wrong now. There will be a small change in the order of going to oblivion. He wished it would not add to her pain.

"You must be tired after the journey," Teena told him without expecting a reply or confirmation. "You can take the upstairs room." She was slightly hesitant because she knew that the guest was the elder brother of her boss and had sufficient liberty to occupy any room without direction from a caretaker.

4

THOBIAS DID NOT SPEND much time in the room. He put the suitcase over the wooden table and moved towards the basement of the old house.

It was covered with a plant locally known as *communist pacha*. This was a medium sized shrub which could multiply fast and spread in spite of obstacles, hence the nickname, *communist* plant. The basement was a few inches above the ground and Thobias spent a few minutes searching for a vacant entry point to place his foot without troubling the present occupants.

He could sense movement inside the shrubs as soon as he intruded into the otherwise undisturbed natural habitat of rats, wild lizards and even snakes. He mentally aligned the rooms of the old house on the basement. He could locate the drawing room facing the road, the room on the eastern side where Pappu and Thobias slept and the other bedroom where smaller children and ladies used to stay. The dining room and kitchen were in the second row, he guessed, along with the veranda behind. They were big rooms in those days, but now the basement partition showed them as small match box rooms.

The original house had been a toddy shop, before his birth. Pappu was against any type of adulteration and naturally the business became unprofitable, forcing him to close it down. The basement was later elevated in a novel way, by collecting muddy water from the elevated road during the heavy rains and allowing it to settle in the basement, leaving the mud behind and allowing the water to percolate down.

As the house was very close to the road and because of its alignment, the sunrays heated the front rooms throughout the day. In summer, it was difficult to spend theafternoons inside the house. Pappu was used to the scorching sun; even then, he escaped to the nearby toddy shop to beat the heat. The sons used to go to the nearest junction, leaving the ladies and small children to get heated. They too sometimes moved out to the farm land in search of natural shade.

Evenings were study time. There would be four or five kerosene lamps in the house. One would be permanently placed in the drawing room, where Thobias used to sit and read along with his sisters. One would be in the kitchen where cooking was a continuous process, one in the ladies room, and another one on the floor for general use. Getting kerosene was a costly affair and naturally Pappu had to effect restrictions on the number of lamps. But on entering High School, one could claim a lamp exclusively for oneself.

The nights were silent except for the shrill sounds of crickets, or at times, the deep hooting of owls. There used to be long intervals between two consecutive hoots, giving the impression that the owl had to recoup a lot of energy for its next hoot.

"Take the kids inside and close the doors," Amma used to say whenever she heard the hooting of owls in the evenings. She believed that it was a bad omen and she had absolute proof to substantiate it. She had heard the repeated deep hooting of owls very close to the house when Laila,

Thobias' elder sister, had died immediately after she was born.

The hooting was repeated, this time by two owls sitting on a mango tree near the courtyard when Susy, his younger sister, died while she was still a angel. Thobias too started fearing owls.

In those days, childbirth took place at home; only those who had substantial means could take a pregnant lady to the hospital. Experienced ladies called *pathichis* acted as midwives. In case of any complications, they used to attempt to save the mother over the baby. This way, a lot of newborns ended up receiving God's call.

Pappu never believed in the owl's great capacity for distributing misfortune. If his mood was good, he would take his old single barrel country gun and torch and move out into the darkness. If he found the eyes of the owl as bright spots, one could hear a shot and could have a non-vegetarian dinner. But at times, the bird would be lucky enough to fly away to the next unlucky house to add to their ill luck further.

Thobias returned to the location of the old room where Pappu and he used to sleep. Pappu's cot was near the wall, closer to the road, while he slept on the other side with a steel-framed centre table in between. Pappu would be slightly intoxicated with his usual quota of toddy, but he would still read books for Thobias loudly.

"Try, you can go up, Plant, you can harvest, Give, you will get, We make our heaven, Hell too, in the same way," once he read out from a thick book, and Thobias learned it by heart immediately.

Most of the other children preferred to go to bed before Pappu came from the toddy shop to avoid hearing his lectures.

"I am not happy. Your Pappu was a topper in SSC in his time and all his classmates are big officials now. He ended up in a toddy shop. You are following his footsteps," Amma said when Thobias showed her the gold medal he had received for being the topper in SSC in the *taluka*. Amma had seen Thobias drinking toddy along with Pappu many times.

"His life has not ended so far. Pappu says everybody's life ends in the cemetery," Thobias revealed Pappu's mind only to defend him.

There were only a very few occasions in those days when Thobias could not sleep with Pappu in that room; once, when a deadly spider called *irukoli* stung Pappu. The excruciating pain made the victim creep and crouch like a spider.

"Yeah, he will become a big spider-like creature," one of the many visitors who poured in predicted loudly.

Thobias did not believe it initially, but when Pappu started crying loudly in pain and crawled on the floor mat like a spider, an element of doubt crept into his mind, as he had never seen Pappu crying earlier.

"Take this kid to the back room," someone from the crowd commanded.

Thobias understood his insignificance, but he did not leave the place because Pappu was more important to him than the unknown who commanded.

"The poison has to be sucked out," a tall man with a turban on his head took command of the situation.

"Bring twenty-one hens immediately," he directed, without pinpointing responsibility on anybody.

"He can count up to twenty-one," Thobias thought in admiration.

Eleven hens came from Amma's small hen coop and the rest were brought in by neighbours. They were beheaded one by one, and the neck with gushing blood was held to the wound for a few seconds, amid chanting of certain *mantras*. Pappu went to sleep after that. Thobias watched him through the window for some more time before retiring to the dining room to sleep on the table there.

"Where were you last night?" Pappu asked in the morning. Thobias could not reply immediately. He was enjoying the sight of Pappu who was still in human form.

"They said I'm a kid and sent me out," Thobias complained.

"No, no. You are not a kid. You are my best friend. I want you always with me. Always."

Thobias too wished it. But God disposed it unfavourably.

"Please come. Tea is ready," Teena came up to the wall of the new courtyard and reminded the guest. She led him to the dining table and stood at a distance, alternating her attention to the dining table and the television which was airing a serial in the local language. Thobias finished his tea silently and withdrew to his room.

5

THE FRONT WINDOW opened towards the courtyard of the old house. Thobias watched the plants that grew in his one-time playground.

It was the place where paddy was stacked during the harvest season. The courtyard would be thoroughly cleaned and smeared with cow dung to receive the harvested paddy. It was okay for Thobias to pick fresh dung with his hands. It gave him a sense of warmth. When the dung was old and partly decayed, he used to close his eyes while picking it with his tender hands. It was then mixed with water and poured into a bucket, which Thobias would carry to the courtyard. Pappu would smear it there, using a broom made of the ribs of coconut leaves.

Harvested paddy would be stacked in squares, the height of which depended on the effort put in by the labourer. It was fun to jump from one heap to another. The most popular game at that time was hide and seek, as the stacked hay provided enough hiding places. The games used to start after the sunrays had reduced their intensity and then vanished, prior to Pappu's arrival. In between, there would be continuous reprimanding from the kitchen for jumping over the paddy stacks, an activity that was regarded as disrespectful to the staple food.

If one bathed immediately after the game, one would suffer severe itching all over the body from the small bruises caused by the sharp hay. Hence bathing would be postponed, or at times, done away with for that day.

After threshing, Pappu would measure the paddy grains using a basket made of cane. A basketful would go to the labourer after counting nine baskets in his own favour. Pappu was generous and always gave a little more at the end, as many of the labourers were his own friends, and the goodwill gesture spread smiles all around. That was the maximum possible benevolence from Pappu.

Once the courtyard became vacant, the drying of paddy started, followed by the boiling and the milling. Thobias was lucky, for there were many in the area who did not get this opportunity as they never owned paddy land.

The only entertainment in the evening was listening to Varunni. He was in his late forties and was well known in the area as an expert in building walls with local stone. He would sing songs loudly. They were his own compositions, based on contemporary issues faced in the village. Sometimes, it would be speeches covering politics, religion, philosophy or sometimes a mouthful of ugly words that kids should not hear. His legs would be shaky depending upon the level of toddy inside him.

Thobias moved to the second window to get a complete view of the old courtyard. He could not stand there for long. He moved downstairs and reached the extreme left corner of the courtyard. The old cowshed was still kept intact.

Pappu had only one cow. It fed his entire family till its life permitted, sparing some for its own kids who too came into the world every year. Later, it was given to a butcher when the quantity of milk became uneconomical. Thobias was in tears when the black cow with small curved horns looked back at its old master and one time playmate, resisting the strong tugging by the new owner.

The cowshed was now used for storing items retrieved from the dismantled old home. Thobias searched for a small sized green trunk in the heap. It contained a few childhood items, which he had put by when he went out to join Smile Bank. He had been so busy that he had forgotten about those things in those days.

After moving a few wooden pieces and jute bags, Thobias was able to locate parts of the trunk, crushed in the middle. The top portion came out when he inserted his hands through the corroded partortion to lift it up. He pulled out the lower portion from the heap. All papers had become small bits and got coated with reddish rust from the box.

The childhood treasure box was intact, but it had turned black in colour and the lid was held fast to the body due to corrosion. The box contained Master Thobias' hard earned coins. Thobias took the box out and observed it, turning it around from the back to the front. Curiosity made him open it in a hurry, using force. But the already corroded box was crushed and the valuables fell down. There were eight fifty-paise coins, four twenty-five paise coins and a round medal which he had received when he topped the school leaving examination.

Fifty paise was not a small sum in those days. One could buy ten ice candy sticks with it. The coins were earned by locating the rubber sap which deviated from the allotted route like a rebel, refusing to fall into the coconut shell kept for collecting it, and went to the soil to get condensed there, spoiling its chances of getting converted into nice rubber sheets. Such condensed sap was dug out, then washed, dried and taken to the shop. One month's collection could even go up to ten rupees, and two fifty paise coins could end up in his treasure box.

Thobias looked at the coins with much curiosity, turning them over in his palm. They had become black and nothing on them was readable. He remembered the pain and mental control that had to be exercised for preserving them. Licking the ice candy stick was his biggest weakness in those days. The ice candy vendor came during the lunch break at the rear end of the school, and there would be a big gathering of students around his bicycle. Some would be able to buy the treat and others used to watch those lucky fellows licking the ice stick.

When the sale was over, the upper lid of the box would be removed and the broken ice sticks and the thick white ice which shielded them would be dumped over the grass. If one was quick enough and willing to risk a few bruises, one could get a few broken pieces from the grass. Such pieces had definitely saved five paise many a time for Thobias Mathai.

The money saved had its use during the school vacation when they went to Amma's ancestral house. It was a dream-come-true when the bus started with Thobias Mathai in it to his dream land. There were as many kids available to play with as in Pappu's home, and it was a privilege to be treated as a guest.

Thobias dropped the medal into his pocket and searched the area further. Pappu's wooden box was still there over the red stool. It contained tools made and used by him in his day-to-day life. Pappu could pull out a shaky tooth using a forceps-like iron tool which was bent inwards to get a grip on the tooth. It also helped many, when fish bones got stuck in their throats. A sharp knife-like pointed bar was meant for pulling out thorns from the legs of children. Discarded rubber tapping tools, the headlight made by him for tapping in the early morning, the plastic suction pipe to transfer liquid from one vessel to another and a few half finished and finished wooden toys of different sizes were all still intact there.

Toy-making was his pastime, and he liked to display his craftsmanship. The toys would be lying here and there for some time or would end up in a corner of the barn, where Pappu used to keep his tools. Some of the kids would take them to the backyard to play with them. They would then be left unattended, and then the heavy rain would take them to the sloping farm land.

6

THOBIAS MADE HIS SECOND VISIT to Amma's room. She was still sleeping under medication. "Call me when she wakes up," he left instructions with Teena and moved towards the farm.

He took a minute to look for the old pathways which had been fully covered by bushes. People traversing along the farm must be rare after Pappu's death. This was the land that had fed and educated a family of ten children. Pappu used every inch of this fertile land to make both ends meet.

Thobias' grandfather had migrated to Panamkara, attracted by the availability of water and the fertility of the land. He prospered here and his son Pappu married Thresiakutty from Thodupuzha, and she became mother to Thobias.

"You know, being born in this world is the luckiest thing to happen to anyone," Sister Clara used to teach in Catechism class. "One gets a chance to live on this beautiful earth, gets love and then one can join God in heaven."

"What is life in heaven like, Sister?" It was an innocent question from Thobias and she paused for a moment to reply.

"It's a garden. A very big garden!" Sister widened her eyeballs. "There will be God and a lot of angels singing songs." Thobias understood that God likes songs, probably the same ones that the sisters sang in church. Thobias was also familiar with Varunni's songs. But Varunni was an atheist and sang only under intoxication. It cannot be the nature of songs in heaven.

"Anyhow, all doubts will be cleared in a few months," Thobias said to himself while searching for the bent coconut tree in the middle of the farm. It had begun to grow vertically after falling mid way. There were two areca trees close to it, which would extend support to those who felt like falling while climbing the coconut tree. It was the playing area of kids. That coconut tree must have witnessed a lot of fun, a lot of quarrels, a lot of crying and a lot of laughter and must have enjoyed its life far better than those trees which never fell down and grew thereafter. The tree was not there anymore.

The coconut trees around were old; they tapered towards the top and the crown seemed ready to fall off at any time. The rubber trees of that time had disappeared. In those days, he would find it unexciting to accompany Pappu for rubber tapping in the early morning. After breakfast they would visit each tree again to collect the sap which had oozed out into the coconut shell. Pouring it into aluminium dishes for condensation, taking it for pressing in the evening, bringing back and drying; all these activities comprised the productive work of childhood.

The only unproductive work was the peeling of the thin rubber patches from the hands and legs. Thobias used to do the peeling exercise during his social studies class. A majority of the students would be engaged in gossip when Miss Alice harped on the greatness of Akbar or the administrative reforms of Muhammed bin Tughlaq or on how the Kalinga War brought Ashoka renown. Thobias used the time effectively.

Now he could hear the movement of creatures disturbed by his entry. The squirrel which was relishing the cocoa nut on the slanting branch of a cocoa tree raised its tail, signalling about the entry of an unfamiliar face to the farm. It watched the intruder for some time and then put down its tail, indicating to its group that there was no problem.

There used to be a big rat snake which roamed around the farm, and was frequently spotted by Thobias and Pappu when they went out for rubber tapping.

"Why don't we kill it?" Thobias had once suggested.

"It is harmless and helps us to control rats," Pappu explained the political equation of the nature.

"Can you kill a snake?" Pappu tested Thobias' bravery once. "Mmmm . . . ."

"I too feared killing snakes for a long time," Pappu continued. "But I had to live here. So I was forced to kill cobras."

"When it comes to survival, all learn their tricks. Here I've got a rat, a big one. It has made its burrows near the border of our farm with escape routes spreading to our neighbour's farm. I tried to smoke it out so many times but always the smoke escaped somewhere and I could not lay my hands on it. I have to appreciate its trick," he continued. "All play tricks to survive. Society classifies some tricks as lawful and others as unlawful."

"You study and escape. I made the mistake of choosing farming and I live a life of toil. Study alone cannot grant you success in life. Still, there is a better chance. Watch the front benchers who are intelligent. They become engineers and doctors and lead a silent life. The group just behind, who are not prepared to apply their full brain but realize their mistakes later, become civil servants and police officials and rule over the first group. The third group which sits in the middle row is not good in mathematics and science, but is very much concerned about the colour of the uniform and the behaviour of the class teacher. They become leaders and rule over the first two classes. Backbenchers who do not listen to anything and forget to bring textbooks become money lenders and dons, and they control the leaders."

"There will be another group sitting silently in the front bench, not understanding things as the intelligent ones. They become the clergy and rule over both the worlds. Everybody has got a room here in this world to grow and expand."

Thobias began to recall more of Pappu's words and they made him emotional. He decided to return to Amma's room. He took a shortcut through the area where banana plants were grown earlier. Still the thoughts chased him.

"Watch this plantain. It yields its bunch and gets decayed to become manure for the new sprouts. I will be happy if my life too ends like that," Pappu told him once, much before he actually ended like that. Thobias increased his pace as the day was getting darker and he feared the prospect of a snake-bite even though he didn't have more than a few months at risk.

"Hello." It was the much awaited call from Teena. This time the call was much louder and she crossed the courtyard and entered the farm. "Amma has woken up. She is waiting for you."

7

"DID YOU TELL Amma about my arrival?" Thobias asked Teena.

"Yeah, she has become energetic now." Teena was concerned about Amma.

Thobias entered Amma's room. She was sitting on the bed supported by two pillows on a wooden slanting platform, the height of which could be adjusted. She looked cheerful and radiated a charm that reminded Thobias of the old days, though time had taken its toll on her smile. Her eyes were overflowing with the joy of meeting her son after two decades. Amma extended her hands towards him. Thobias caught the hands, which were very soft and trembling slightly.

"Sit by my side," she said, softly. "Finally, I can see you. I thought my end would also be like that of Pappu, without anybody near and without seeing you." She stopped for a moment as she was unable to talk continuously.

"You came all of a sudden. Why didn't you bring Theresa and the kids? I was longing to see them."

Thobias did not answer that question but continued holding her hands.

"What kept you away from me for the last twenty years?" The question was expected.

"Many things happen without a reason." This time Thobias opened his mouth.

"I know," she smiled. "I expected only philosophical answers from you."

"How are you, Amma?" Thobias enquired.

"Just as you see." She smiled again.

A few seconds elapsed in silence except for the ticking of the old wall clock. Thobias turned his head and looked at the clock which was placed above the entrance.

"You remember that clock?"

"How can I forget it? My problem is that I cannot forget things," Thobias revealed.

The clock had been gifted to Pappu by one of his close friends, Chathukutty, for the help Pappu rendered to him in finding a buyer for his ten cents of rocky land. The clock was placed in the drawing room of the old house so that it could be seen from the road. Clocks or watches were not common in those days at Panamkara. Its perfect black cover with a white dial gave clear visibility from the road and many, for whom time mattered, used to stop there to have a peep at it.

One day, a quarrel broke out between the close friends. Nobody knew the exact reason for the quarrel. Pappu offered the cost of the clock but Chathukutty refused to accept it. He felt insulted and sought the clock back, which Pappu refused.

The case went to the police first and then to the court at Muvattupuzha. Pappu was no match to fight a court case with Chathukutty. He took the clock to the court and placed it on the big table of the judge and narrated his version of the dispute. The judge watched the emotions flowing from an innocent farmer and ordered its release to Pappu. It came back to the same place on the wall and

Pappu inscribed Amma's name, Thresiakutty, on it as a gratitude for her support in the entire episode.

Pappu was very attached to this clock after this incident. It was a symbol of victory for him, probably the only victory he had in his lifetime. He never forgot to wind the clock every week. Even when he was bedridden, he would climb over a stool and wind the clock, holding the wall for support. This routine continued till he became immobile due to a leg fracture.

Both Pappu and Chathukutty are no more but the clock still ticks.

"Who is winding the clock now?" Thobias asked, his eyes still fixed on it.

"Madhumon comes on Sundays." Madhumon was the male attendant who used to come on Sundays just to rekindle his attachment with Pappu, whom he loved ever since he had come there in search of a job.

"How are the kids?" Amma brought Thobias back from the clock and Chathukutty.

"Not kids. They've grown up. They are a lady and gentlemen now, and they are fine."

"And how is Theresa? Did she get a good life over there?" Amma still seemed to have a lot of attachment to her. For that matter, she had an attachment to anything that was feminine. She was very familiar with the sufferings of women. She believed that boys would get a life or at least get somebody whose life could be spoiled.

"Must have. She must be happy. I have managed things well." The reply from Thobias was not to the point, but it was better than avoiding a direct answer and conveying unnecessary meanings.

"Managed or loved?" she asked with a smile.

It was Amma who had selected Theresa for Thobias. Amma was looking for a girl who would care for the less fortunate ones in the family. Thobias always went for the beauty of the girl and he was unable to adjust to the nose of the girl if it did not match with that of Cleopatra, or the shape of the chin not matching to that in a Ravi Varma painting.

"Beauty is only skin deep," Amma tried to convince her son at that time. "A happy life does not last long," she brought in another point to convince him fully and Thobias believed her as he used to in his childhood.

It was silence for a while. She might be aware of the pain of acting in life.

"When are you going back?" Amma broke the silence.

"I may not."

"Really?" A big relief overtook her even as she was taken by surprise. Thobias watched Amma regaining her energy levels and she tried to sit without the support of the pillow.

"You are not joking? Are you?" Her eyes were sparkling.

"Not joking, Amma. This is my last coming and I'm not going back," Thobias was not acting.

"Bringing Theresa and the kids too?" Amma knew that the family has to follow the leader.

"Not decided yet," Thobias was as brief as possible.

"Something happened between you two?" Her doubt was natural.

"No, no. Ours is a perfect family. After all, what is there to happen at this age? I just wanted to spend some time with the memories of my old days. I am also nearing my end," Thobias tried to erase the doubts in her mind.

"I am ninety, my boy. You are still young. Don't say you are old when your mother is alive. It can make me too old." She laughed heartily.

Amma made an attempt to stand up on her own. Seeing the action through the window, Teena rushed in and stood guard.

"What is there for dinner?" She looked at Teena. "Can you make fish fry with *puli* leaves? Thobias likes it very much."

"Building one more house or staying with me?" Amma asked during dinner.

"With you now." She loved that answer.

"I can sense some tension in you. What is it?" It was very difficult to hide things from her right from his childhood.

"Nothing. Just nostalgic about my childhood and the memory of Pappu," he tried to escape.

"Only Pappu? Am I not there?" Thobias was caught off guard. "I know you have become indifferent after his departure, or is it that your importance diminished when others grew up?" She was blunt and Thobias could not answer that easily, because he needed time to admit the truth.

"Something is worrying you. What is it?" She seemed to have detected something unusual on his face.

"Nothing." The reply was not emphatic enough to convince her.

"Thobias, everything happens for a reason; illness, poverty, lost glory, all occur to test the limits of your soul. Without these tests, life would be meaningless and utterly boring." Amma was becoming Amma again.

"Thobias, your mind is wandering," she started again. "Pray to God to make you a believer. At this age, there is a tendency to search for the meaning of life." She made an assumption about the cause of her son's listlessness and Thobias felt relieved.

"Don't waste your time and energy on it as Pappu did," she continued. "A lot of intellectuals with much bigger brains than yours have thought about it without getting any answers. So, just live happily the little time you get here in this world." Thobias was still silent.

"You are not arguing as you used to earlier. I am saying this because I find you tense and your silence is telling me a lot of things," she paused.

"I am a little tired after the journey," Thobias tried to escape again.

"Forget those things over which you don't have any control, and be happy with what you have got. Just look down. There are people who are suffering far more than us. Always pray to God and thank Him for the blessings he has showered on this family.

"You are a lucky man. You will find many people in Panamkara without any story to tell in the dark corners of their houses. Most of them exhale a deep sigh for those good things which did not happen in their lives. Just think about them. It is a small life, my son; only you can make it big."

She paused again and searched his face for the effect of her lecture, but it was not as easily readable as earlier. The dinner ended in silence and Thobias withdrew to his room upstairs.

8

THOBIAS WOKE UP when the sunrays fell on the bed through the gaps in the window curtains. It was a deep sleep in the lap of childhood memories and feelings, undisturbed by life's tensions. But there were no crickets chirping or owls hooting to re-enact the old days.

Thobias opened the rear window of the room; it wasn't easy to unfasten the disused and corroded latches which had made a permanent association with the hooks on the frame. However, the view of Mulliri Mountain through it was worth the effort taken. The mountain's top had the shape of an elephant, with a curved body sloping and rising again to form the head. Thobias felt that the mountain had come closer and the height had reduced. The greenery had vanished, exposing hard black rocks. A number of small streams that originated from its top had also vanished. They had either gone forever, or would reappear during the monsoon. Paddyfields down the valley had given way to pineapple gardens and the small hillocks had become flatter.

The Mulliri mountain never knew that it had an ardent lover who loved its majesty, the water streaks that decorated its top like silver ribbons when the sun shone over it, its steep valley covered with a thick green coating, the gentle breeze that kissed the fragile paddy all the way. Thobias was just one among the many who loved the beauty of the mountain without its knowledge.

Mulliri mountain was a thick forest in those days. Now houses were visible even at the top. Thobias remembered something that Pappu had once told him.

"Thobias," Pappu said, "this entire area was a forest in my childhood. At that time, there were only two forest guards supervising the area. No leaf used to fall without their knowledge. After that a Forest Office started functioning here, along with a lot of guards and officers. However, the forest thinned out and vanished. You know why?" Pappu did not explain the reason, but only said, "You will come to know about it when you too become a government officer." In those days the government was the sole employer.

Thobias could see the Akkara house from there. It was the house of his cousins and a considerable part of his childhood had been spent in playing there.

"I will visit Akkara and come," Thobias told Amma after breakfast. In his childhood, it was tough to get permission to go to Akkara. One had to complete all allotted tasks and finish one's homework before seeking permission.

Thobias took a shortcut to Akkara through the neighbour's plot as in the old days. It was not a safe route to take while returning in the evening. There was a big *pala* tree near the pathway. Some people had seen a female ghost in the evenings, dressed in a pure white *sari*. Thobias did not believe in ghosts; still he gave it the benefit of the doubt. She was finally nailed by a *tantrik*, who spent a full Friday night alone near the *pala* tree and talked to the ghost in an unknown language. He commanded her to confine herself to the tree. The ghost obeyed him, and he pushed a six-inch long nail into the tree as soon as the ghost entered it. The successful nailing of the ghost was the talk of the town at Panamkara the next day.

Even so, people used to avoid that path. Thobias too wished to avoid it. But after the evening games he had to reach home early, before Pappu returned from the toddy shop. The journey always followed a definite pattern. Thobias' pace would be slow until he reached the *pala* tree. Then his legs would pick up momentum automatically, as if he were participating in a walking race. The speed would increase further, ending in a sprint, along the short stretch where the *pala* tree stood majestically. Thereafter, his speed would come down automatically once he realised that he had crossed the ghost tree without harm. Then he would be relieved, but would still look backwards a few times to ensure that there was no white *sari* chasing him for soft blood.

"Hello, this is not a public road," a tall man, perhaps the new owner of the land, said, coming out of nowhere as Thobias was trying to locate the familiar childhood route to Akkara, pushing the shrubs sideways.

"Oh, sorry." Thobias withdrew his steps.

"Where do you want to go?" The man appreciated the quick obedience of the intruder.

"I thought there is a pathway here towards the paddy field." The land owner understood the intruder's familiarity with the route.

"You are . . . ?" he asked.

"I am Thobias, second son of Pappu." Thobias understood that he did not have an address of his own.

"Oh, sorry. Please don't feel bad. I did not recognise you." That address had a value.

Thobias moved on, stamping his feet occasionally on the ground to scare away snakes. The *pala* tree was no longer there. Its place has been taken over by big rubber trees, indicating its death long ago.

Thobias crossed the bushy area and reached the one-time paddy fields. He did not like the new crop that came up there. There was no provision to play there anymore. In those days, it was a big event starting from the wait for the harvest season, preparing big balls and keeping them in hiding. The balls were made without the knowledge of Pappu. Paper would be rolled thickly like a small ball. It would be wrapped with rubber threads which would then be covered with a piece of cloth and dipped in rubber sap, without anybody noticing. Rolling it on the ground and giving it another coat of rubber would add more bounce to the ball.

The games used to continue till the sun disappeared from the red sky. Sometimes there wouldn't be the required quorum to play. The disheartened group would then move to the big gooseberry tree overlooking the fields. That too was fun; collecting ripe gooseberries, sitting in the shade of the tree, enjoying the gooseberry and drinking water from the stream to get that sweet aftertaste.

It was the growing age too. The boy Thobias was wonderstruck with the secrets of the universe and human life. The group consisted of six or seven boys in the age group of ten to eighteen years. The discussions were about the universe without boundaries, earth's meticulous revolving around the sun and its insignificance in the galaxy, the depth of the sea, life after death, the wonder of electricity, an equipment called television, and a battery operated equipment called transistor which could bring sound from a distance, and all sorts of weighty subjects. Thobias was puzzled and baffled by the extent of his ignorance and looked towards a bright energetic world where things could be better than mere tapping of rubber in the morning and going to school.

"We are insignificant in this universe." It was a while before Thobias believed it.

"Yeah, there may be planets with better and stronger people." Thoma was the eldest encyclopedia of the group.

"Where is heaven?" Thobias' obsession with heaven had started in his catechism class.

"Ha, ha." The group found something worth laughing at.

"It is a belief," Thoma clarified. "And all unknown places are more beautiful and gracious."

Master Thobias was not satisfied with such answers. Pappu was the best friend to depend on for a serious answer. But his words too were not encouraging.

"How the universe was formed and what happens after life on earth are matters for those who can afford the luxury of time to think about it. For me, how to live here is the most important subject and I spend much time thinking about it, my son." He was practical.

Thobias was not sure as to which were the best days of his life; the innocent childhood days of searching for stray paddy in the field after harvest, collecting it in a small cane basket and presenting it to Amma to make her eyes wet, or getting drunk and sleeping over the wooden bench at Tarseen Bar or chasing the mirage called a happy life?

Each age had its own answers.

He crossed the pineapple garden and started climbing a small hillock. Suddenly, he realised that he was a patient. It was difficult to breathe and he was puffing and panting, till he sat on the steps and rested for a while.

It was dead silent at Akkara house, except for the barking of a few fierce dogs which were properly caged. Younger cousin Boban used to live there. He had remained a bachelor while the others were settled abroad. The old home still remained intact, untouched by the change of lifestyle, except for the widened courtyard and a polished guest room to suit the occasional visit of the legal heirs from abroad.

Thobias did not like the silence and started the downhill journey. It was easy and enjoyable.

He avoided the shortcut while returning. The lengthier route was wider too. On both sides of the road were paddy cultivators who tried their luck in patches here and there. Pappu used to own one acre of paddy land there. This road had been constructed by him and his brothers to enable the entry of tractors when the law of 'land to tiller' was enacted, forcing farmers to cultivate land without hiring labour. Ploughing was a tough job especially for the first crop when the land was hard after the summer.

But the tractor was not welcome in Panamkara. A group of people came shouting slogans and told Pappu that it would eliminate labour opportunities. They also told him that ploughing the land with a tractor was against their theories and that those who disobeyed their theories did not have a place on earth. Pappu surrendered there because he did not know any place other than earth, and sold the paddy land dirt cheap to the one who shouted at the maximum pitch.

Thereafter, life was dependent on the ration shop like that of the majority in the area. It was Thobias' job to be in the queue one hour prior to opening the shop as an early bird, because there were chances that the stock would get exhausted early.

The pathway led Thobias to Panamkara junction. The junction had a few petty shops, one room for playing cards, a volleyball court and a toddy shop down the line. The roads were desolate, maybe due to the summer, when people come out only in the evening for a stroll and some chit-chatting. Thobias could feel the heat after the short walk and sat on a bench in front of the second petty shop.

All the shopkeepers were new-generation boys. Nobody recognised Thobias who had spent nearly 25 years in this junction wandering without purpose. The alienation from his roots caused him more fatigue than the summer heat did.

"Does Peekeri Rajan come here?" Thobias asked the shop owner.

"He is more or less confined to his home, and comes out only occasionally." Thobias was happy to know that Rajan was alive.

"Who are you?" It was a regular question posed to strangers in villages, and Thobias repeated the same introduction he had given to the land owner.

"Oh! The one in USA? You want me to send somebody for Rajan?" the boy offered his help.

"No, thanks. I will go to him in the evening." Thobias walked back.

9

THE WALKING EXERCISE in the morning gave Thobias an insight into the state of his health and he decided to take the car out in the evening. Rajan's house was not far and he could locate it without much effort, though the landscape had undergone much change. Several new brick red houses had changed the area, replacing the old lush green background. The house had been modified in the front; adding two rooms, a sit-out and a car porch. The courtyard had been narrowed and a few rubber sheets, hung on a wire to dry, decorated the courtyard.

Thobias stopped the car on the road and walked up to the sit-out. The man lying on the armed chair placed his hands on his forehead to shade his eyes from the sunrays and have a better look at the visitor.

"My eyesight is bad," he said, inviting the visitor to introduce himself.

The reply did not come instantly, giving him time to recognise the visitor.

"Thobias!" The host finally recognised him. "Wow!" Rajan opened his mouth wide. "I thought it was you, but a wrong guess would have been insulting. That is why I did not take the chance immediately," he laughed. "You still look young, but age has caught up with me." Rajan had changed into an old man; his eyes had lost their glitter and sunk into the sockets, the skin was wrinkled, the muscles loose and the beard and moustache were snow white.

"I never thought we would meet again. Amma told me that you had settled there and may not come back. I have a small chicken farm; my son Sivan is looking after it. I seldom go out; instead I sit here and watch the people who stroll on the road," Rajan explained his life in brief.

"What made you come back? Settling here?" Rajan asked, the surprise still visible on his face.

"The smell of this soil and the love for my roots," Thobias told a half-truth.

"There is no smell of the soil in USA?" Rajan laughed heartily. "What will you take? Tea, coffee or our old friend?"

"I forgot to tell you," Rajan paused for a second and looked towards his old bedroom. "She passed away three years ago. Now there is nobody to scold me if I booze too much, and I too lost interest in it." Thobias knew restrictions were needed to get the thrill of breaking them.

"Old friend will be fine for me. Why don't we go to our old place, the rocks near the paddy fields overlooking the river?"

"You still remember them?" Rajan was happy to hear that.

"I never forgot it, to remember again," Thobias revealed his weakness.

"I have to take permission from Sivan to go out. Love brings in strange patterns of behaviour; it was he who used to take permission from me. Anyhow, this is a nice feeling." Thobias felt slightly jealous.

The car retraced its route towards Panamkara, so that they could get a few eatables.

"Hey, what happened to our study class room?" Thobias asked Rajan, when they reached the junction.

There was a room upstairs, in the tiled two-storied building near the junction. Rajan had once taken Thobias there after class. There were seven students in that room when they entered. All were from the Panamkara government school and one lean man, with a black beard and sparkling eyes, was talking to the assembled students in a low voice but emphatically. He stopped for a moment when Thobias entered and looked questioningly at a person standing nearby. The person tilted his head and smiled, indicating that Thobias was welcome.

The gathering was about launching a students' movement in school. Thobias sat in a corner and listened to the man's talk about the exploitation happening around, how unity could prevent it, how the wealth should be distributed to eradicate poverty, how labour is perishable, how students should participate in this noble cause of fighting the bourgeoisie.

The classes continued the next day too with questions from the previous class. Only Thobias could answer them fully and he was liked by the teacher. He patted Thobias on his back and asked him to stay back.

"Who taught you all these things?"

"Pappu, my father," Thobias felt proud.

"What else do you know about our noble cause?" His eyes were shining.

"Nothing much. Pappu used to talk about it." The answer did not satisfy the teacher.

"Why don't you come with me and teach your fellow students? You can also explain things as I do."

"But Pappu told me something more," Thobias did not know how to reject the offer.

"Like mixed economy, dictatorship of proletariat, killings in the name of ideologies, distribution of poverty and . . . ."

"What do you think about all those?" the teacher interrupted.

"I did not think anything about those things so far on my own. My aim is to make a living for others in the family." The reply was from his heart.

"Try to think big. Don't narrow down to yourself. All have got families," the teacher also said from his heart. The man standing near him signalled something to Rajan and he led Thobias downstairs.

Thobias met him again near the school gate for the inauguration of the students' movement in the school.

"Hello, Thobias," he called. "Did you tell your Pappu about our meeting?"

"Yes."

"What did he say?" he persisted.

"Not to get the vision coloured by ideologies. It is for people who are unable to develop their own opinion," Thobias repeated the words of Pappu without any hesitation. The face of the teacher became pale for a moment, but later he brought a smile on to it.

"I would like to meet your Pappu sometime."

"Sure. He too will be happy," Thobias told him but he never came.

Rajan ordered a packet of chilli flavoured groundnuts, banana chips, a half-litre bottle of soda and a packet of cigarettes from a shop, without getting down from the car.

The boy obediently supplied it. Thobias took out his wallet to pay for the purchases but Rajan intervened.

"Put it in my account," Rajan told the boy and he withdrew to the shop.

"You remember the study classes over there and the teacher?" Thobias asked Rajan and he took a few seconds to scan his memory, covering it in steps of decades.

"That plenum Paily?" Rajan asked. *Plenum* was the nomenclature for the annual meeting of the students' movement of the party. Paily was a hero in plenum speeches and the nickname stuck with him for his commitment to the party ideology and the hard work he was putting in to propagate it.

"Your memory is great," Rajan was more interested in appreciating the memory of Thobias than giving an answer.

"I don't know his present whereabouts. He has not come up in the Party," Rajan said.

"You never met him again?" Thobias asked in disbelief.

"Just a few times. He was always on tour, and finally the college authorities expelled him for insufficient attendance. I don't know what happened to him after that."

"Happily lived on ideology and perished?" It was a harsh observation from Thobias and Rajan did not relish it.

"Everything is a matter of time. Remember those big processions we undertook tickling the very air of Panamkara? Those slogans? Those songs? Those flags and the feeling when volunteers marched in their uniform with the beating of left-right-left, left-right-left? Those ideologies helped us to live in hope. Otherwise what was there to live for?" Rajan defended.

Thobias decided not to continue with that subject, as the economy had changed much since then and the old theories had given way to new ones.

"Stop here. Can't you recognise our old place?"

"Oh, no." Thobias could not recognise it. The old rocks had disappeared due to the construction boom and the paddy field had become grassland, with frogs and possibly snakes too around. The location of the old toddy shop had become unrecognisable and the river nearby was not even a river.

Both sat inside the car and opened the Scotch bottle.

"You remember the murder of Benoy? It was much before your departure to USA." Rajan broke the silence.

"He aspired to become a don. Didn't he?" Thobias had a faint memory about the incident.

"Yes, recruiting under-trials from jail and threatening respectable people. Even the police started fearing him. He even manhandled our Society President. Only then did we make up our mind to eliminate him through his own friend-turned-foe, as advised by the police. We could save the murderer from hanging but with much difficulty." Rajan looked into Thobias' eyes and gauged his interest in the subject.

"But it could have been avoided," Rajan continued. "None of us has escaped the wrath of God; my wife was bedridden for years, Nathan got cancer in the neck, Adappan lost his business and the list is endless. And now, guilt is chasing me."

"Don't run; it will chase you further. All have got their own share of guilt. You helped killing a don. I killed a lot of loved ones mentally," Thobias reduced the gravity of the subject.

They were silent for some time, occasionally throwing small stones at the small body of water which was stagnant and looked dirty.

"When are you returning?" That was a customary question to visiting non-residents in India.

"No plan yet." That was a very different answer, coming from a non-resident Indian.

"Any family problems?" Rajan tried to peep into the married life of Thobias.

Thobias smiled and just shook his shoulders indicating that there were no such problems.

"I have got a strong feeling now that there is a God, and killing, even if for a good cause, is a sin," Rajan was allowing the guilt to chase him further.

"*Thy belief saveth thee.*" Soon the evening turned to night.

10

THOBIAS WALKED to Parakad church early next morning. He entered the church premises through the left gate to avoid crossing the central door. Believers often bow with respect towards the direction of the big crucifix on the altar when they cross the open main door. The central door is closed most of the time. Still, Thobias did not take a chance.

The cemetery was desolate as expected and the granite tops were reflecting the sunrays. Thobias could locate the third one at the fourth row from the gate itself. It appeared brownish by the laterite particles brought over it by heavy rainfall. Small shrubs growing in the narrow patch of soil between the tombs had covered its periphery.

His mind was blank for some time. Was it due to a surge of too many emotions choking the routes, or was it because he would be meeting Pappu soon, or due to guilt for not having visited the tomb for twenty years, or was he in no mood to pick up the emotional threads which were cut while chasing the mirage called success? Maybe his mind was trying to reason with Pappu that it was all fate. He liked the blankness of the mind and the silence of the cemetery. He sat on the tomb, reading the names of his would-be neighbours. The mind took a lot of time to come out of that lethargy.

Pappu was a good father like any other father, but unable to do much about his own life or the lives of his children in a way he wished to.

He feared so many things; fear of the future, fear of hunger, fear of school bills, fear of neighbours encroaching upon his farm, fear of God, fear of growing children turning against him, fear of rain clouds at harvest time, fear of rats eating the tapioca crop, fear of seeing the tears of children, fear of leaving this world even when there was nothing in it for him.

Pappu liked to escape from all these fears, but was unable to do so in his lifetime. The choices were limited, and one had to lead the life one was allotted even if one could not enjoy it. But at the same time, there were many around him watching and directing without responsibility and finally slapping the award of failure on him.

"I used your sentiments too much," Thobias confessed in silence, "and returned nothing to you."

The emotionally charged words of Amma came to his mind. It had happened on a Sunday just before going to bed and Pappu had gone to bed already.

"Why do you want to get out of your job?" she was controlling her anger. "Your plans are affecting everyone. You are venturing too much and Pappu and we are the sufferers." It was a truth, and Thobias was unable to explain why such a lucrative job was unattractive to him.

At that time, Thobias was working in Smile Bank and Investments at Marcardia. The job was attractive initially, but turned hot later and was absolutely boiling further on. Thobias was trying escape routes thereafter. There was only Pappu to bank upon.

Agriculture was the first option. Pappu started running for cheap land. Thobias located it at the top of a mountain, a few hundred kilometres away from home.

"You buy it. I will make it a success," Pappu was confident and extended full support.

It was a five-kilometre walk from the nearest bus stop, over untarred roads filled with loose red soil, covering more than three barren hillocks. Dry wind blew throughout, and water was a luxury for the greater part of the year.

The area was known as Asinus land, a name coined by the erstwhile white ruler, who was a postgraduate in zoology, when he saw herds and herds of donkeys moving on the road among a few human beings. People used to bring donkeys in herds of fifteen to twenty, all connected by a single rope. Once the goods are purchased and laden on the backs of the donkeys, the herd starts its return journey covering hillock after hillock. A few donkeys, in between, who do not put in their best efforts, would get beaten up severely, till they fell in line with the other donkeys. The man leading the donkeys would be holding a bunch of Sudanese grass to ensure that the first donkey stayed on track. At times, all of them would stop walking and stand in the middle of the road, thinking about their donkey lives.

Pappu was happy to get a larger area for farming. He stretched his skeletal body and climbed the hilltop several times. He hired labourers and started planting rubber trees in right earnest. At night, he stayed in a half-thatched shed and during the day, under the scorching sun. Both were equally comfortable for him.

"I found water," he wrote a letter to Thobias one day. "It is a small outlet, but we can survive and you can quit your job in another few years."

"You are committing a crime, exploiting the remaining blood of Pappu," Amma was angry about the project from the start.

"He himself suggested it and agreed to do the hard work," Thobias tried to evade responsibility.

"That is because of his love for you. He did not earn anything for you and is trying to do something now with his sweat." Thobias decided to end the project.

"We will stop it," Thobias suggested. "You are working too hard for me." But Pappu was not ready for an early exit as he had made a lot of efforts with the borrowed money. He had planted a lot of dreams along with the rubber saplings.

"My life was full of failures; I don't mind adding one more," Pappu said from his heart. "I thought you would appreciate my hard work. Instead, you are telling me to get out from there.

"I toiled because of my love for you, Thobias. I imagined the number of trips you made to the peak of that mountain. It gave me the power to crawl, stretching my body." Pappu was nearly in tears. Thobias took time to understand the difference between who he loved and who loved him.

"It was for different reasons. I can't take the blame for spoiling your health further," Thobias pleaded.

"What about my labour in our three-acre land? I was toiling there too with the same intensity, spoiling my health for all, but nobody said anything about it. Then why are all bothering about me now?" Thobias had no answer.

"You do not know the love that a farmer has for his land. I started loving those barren hills, the discovery of water there, the wind which takes away my sweat as soon as it comes out and the scenic beauty far away from the crowd." Tears rolled down his reddish eyes and flowed all the way down to his lungi.

"But, you are exerting yourself too much and it can ruin you; all because of me," Thobias persisted.

"Maybe," Pappu said. "After all, a short useful life is better than a long useless life."

"I have decided to sell it off to our neighbour," Thobias was firm.

"You too are defeating me?" Pappu folded his hands before Thobias as if he were praying.

It was a sleepless night for Thobias, Pappu and the land. Fire engulfed the entire estate; all the innocent rubber saplings so loved by Pappu turned black and the partially thatched shed disappeared into thin air.

"I am innocent," said the neighbour. "I do not know how the fire broke out. Anyhow, I cannot give you the agreed price now. I can give half the value of it." The neighbour smiled.

"It can be a curse. I heard that you're selling it against the wishes of your father," the neighbour tried to discover the cause of the fire.

Pappu might have lived for a few more years and enjoyed the much postponed *living*, had Thobias not ventured into this enterprise.

Thobias never expected Pappu's eternal journey that fast. He always thought that there was time to live and time to attend to him. He was ready to fulfil his dream; his dream of walking through the roads of Panamkara holding the hands of Thobias Mathai, permitting the innocent rural folk of Panamkara to generate sufficient envy.

But Pappu was sure that it was not going to happen. It came as a dream to him in the early morning of an ordinary day.

"Thobias, I saw a dream today. I was looking for fish in the big canal on the east end of the paddy field. I could not catch any of them even when a lot of fish were moving very close to me, occasionally flipping in the air. I was there for many days, till one day when I noticed that the canal was dry and fish were freely available for picking. However, I found that I had aged and my hands were unable to move like my legs. It was a morning dream and may come true." It did.

Thobias had no explanation for Pappu's sufferings in this world. After these intense sufferings, God may want to ease his entry into heaven. But Thobias was not sure why God has concentrated so much on this skeletal Pappu of Panamkara. Maybe God's list was very long and need not be revealed to an ordinary man like Thobias.

In a way, he was lucky. He had lost many of his brain cells in the frontal area before the start of the senile phase. It was not possible for him to connect to the past. He would easily forget the hard work he had put in to bring up a bunch of thankless children. He could not remember the smell of the sweat that came out of his body while trying to feed those mouths. But the loss of memory did not go well with the polished generation. The half doctor in Thobias diagnosed him a lunatic. He was kind enough to take him to a lunatic asylum for a check up.

"I wish your children do not do this to you," Pappu told Thobias when he saw the hospital board through the thin layer of casuarina trees. Thobias also understood that the patients there were a happy lot and Pappu could not fit in with them.

"His frontal cells are gone due to hard labour. Give him a bit of love and care, and don't bring loved ones to such places that fast," the doctor advised.

Thobias started pulling out the shrubs that were covering the dusty slab of the tomb and almost completed the cleaning work.

Suddenly it came as a flash in Thobias' mind, and hence it must be correct. Thobias understood why Pappu had led a torturous life. It was due to the acceptance of his own prayers.

"Oh, God," he used to pray daily, "give my children a better life than you gave me."

He was not aware of the inability of God to give a better life to all his ten children. At the same time, God was compelled to respond to the melting prayers coming from the loving heart of a father. God kept the relativity. He gave additional sufferings to Pappu and the children's lives were better than that.

The last touching discussion Thobias had with him was about his departure.

"Thobias," he said, "you're middle-aged now. It is a dog's life; aged parents on one side, grown up kids and wife on another side, the employer and the pressure of work on another side and your own personal ambitions on yet another side. I will try to give you a reprieve from one side at the earliest." And he kept his word.

A few tears trickled down Thobias' face and they too contributed to cleaning the granite top. The final touch was not possible without water. Thobias knocked on the door of the parish office and a boy gave him a bucket and showed him the water tap. With three washes, the tomb became the cleanest in the cemetery.

"I did not get you," said the vicar, who was in the office when Thobias knocked on the office door to return the bucket.

"I am the son of Pappu, the second one," his address was the same everywhere.

"I have never seen you in this parish so far." There was an element of complaint.

"I was not here. I was in the USA," Thobias replied humbly.

"Settled at?" Father was expecting an additional family to the parish.

"Not yet settled. Want to settle here." Thobias pointed towards the tomb.

"Where? In the cemetery?" A smile appeared on the vicar's face.

"Come inside," the vicar liked the conversation. "I saw you sitting on that tomb for long." The priest looked at Thobias, trying to discover the inner turmoil within him.

"I am serious, Father. I want to be in that tomb when I die," Thobias was categorical.

"You are ten children? Right? And five are boys? Suppose all the children want to be with the parents and their wives and kids too want to be with their husbands and fathers, we may not get time to close the tomb," Father reduced the gravity of the air with a joke.

"I have not applied my mind that far. But I want to be there," Thobias revealed his attachment.

"It's not very important as to where your body stays after death. What matters is the soul," Father tried to lead Thobias to a point where he was proficient.

"It matters to me, Father. We were friends and probably he was the only person who loved me without expecting anything. I came here only to lie with him after my end," Thobias was sure about it. He was also thinking that the Father would be impressed with that attachment.

"Ha, ha," he was not impressed at all. "When he was alive, how many days did you stay with him?" It was a hard question and Thobias sat on the wooden chair without permission, without any reply.

"It's natural to think about the good deeds of the loved ones when they depart. You need not be an exception. All the skeletons lying down under there belong to people like Pappu. Some were even more laborious, but still died in poverty. Many could not make a tomb, but that does not mean that they are less affectionate to their departed ones." Thobias liked the mature advice from the priest.

Thobias knew that many became unknowns while toiling to meet both ends. Their feelings went unnoticed and unreciprocated.

"I appreciate your love for him," Father was guessing Thobias' thoughts. "There are some underneath, who are not remembered by their kin. Their stories are never told, and maybe, they were without any stories. That was the generation that went by, just toiled in this area and brought up people like you and vanished from the scene, unknown and unheard." Father stopped for a moment.

"Be happy if somebody tells your son something like this, later. This is the game of life. Take it lightly and believe in God; He has got a plan for all," he summed up.

"Thanks," Thobias nodded and stood up.

"Wait a minute. This is a poor church. You too can contribute to our renovation fund." Father smiled hesitantly.

"Sure, I will." Thobias moved towards the door.

"Your mind is highly agitated." Father accompanied him to the door. Thobias stood there for a moment expecting to hear something more. Father was silent but smilingly came closer and put his right arm over his shoulders and whispered, "I will pray for you."

11

THOBIAS STARTED FACING THE MONOTONY of nothingness soon after the euphoria of revisiting his childhood ended.

He confined himself to the upstairs room, watching the road and the vehicles that carried busy people to their destinations. He kept the vernacular newspaper in his hand, occasionally glancing through its seventh page, listing those souls who had departed this beautiful earth during its last rotation.

It was around noon, the musical note of the calling bell signalled a visitor.

"I have to talk to you on behalf of Marcardia State Investigation Bureau," a well-built man in his early forties extended his identity card to Thobias. There was a hidden air of authority behind the polished introduction.

Marcardia was a large country in the tropics, where the heat and dust varied from place to place like its people, gods, flora and fauna. Still they were together, because the founders gave democracy and freedom of speech to its people.

Democracy in Marcardia was very vibrant. One could see its vibrations everywhere. Even the hands of their citizens would be vibrating in the air like a steel rod when stuck at the loose end. The vibrations ensured that they always got a government which they deserved.

Freedom of expression was also given to them. It was a feeling that one could speak the truth, at least till the damaging truth reached a few metres away from the powerful man who was responsible for making somebody tell the truth.

In Marcardia, the people in general didn't mind suffering to any extent, and that too without any complaint. This norm was established over a long period, starting from ancient local rulers, carried over by the local invaders and later followed by the white rulers who came there after crossing many seas.

This norm was maintained later under its own brown rulers. There were many reasons for this. The country did not have any agency of repute to listen to its citizens' complaints. Even if a complaint was made to its ruler, nothing came of it. Hence, they did not waste their time making complaints. A number of people used to complain loudly about nothing in particular. Their complaints confused the situation in the thickly populated country. All were eligible to complain and nobody on earth could solve their problems. God was the only soothing agent that could reduce their blood pressure. God listened to their complaints in silence. It was a big relief for its citizens and they became very religious.

Even the founders were aware that they could not make their citizens happy. Hence, they did not include the Right to the Pursuit of Happiness as a fundamental right in their Constitution, as in some developed countries. Pursuing happiness was considered more or less a sin, like making money. One had to be neutral; neither happy nor sad. That was the accepted norm. Happiness was measured in a negative scale, and if life went by without many sufferings, it was considered a great life.

The common people were highly religious and generally pious except in cases which affected them. Family relations were much admired and valued over generations, and it had created good citizens for their country.

Although the Right to Happiness was not enshrined in its constitution, the people of Marcardia were a happy lot. Happiness came to them easily. They were happy when electricity cut was reduced from five hours to four hours. They were happy when the municipality picked up the waste after two days instead of three days. They were happy when the delayed train finally arrived trembling on to the platform. Imagine their happiness when a seat that they had reserved was finally vacated by the intruder. They got the same intense happiness when they reached their destination without an accident.

They were equally happy when they get out of a traffic jam a few minutes earlier than usual. They were happy when the death toll in a flood was lesser than that in earlier years. They were happy when the drought spared human lives, even if it spoiled the crops. They were happy when they foud the government *babu* in the office seat, even though he did not accept their application for their family pension. They were happy when they found the correct person to pay the bribe, and their happiness was unfathomable when they got a discount on the bribe rate.

They were happy when the petrol price was reduced by one Lian just after it had been hiked up by five Lians. They were happy when leaders begged them for votes. They were happy when they heard about their promises for the future. They were happy when political parties ordered *bandhs,* bringing everything to a standstill, exactly like the unexpected holiday they received when their not-so-beloved leaders departed this world, requiring them to mourn their passing.

But there were a lot of things which could make them unhappy easily. The nation wept when their cricket hero missed his century by giving a simple catch at leg side, as had happened the last time. They murmured and cursed when asked to stand in queue, instead of exhibiting their muscle power to get into the bus. Don't tell them to switch off their loudspeakers at midnight. They know that it is the best time to pray loudly to wake up the sleeping gods.

People of Marcardia are known by designations instead of names. Those who do not chase designations are called common men. Honesty is widespread among them. Others live on borrowed honesty and some even without that.

Southern Marcardians prefer to study well and work hard under somebody, without taking risks. They lead a disciplined life attached to their families and peer groups, especially if they are living outside their home state. The phenomenon of working away from home had strengthened family bonds, as family reunions were short and each moment was used to please the other. Northern Marcardians, on the other hand, were risk takers and enjoyed making money rather than working under somebody.

Unlawful corruption was never tolerated in Marcardia. There were certain rules in place to ensure lawful corruption. One had to know them thoroughly, or had to engage an expert who exclusively dealt with corruption. It was a cat-and-mouse game, and there were various agencies to catch the corrupt, if the level of corruption fell below a prescribed standard. There were also sufficient laws to protect the corrupt, and ensure that the dignity of corruption was maintained.

They got their independence from the minority white rulers, who made laws for the people in return for the tax paid by the citizens. The tax was not a tiny sum. The citizens paid it after toiling in the dusty fields and tightening their belts over their flat stomachs. The rulers enjoyed it and imagined things for them. They were more imaginative than their citizens, because they got time to imagine things. They even imagined a situation where the state had a responsibility towards the citizens.

They also tried to convert the citizens to their way of reaching heaven, to compensate for the hellish life they let them live in Marcardia. The people at large were not against accepting one more God to reach heaven. But the new religion did not formulate a hierarchical system to replace the existing one. People in general never liked equality, as they felt that they were inferior to their neighbour.

Politics was the largest industry in Marcardia, employing and providing livelihood to millions and still counting. Parties were numerous, and newer parties could be formed at any time if the booty was not evenly distributed among the functionaries. Each party had numerous posts and committees, at the national, regional, state, district, taluka, panchayat, village and family levels. All party members had to live with the meagre income they earned from serving others. Hence, corruption had to be allowed. A person who did not get the chance to indulge in corruption would be constantly accusing the other of being corrupt, till he attained the ruling chair and became corrupt himself.

The nation progressed well under its visionary first ruler, who selected a mixed path to progress. The notes printed at that time were mainly used for building knowledge centres, dams, big industries, and institutions of repute. Later, the country turned a bit to the left and concentrated on equal distribution of poverty. Now they are experimenting with fair concentration of wealth.

An election was the national festival of Marcardia. However the intensity of celebration was more at the lower strata of society, since they had higher hopes than those in the upper strata. During this period, they were pampered and treated to promises about the future. They also understood the biggest secret of democracy: that all parties are good and are eligible to get votes.

Various methods were used to please the electorate of Marcardia. One had to exercise one's imagination and promise solutions and projects. The person who promised the maximum got elected, and ruled over those who were incapable of making false promises.

The elected leader often converted the promises to foundation laying ceremonies and inaugurations and travelled the length and breadth of Marcardia. Inaugural ceremonies were not so easy to organise. One had to make arrangements for mammoth crowds by bringing party workers in trucks and buses after collecting donations from work contractors, liquor dealers, moneylenders, sand smugglers, unlawful spirit dealers and without paying for the hired vehicles. Then they errect a big dais to house the entire Who's Who of the area, seating them front-to-back in the order of hierarchy. There will be a sound system, which can withstand the fiery speeches. The names of the people on the dais will be engraved on a marble stone, which is expected to convey this message to generation after generation. The decorated cloth over the marble stone will be removed in the official ceremony, giving the people a permanent record of the hierarchy of the people present on the dais.

The stone would stay in place for some time as a symbol of hope for the people, and would be used for tying the cows, till it got covered by grasses and later by bushes and then by trees.

Intelligent voters remember next time to vote for the new candidate who promises yet another set of projects, to get the act repeated all over again, with better foundation stones and another list of VIPs, engraved in better style.

In between, a few good things also happened as a matter of course, which rekindled hope and allowed the people to dream of a better Marcardia.

The Government was busy with business in the initial years, reserving and promoting sector by sector. Luckily, they forgot to promote the new sectors that came up after writing the sector list, permitting them uninhibited growth, helping Marcardians to discover their capabilities.

After the success stories, they started permitting more than one agency to provide telephone, electricity and flight services, giving the people a chance to reject the worst. However, such a luxury was yet to be permitted in the case of policing and government services. There was still only one municipality, one corporation, one government and one police and the people had no option but to suffer under them. The police was the visible symbol of the state for most of the people. And they effectively prevented the wrath of the people from reaching the rulers.

There were many big cities in Marcardia. In some big cities, ruling was subcontracted to dons, without bothering about the ward bifurcation or jurisdiction of the police stations. These dons dispensed justice faster, and sometimes even cheaper. In the interior parts of Marcardia too, the ruling was outsourced without any governing expenses.

The police was a very useful force. It was like God for many. It used to be a point of reference for the weaker lot to threaten and escape. Others allowed them to escape when the name of the police was uttered, even when they knew that the police were their own men. They also knew that dealing with their own men was often costlier when the cost benefit analysis was done.

Law and order was maintained satisfactorily by a few full-time politicians, part-time liquor vendors, full-time toddy drinkers, part-time money lenders and a few people who were blessed by God. A few in uniform performed their duty by day in the cities. The robbers and petty thieves did theirs at night, taking care of the vacant and semi-vacant houses in remote areas.

Thobias had worked in the *Hartal* state of southern Marcardia during most of his Smile Bank service period. The state was named thus after its famous celebration, '*hartal*'. This festival was a celebration against the evil happening in the world. A group of people, representing the evil, would show up with *lathis,* swords, knives and stones, blocking the highways, threatening the pedestrians, smashing vehicles and closing the shops. Their sacred drama would be protected by a battalion of armed police, who also moved with the *hartalites*.

The common man celebrated the festival with a bottle of rum and tandoori chicken over a game of cards. It was not due to disrespect to this sacred ritual. They were a tired lot, tired of running to escape from the suffocating embrace of the people who preached from holy books on the one hand and from *Das Capital* on the other.

The drama went on till the sun got hotter. This symbolic act helped the world to move on the right track. The Americans withdrew from Vietnam on the third day after the celebration of a *hartal*. They did the same from Kuwait immediately after another *hartal*. The crude price went down by half in the international market when a *hartal* was celebrated in its full gaiety.

There were certain rules to ensure that the festival was celebrated in the right spirit. Only political parties could order its celebration. The parties had to have a president, a secretary, a treasurer, a minimum of one hundred followers and a flagt. The participants and police could remain the same.

Thobias joined Smile Bank and Investments at a time when Marcardia did not have many job opportunities and its economy was measured in terms of poverty slabs. It was one of the very rewarding jobs at that time. It was difficult to separate life from a bank job in Marcardia. It was one and the same, and if ever differentiated, one's job was far more important than life. There was a continuous increase in salary based on the official inflation index. A bit more would be added to it every five years, to take care of the black money inflation. This ensured that one was at the same place in terms of relative standard of living.

"I am here to ascertain your present address and to hand over the acknowledgement for the impounded passport," the visitor expressed his displeasure at the long silence of Thobias.

"I would like to know the reason for the impounding," Thobias was eager to know.

"There is a serious case pending against you. I do not know the exact nature of the case." He did not reveal the details.

"Case? I'd like to know about it." Thobias could not believe that there could be a case against him initiated by his erstwhile employer. Thobias was a meticulous, sincere and hard working employee in those days and a lot of his superiors had even issued certificates for that.

"I do not know much about it. You were working in Smile Bank twenty years ago?"

"Yes."

"They've filed a case against you. Mr. Tejaram is the investigating officer. He will tell you about it in detail. The passport will be with him," the visitor readied himself to leave the house.

"Was it filed recently?" Thobias enquired. "Or twenty years ago?"

"I do not know exactly. I only know that the case is a very serious one; otherwise your entry would not have been detected that fast and Mr. Tejaram would not have been entrusted with this case. He is a very senior officer and attends only serious ones." That was a good description about Tejaram.

"If serious, why didn't you pursue it when I was in the USA?" That was a genuine doubt from Thobias.

"It was difficult, Sir." He was defensive. "We have to prove a case to seek deportation from the US. Now you are here and you have to prove your innocence to escape punishment. This route is much easier, because we have got a treaty with your country."

"Can I get the phone number of Mr. Tejaram, just to know the details of the case?"

"Ha, ha. No way."

The visitor went out closing the gate behind him, and his blue car took a westward journey. Thobias was left confused, and he sat brooding over the possible errors that could have happened during his service there.

12

"I CAN'T UNDERSTAND why the bank is after you," Amma showed her irritation and avoided Thobias' eyes. She always avoided eye contact whenever answers were not expected.

"This is normal with Smile Bank; one need not do any mistake to be under investigation," Thobias educated her. "An upbringing problem is also there. Pappu advised us to keep the vertebral column intact at ninety degrees. But Smile Bank never liked that body part even if the degree of inclination was far less. Naturally, there might be some problems here and there." There was an air of disappointment.

Thobias decided to visit the Smile Bank headquarters in Marcardia to know about the case. Escaping punishment was not very important, as the pace of Marcardian law delivery would not overtake the remaining lifespan of Thobias. At times, it even took the full lifetime of a healthy individual. But if some false charges are later proved in absentia, it might create news and Theresa and the kids would have to live in society with that stigma, if they ever returned.

Thobias withdrew to his room and sat before a solitaire game on the computer to divert his mind. But it was not an easy task and the computer took the opportunity to defeat him continuously until he switched it off.

Joining Smile Bank and Investments was a proud moment in Thobias' life. It was a plum job at that time, with an enviable pay. It improved his life and took Pappu's dreams to a higher level.

The working environment was very good. There was full freedom to improve the business. Thobias was full of energy and enthusiasm to excel, to serve the poor, and to run around and canvass business. His immediate boss, Murugendran, was very happy to get a good officer.

Ravikiran was his close colleague in those days. He had joined Smile Bank fifteen years earlier and believed in working as per the rules.

"You know, Thobias," Ravikiran once tried to educate him "Smile Bank is a big hollow cylinder. You can put anything into it but you won't get anything back. Don't exert much. Salary will be the same for you and me." He winked his right eye and laughed loudly without bothering about the sanctity of the office.

"You carry on," he continued. "It takes time to understand things. Whatever be your efforts, the profit will be transferred to the Head Office at year-end and you will get a smile extra. A few files will remain with them, to catch you at a later date if anything goes bad. At that time, nobody sees how much profit you made for getting that extra smile."

"I am getting paid handsomely and my duty is to work in the best way possible," Thobias did not like the advice.

"Don't forget to live." That was the last bit of advice from Ravikiran.

Newfound status, social acceptability and a circle of influential friends, all opened new horizons for the gullible Thobias.

Pappu had cautioned Thobias once, "I loved you from the day you came to this world. And I wanted nothing back from you. All your friends became friends after you became you. And they will remain friends as long as you remain useful to them. When you find it difficult to get a sincere friend, you will remember me. I may not be there at that time."

"You've stopped searching for a new job?" Ravikiran asked once. "You have got the capacity. I've become old and nobody wants me now. You know frog's behaviour?"

"If it's put into cold water which is gently heated, it will enjoy the warmth. It will not know the water is getting hotter and it is going to boil. It will always be in a state of indecisiveness whether to escape or not. Finally, it dies when the water boils. But you know what happens if you put the frog into hot water?"

"It escapes?"

"Exactly. It jumps out and lives longer." But the story did not impress Thobias as he was determined to work hard and go up the ladder.

"Management is an art and science," the middle-aged Murugendran taught the enthusiastic young officer who was impatient to study lessons one after another. "You want to see the live demonstration of a man-management technique? Watch the next staff meeting of our branch." It was an offer without any request.

The branch had a total staff of thirty and all were very obedient except for the typist, Josean. He was a postgraduate in economics with a sharp brain. He knew the rule book by heart and it was very difficult to extract additional work from him.

"Look, Thobias, your scholar friend is working at the counter today." The Manager winked.

"Yeah! I too was wondering what had happened to him," Thobias became curious.

"I promised him the cash department in the next job rotation after a satisfactory working at the counter," Murugendran explained the nature of the carrot he had dangled in front of the typist. The cashier got special allowances and all the clerks were eager to get that duty.

"But a typist is not eligible for that," Thobias opened the rule book, "and others will object to it."

"That's why I asked you to watch the next staff meeting," Murugendran straightened his posture and expanded his chest with an eerie smile. "Now he will ask for cashier duty from the next month in the staff meeting."

The day came and the staff meeting started at 4 o'clock in the banking hall. The Manager took a very serious posture, unshaven and devoid of any warmth as if he were ill. At the meeting, the Manager talked first about the branch in general, business position, shortcomings of the branch and the role of employees in business growth. Then, he permitted the open forum.

It was Josean who stood up first with a white piece of paper in his hand, looking into it again and again so as not to leave out any point while reading. He wanted to make sure that he used the best words. But something happened in between.

"Aow, oh, aow . . . ." The cry was from the Manager, Murugendran. He was struggling to breathe and was keeping his hands close to his chest.

"What happened?" Thobias rushed to him and carried his weight while he was about to fall from the chair in acute pain.

"Take me to the hospital," he said, crying.

Thobias literally carried him to an autorickshaw while the others watched sadly. The meeting ended without any official announcement. And the staff resumed their work.

"We will have some refreshments at my house," Murugendran winked and smiled at Thobias as soon as the rickshaw crossed the main junction a few meters away from the branch. Thobias could not understand the logic behind going home after such a massive heart attack.

"What about your pain?" Thobias could not believe that he had recovered as soon as he left the office.

"If anybody cross-checks, tell them that we had gone to Vinaya hospital. I have already told Dr. Elias to make an entry in the hospital register," Murugendran said. Thobias learned a good lesson in management on that day without any fee.

"Today you have silenced him with superb acting. Suppose he comes with his points again. What acting will you do then?" That was the only doubt Thobias had in the practical lesson.

"The next staff meeting will be after two months on a day when he is on leave. At the meetings thereafter, this will be an old subject, and the emotions attached to it will thin off. Without carrots, it is difficult to get work done. There will be a lot of unfulfilled promises made by Managers. That is why Smile Bank transfers the Managers every three years to install a new face, with a new set of promises." That was the theory part of the practical session.

Thobias could not study further lessons from Murugendran. Smile Bank was taking over Money Bank, and to help this takeover, it was in need of energetic and enthusiastic volunteers.

The carrot offered this time was very big. "For each year you work in Money Bank, you will get additional half year seniority," the white-coloured internal circular of Smile Bank announced.

It was an irresistible offer for Thobias. All promotions and placements were based on seniority in Smile Bank. Thobias filled in the option form with a shivering hand and sent it by registered post to ensure that it was not lost in the mail.

"Only very capable officers are selected for this takeover assignment. The task ahead of you is not an easy one. You have to forget your life for another three years. You are getting additional seniority and when you overtake me, don't teach me management lessons," Murugendran joked half heartedly, and wished him good luck for the new assignment.

Thobias jumped into the train bogey, which carried him to the Money Bank branch at Unar. Even while he was travelling, he was getting a second of additional seniority for every two seconds travelled.

Thobias forgot to inform Pappu about the transfer to a very distant place with an unfamiliar language. It was not exactly forgetfulness. Thobias could not risk a negative suggestion for the very intelligent choice he had taken.

"You did a wonderful job here, and I am proud of your achievements!" Assistant Principal Manager Mr. Bachaloran patted Thobias on his back, after the three-year term at Unar. "You are very young and have already overtaken hundreds of your fellow officers. Now the sky is the limit for you. We have got a special offer for you. If you stay one more year, you can get another four months additional seniority. This offer is only for the selected few to help them to come on top, to enable the succession plan of Smile Bank."

"My parents are waiting for my return," Thobias was reluctant for another year of stay.

"Opportunity never knocks twice on your door. You have to choose between your parents and the glorious life awaiting you in Smile Bank." Thobias chose the latter and continued the same life, though it was not eligible to be called such a respectable title as 'life'.

Life was not different, when Thobias returned to a place near Cohiana.

"Welcome, dear performer!" The APM at the new place, Mr. Dilkhush, smiled nicely. "I am happy that you are posted here. We were looking for an energetic young man to open a new NRI branch. Even though market conditions are tough, it's a small job for you. Our interest rates are a bit low compared to those of other banks. It can adversely affect your deposit growth. We have got some software problems too. Only you can take up both these challenges. We give lucrative foreign posting to performers after these types of assignments," the APM inflated his ego and Thobias moved southwards crossing a few districts of Marcardia, again without telling Pappu.

This time, his wife and kids too were to be taken along. It was a hindrance for one who aimed high. Thobias tried to persuade them to stay with his father-in-law, who was leading a comfortable retired life. But Theresa, alongwith the kids, joined him with a wild explanation that it is better to live with one's husband than one's father. It was a distraction for his career. However, there was no escape either. Marriage is forever, surpassing the jurisdiction of planet earth and carried over from birth to rebirths.

"What a great job, Thobias Mathai!" APM Mr. Dilkhush finally caught up with reality and was struggling for words to congratulate the Man of the Region. "I'm under transfer to Rulers city. I have recommended your name for foreign posting. But I know it is difficult because there are many performers this year. See you some time in life, somewhere." He avoided direct eye contact with Thobias. Instead, he looked far above him to the sky, counting the number of crows that came to teach a young one flying. He was unhappy about his workload that only one APM was available to teach Thobias Mathai the entire gamut of business ethics of Smile Bank.

"I can't avoid giving you another challenging assignment," Mr. Dilkhush expressed one of his major inabilities of life.

"Yes, Sir," Thobias was all eyes and ears.

"Our aim is to serve the people. There is a place called Kakkadam where people do not have electricity, water or roads. We want to open a branch there and show to the country our commitment to rural people. Anyhow, you are going to the top of the ladder and it is better to experience the pulse of rural Marcardia. This can come handy in discharging your duties towards the great nation of Marcardia."

"The only difficulty is that," the APM continued, "you have to walk about twenty kilometres to reach that place from the nearest bus stop. But the air there won't be polluted and the water is as pure as tears. Sleeping in the open air can give you a big thrill that you won't forget."

There was no time for Thobias to think about his life for the next three years. They just vanished leaving behind a few Lians, as there was no avenue to spend it except for a petty shop and an illicit liquor outlet a few metres away from it, which opened when the sun closed its watchful eyes.

A knock on the door disturbed Thobias from the revisit to his enthusiastic days.

"Amma was asking why you are not having dinner," Teena passed on the message and left without waiting for his response.

13

THOBIAS, IN HIS POOR HEALTH, was hesitant to make a long and lonely trip to Marcardia. That was why he requested Rajan to be with him on his trip to Trivania, where the headquarters of Smile Bank was situated.

"Suppose something happens to me, just read this small file," Thobias showed Rajan a thin file with a red cover from his suitcase.

"What can happen to us on this journey?" Rajan was not amused at the instruction.

"Nothing, nothing at all. Just a small precaution," Thobias eased his friend's anxiety.

"Here is a Smile Bank branch," Rajan pointed towards a blue board on the first floor of a building on the busy S.R. Road, soon after they crossed the border and entered the great country of Marcardia.

"This one is open at late night!" Rajan exclaimed. It was new to him.

"It's a norm fixed by someone and enforced later by the management. Nobody dared to break it," Thobias clarified.

"Did you get allowance for that?" Rajan asked naively.

"Ha, ha! Forget about it in Smile Bank; instead, it exposes you to more work, more errors and more punishments." Rajan did not follow the short explanation and Thobias was not ready to remember a sad part of his life on such a good evening.

"It won't happen in our area. Our farm labourers are very clever; they always want to work less for their wages. It's a tough time managing them." Rajan was an experienced agriculturist. "I can't imagine people sitting late and increasing their workload and risk without any additional benefit."

"It is made possible through *asinisation*."

"*Asinisation*? I'm hearing this word for the first time."

"It's a word coined by a friend of mine to illustrate how an officer could be made to work like an ass," Thobias remembered the classes of Velevendran. "It works by utilising an innate human weakness and is beautifully crafted over a period, researched and improved by the best brains, and practised by employers the world over."

"See the donkeys in the milling stone. Their eyes will be blindfolded and will be tied to the long pole of the crushing mill. They move round and round crushing the oil seeds, as long as they get food and water. At the end, they will be auctioned for their skin," he illustrated further.

"But in a big bank like this all must be educated and must have good brains to escape what you call . . . ." Rajan wondered how his brilliant classmate could be asinised.

"Anybody can be asinised by better brains," Thobias laughed. "Nobody recognises it as long as he is inside the system."

"I do not get you," Rajan revealed the capacity of his grey matter.

"Everybody thinks that they deserve a better life than others," Thobias tried to explain human nature. "Institutions sell it in the form of ambition."

"What ambition is there in a bank?" Rajan was ignorant about the hierarchy inside the bank and it was immaterial to him as long as his loan was passed before the onset of monsoon.

"Who sits on which chair is important for an insider. Like a game of musical chairs. The number of chairs will be limited and the eligible people will be running around them, and in this running, Smile Bank gets its work done. There are many types of ambitions; ambitions for recognition, for promotion, for gifts and bribes, for making others listen to you, for giving orders, for getting an air-conditioned cabin, for ensuring that others stand up when you arrive, for getting saluted by an armed guard, for getting a pretty lady secretary, or a chauffeur driven car . . . Oh! The list is endless, my friend. The main part of asinisation is identifying the ambition in an individual and selling it to him," Thobias stopped for a moment, to allow Rajan to catch up with him.

"We will stop here and eat something," Rajan pointed to a hotel.

"The next part of asinisation," Thobias continued after ordering two pegs of vodka and *parotta* with chicken curry, "is effective utilisation of the ego."

"All have got ego," Rajan commented casually, while adding lime cordial and soda to his drink.

"True," Thobias watched the gas bubbles rising from the bottom of the glass, expanding on the way, and finally bursting at the top. "But you know your limitations and settle down to it, whereas a big institution shows you a very big world and makes you look at persons sitting in plush cabins giving orders. Naturally, one wishes to become like that. You will be on the run thereafter, with fire in the abdomen, crossing targets after targets, forgetting loved ones, skipping marriage anniversaries and birthday celebrations, avoiding funerals and everything personal, till you understand that the chase was a mirage. By that time, you will be ripe for the next world and you will be hesitant to reveal the foolishness even to your loved ones." Thobias paused for a moment looking at his friend who was expressionless.

"I don't get you, Thobias," Rajan looked into the eyes of Thobias. "You've changed a lot since we met last time."

"I was a happy donkey at that time," Thobias laughed. "Donkeys are not unhappy till they see something better than Sudanese grass."

"You are talking big things that a farmer like me cannot understand," Rajan said, while negotiating with the chicken leg.

"Then I will tell you a story told by a farmer called Pappu," Thobias laughed.

"Once all the birds came to Solomon the Wise, to settle their dispute as to who was the king of birds. The crow put forward its points loudly.

"'We have the largest population on earth; we follow a meticulous time table of getting up in the morning and going home at night; ours is an unenviable social life of helping each other in distress, and . . .'

"'Good!' King Solomon intervened and stopped the crow from further explanations.

"'You are the king of birds,' he proclaimed much to the chagrin of others who didn't even get a chance to explain their virtues. 'Take this crown.' The king decorated the crow with a golden crown.

"The crow started flying with the heavy crown on its head, above all other birds, without rest. It forgot to collect food and did not like to come down to earth even to drink water. After three days of flying, it came down from the air as a dead body."

"I understood it. But can you swear that you have never worn such crowns in your life?" Rajan took a snipe at Thobias.

Both of them laughed together.

Thobias watched the city lights till the car stopped in front of a big hotel. Rajan bent to his right side to view it. "Hotel Feelings," he read out its name.

"You can see the entire city of Trivania from its top," Thobias introduced the hotel to Rajan. "And the Headquarters of Smile Bank is just opposite to it."

"I want a room with a view," Thobias told the pretty receptionist.

"View what?" The receptionist did not like the unspecific request.

"View of Smile Bank building," Thobias was sure about what he wanted.

"You are from the police?" she asked respectfully.

"Oh, no," Thobias understood his mistake.

"I thought you were investigating a case and want to look at the building at night," she teased.

"No, no. I am on the other side; chased by them," Thobias said before entering the lift along with Rajan and the room boy.

14

THOBIAS WATCHED Smile Bank's emblem, neatly set in brass, illuminated by two spotlights. Earlier the emblem was an arrow pointed upwards. The change of emblem and motto became a hot issue among the staff and the public because the earlier one was more meaningful. The reason was later explained to Thobias by Mr. Pannaverse, the leader of the Revolutionary Association of Smile Bank and a member of the Board of Directors.

"This emblem does not represent us in this era of competition," Mr. Bahulian, one of the eight directors of the board, said during the Balance Sheet finalisation meeting of Smile Bank. He was a government nominee and a prawn exporter from Cohiana. He was also the classmate of the Assistant Minister of Finance, Marcardia. He was not sure about the imaginary calculations and predictions of the balance sheet, and slipped into a doze after a heavy lunch with fried prawns which was his weakness. He wanted to somehow impress the forum, as it was his first meeting.

"We have to give a strong message to the public that they are welcome, whatever be our preoccupation. Also, the present emblem does not represent smile anywhere."

"The emblem should convey a strong meaning. Your suggestions are welcome," Principal Manager, Mr. Vadivelu Rao, was very happy about the suggestion from the government nominee. He supported the move immediately by calling a meeting of the intellectuals of Smile Bank.

"We will entrust an agency to suggest something in modern art," a young Deputy Principal Manager in the second row from back, who was sure about his high IQ, made the first suggestion.

"Who will understand modern art? Those with that much IQ have got better banks to go to," remarked Mr. Vadivelu Rao, maybe to make the DPM understand his ignorance level, and the entire group laughed.

"I suggest a donkey as the emblem." The voice came from the back of the audience. He was familiar with the nature of a donkey and put his head down to avoid being detected.

"Other animals have already been taken as emblems by other banks. If we are fast enough, we can get this animal at least," the Vice Principal Manager Mr. Actoriose brought to the attention of the meeting the shortage of animals in a world monopolised by humans. He was not seeing eye to eye with Vadivelu Rao because that undependable boss had written some bitter truth in his confidential file that cost him a promotion as Principal Manager and a posting in Bank of Paradise, spoiling his chance to make it a bank of hell. It was meant as a joke. Still, nobody laughed because Vadivelu Rao did not laugh.

It was not because there was nothing to laugh in it. In Marcardia, nobody laughs when the boss is not laughing, and conversely everybody should laugh when the boss laughs even if there is nothing to laughin it. Laughing illustrates the hierarchy to an outsider. The superiors are not expected to laugh at the jokes of juniors, but the reverse is compulsory if one is particular about a peaceful life in the institution.

"I know an advertising agency," Vadivelu said. "They can design the emblem at a cheap rate of 100 million Lians." Lian was the currency of Marcardia and Vadivelu was aware of the exact rate for art work.

"Hundred million Lians?" the junior Assistant Principal Manager could not hide his surprise.

"You do not know the value of art in the present world. We got this cheap rate because the crucial man there is a friend of mine and I could influence him. He will also give a suitable motto absolutely free with it," Vadivelu persisted, and nobody doubted him when he said the exact terms of the expected contract. He waited for a second for any response from the audience. It did not come. The Assistant Principal Manager recollected the sale of Picasso's work at two hundred million Lians and sat satisfied that he had made his cost consciousness known to all.

The new emblem came with a well fed donkey smiling violently, displaying four of its teeth, carrying heavy baggage on its back. The motto, *'More Weight More Fun,'* was written near the baggage area of the picture, partially covering the tail which was shown half lifted. The emblem came exactly four days after the award was signed but was kept unopened for the next seven days because Vadivelu Rao did not want the truth to come out that it was an easy job for hundred million Lians.

While handing over the cheque of hundred million Lians, Vadivelu Rao said only one sentence, "My hands are clean." The others just clapped their hands.

There was a meaningful speech from the consultant at the conference hall, which was covered by the media for the peak hour news bulletins. However, there was no live coverage on television, as Smile Bank had not given any advertisements to them that year, unlike the previous year.

"There is a big message in this motto," the consultant said. "The employees are working very hard and we are aware of their workload. They are still smiling without any complaint. This is a certificate and we can gladden those who are working day and night."

He took more than a minute to come to the next point. "Secondly, for the customer they are welcome words. He need not hesitate to request for more work because working more is fun for the staff. Thirdly, the motto is very simple and easily understandable by Smile Bank's customers and staff. Again this can be made a norm in the coming years by your Human Resource Section. If ever a protesting employee happens to be in Smile Bank, the boss can show the emblem and just ask him to imbibe the spirit of it," the consultant paused for a longer period this time, reading the faces of the members of the audience. He was sure that he had completed all the points briefed by his wife in the early morning. She had designed the emblem and the motto after visiting the nearby branch of Smile Bank at R. K. Puram to get an understanding of reality.

"But . . . ." Mr. Actoriose, who was seated next to him, stood up to poke his nose into the exclusive territory of Mr. Vadivelu.

"No *buts* here," Vadivelu Rao signalled him to sit down. "I know what you are going to say. Don't have much soft corner for them. You remember those days when our great country was moving towards the left? At that time, salary was good and the job was more respectable than now. Still, employee unions kept us on our toes. Now, we are moving rightward, mighty unions have lost their steam, became aged, unions have got multiplied and leaders are in our pockets. I am sure that there won't be any protest over this emblem and motto. See, they never protested even when we reduced their Provident Fund interest rate. I did it just to test them. This is the time to set new norms and work culture in Smile Bank." It was a whisper between them but it reached the audience as the loudspeaker was on.

"Are we to issue a tender for replacing the boards and hoardings with the new emblem?" Deputy Principal Manager Mrs. Silkiyamma meant business.

"I will inform you later. I have yet to locate a good contractor who can do these things to my satisfaction." All knew that satisfying Vadivelu Rao was not an easy job. The meeting ended there.

The contract for changing the boards and hoardings was awarded to M/s Makkal Kootam for 600 million Lians. Mr. Actoriose did not sign the order for two weeks. He was angry at Mr. Vadivelu for not taking him into confidence over the sweeter aspects of the contract.

There used to be a pact on the distribution of incentives among the who's who in a contract. The incentives were too low in the case of useful items. Mr. Actoriose would sign the contracts without asking for clarifications and without any delay. In such cases, he wouldn't even read the finer lines of the contract. Instead, he would be looking at the pretty secretary as if asking her to see the heavenly halo at the back of his head.

However, incentives were attractive if one dared and did things like the emblem change and buying useless software packages at the cost of a few more working hours for staff. On those occasions, there used to be a clear-cut understanding on incentive distribution. There would be serious whispers going on in the corners of the corridors and inside the closed cabins. Even the prettiest secretaries were not allowed to enter the cabins at that time without knocking twice.

There was a discussion on the seventh day between Vadivelu Rao and Actoriose.

"The contract is given to somebody in Marcardia politics. That's why I did not discuss it further," Vadivelu tried to pacify Actoriose.

Actoriose was not prepared to believe it. He was aware that when contracts are awarded to people in Marcardian politics, there wouldn't be any incentives but the persons who were responsible for it would be getting lucrative postings or extensions in service period which compensated them for the commission lost. Actoriose came to believe the words of his boss later, when Vadivelu Rao got posted as a director in the Banking Authority of Marcardia immediately after his retirement. The special order signed by the Assistant Minister of Finance praised the business acumen of Vadivelu Rao, and hoped the same expertise would be used in abundance for the progress of the great nation of Marcardia.

"Don't get disheartened," Vadivelu Rao again consoled his junior. "Watch the emblem closely. See the fourth tooth of the donkey. It has not come out nicely and the colour is also too dark. That's for you. You can change it when you become Principal Manager."

"I have observed more points," Actoriose was not an ordinary man. "See the boards, they do not have the name of the branch or address. I know it was left out because all parties to the contract must have been in a hurry, and also those additional words were eating into the profit margins after paying left and right."

Actoriose signed the order awarding the contract, but could not become Principal Manager because his action of holding back the contract was not viewed lightly by somebody in Marcardia Ministry.

"What are you thinking, Thobias?" Rajan was observing Thobias standing near the window and looking at the big Smile Bank building for a long time.

"Oh, nothing. I was just watching the Head Office building."

"My first visit to this office was with a complaint." Thobias turned back from the window.

"There are no complaints in love. It starts when you start hating," Rajan became a philosopher instantly. "What was the complaint like?"

"They offered additional seniority while calling for option to work in Money Bank, at the time of its takeover. I went for that and worked there for four years, running like a leopard starved for weeks together, making business grow manifold. But when I came back, I found a new agreement between Management and Revolutionary Association which completely took away seniority from the promotion process," Thobias explained the reason for his disenchantment.

"Oh, that is cheating and you should have fought it out in court," Rajan found a law point there.

"Litigation will spoil the entire life of an individual in Marcardia. Maybe the Marcardian law system was made in such a way that all must feel that obeying is far better than fighting," Thobias said, while arranging the bed.

"Still, I have great respect for big institutions. They manage thousands of their employees and make them work meticulously. We are finding it difficult to manage even a few labourers on our farm," Rajan's admiration was genuine.

Thobias did not like the eulogy Rajan made up for Smile Bank. "You practice the Smile Bank method next time on the illiterate labourers, and they will beat you up." Thobias could hear Rajan snoring.

Thobias also felt like sleeping and he did not wait further.

15

The SECOND TRIP OF THOBIAS to the Head Office was as an officer to work in the credit department. The section was located on the eighteenth floor of the building, and Prem Chandra Velevendran was in charge of it. He was short, and appeared very young if one did not look at the back of his head, where baldness made a perfect circle. His body appeared muscular and stern but closer scrutiny would reveal its flexibility, especially that of its facial muscles. It was elastic like a chewed gum that could change very fast, expressing varied emotions to suit the occasion, without other body parts knowing about them.

"You're new to administration?" Velevendran asked Thobias when he reported for duty. "This is not like a branch where you pretend to be working, do some circus and go home. Here the job is tough, because your job is to make the people in branches work."

"You can exercise the power of the big boss to extract work," Velevendran continued. He was very serious after those introductory words and Thobias could not detect the smile behind the seriousness.

It did not take more than a few days for Thobias to understand that Mr. Prem Chandra Velevendran was not an individual but an institution. He had different facets and each of them involved the management of different functions, some of them contrary to each other, but in total, the institution called Prem Chandra Velevendran was magnificently managed and would have been eligible for AAA rating by any agency of repute. Management tricks were so well studied and codified by Velevendran that he had even coined the term '*asinisation*' for the process of making employees work like asses. It was the other side of HRD.

It was an accidental meeting on a Saturday evening that changed the relationship between Thobias and Velevendran from official to unofficial. Local arrack was the cheapest liquor available in those days to celebrate lonely Saturdays. The only hitch was securing it without the notice of enlightened citizens, as there was lot of stigma attached to it. Arrack drinkers stood far down in the social hierarchy compared to those who drank other liquors.

Thobias located one arrack shop at Vashuthad in suburban Trivania, where there was a provision to enter through the backdoor, leading to a closed room. On that Saturday, he was taking the first gulp of arrack. He closed his eyes and jerked his head and shoulders to escape from the bitter taste.

Half opening his eyes, Thobias noticed a familiar face keenly watching and evaluating his experience. It was Velevendran. Fellowship in a pub brings the real man out of the mask.

"Got acquainted with all?" Velevendran started the conversation.

"Most of them," Thobias replied politely.

"Did Lohithan open his mouth?" Lohithan was the odd-man-out in the office. He never kept the Smile Bank officers' official posture of a half-bent body, left hand always scratching the head at the back, eyes eliciting compassion, lips stretched both ways, making the corners of the mouth reach the ears, thus exposing a few teeth.

"What happened to him?" Thobias was curious.

"The management tried to bend him. But he understood the process. It broke him instead of bending. He became silent thereafter," Velevendran put it in brief.

"Making people work is not an easy task. It requires big planning. Without motivation, nobody works. We have got a fixed pay system, and if you work day in and day out or don't work at all, you will get the same salary at the end of the month. Even if we pay handsomely, those idlers will always be demanding more. That's human nature, always unsatisfied."

"Lohithan's vertebral column was showing more than the required number of bones. Hence, it was presumed that his earnings were higher than required. They gave him a transfer out of the area, citing an emergency that only he could handle. It was to de-capitalise him. But he did not bend," Velevendran continued.

"A mere threat of transfer is sufficient for the majority. Threats work wonders. Now you came to Trivania on transfer, right? You are expecting a three-year stay here. You have arranged for accommodation, paid donations for the admission of your kids and brought your parents. You found out a good doctor for emergencies, secured a gas connection and arranged a servant. One fine morning, somebody tells you that you are likely to get a transfer. What will you do?" Velevendran laughed.

"You will lick the legs of your boss," Velevendran answered his own question. "Not only legs, even more than that. But I tell you that nobody will come to know as to who licked which part of which person. They are very secretive about that. This is the general transfer rumour route mechanism to make one work like a donkey."

"Won't our Revolutionary Association help officers in distress?" Thobias raised a doubt.

"Ha, ha!" The glass of arrack and soda mix which Velevendran was about to drink spilled over when he began to laugh. It flooded the table and both the bankers exited the shop.

"Where do you think they stand in this big process of making you work?" Velevendran tried to throw further light on the alliance between Revolutionary Association and the non-revolutionary management. "The Secretary of the Association sits on that chair without work near his house due to the blessings of the big boss, the Principal Manager. He has to please him with accurate management information. You will tend to open your heart to them because it is your Association. Whatever you tell them will reach the people who want to hear it."

"If that purpose is not served, the union leader will not be sitting there the next day. He will be replaced by another secretary duly elected by the members. You know the history of our earlier Association Secretary, Mr. Dilrose?"

"He was a bit more upright and did not support the asinisation of the staff. See what happened to him! Big Boss stopped calling him for discussions and instead started talking to his arch rival, our present secretary Mr. Pannaverse, who wanted a permanent stay at Trivania. Pannaverse became prominent and members started coming to him with their problems. Just before the election, Pannaverse was sent to all branches to study the impact of the interest rate on deposit growth. He could meet all the members and canvass votes. They voted him to the post of Secretary."

The discussion stopped there for a few minutes, as both were walking down the road towards Maruthoth Bridge. It was a short bridge of less than a hundred feet, made to connect the banks of Maruthoth canal, which carries the polluted water of the city to the sea. They sat on the round pillars projecting from the sidewalls of the bridge.

Velevendran lit a cigarette and blew small rings of smoke. Thobias also tried to make such rings unsuccessfully many times. He did it finally, which gave him immense satisfaction.

"Where did we stop?" Velevendran asked Thobias, who was looking at the fourth ring he sent out to the air from a single puff.

Velevendran scratched his head for some time. "I was about to tell you something funny just before my glass spilled over. I forgot it."

"Yeah, yeah, I got it," Velevendran recollected it after a few seconds of scratching his bald patch. "Once the background is set, playing the game is easy. Suppose the management gets the news that you are going home at eight o'clock from the branch. They will first verify your performance. If your performance is average, they have a reason to ask why you go home so early, and how much time you require in bed at this age."

"From then on, you become the targeted man of the APM. Rumours will be spreading from one end to the other without anybody knowing from where they originated.

"'He is arrogant,' APM will tell me.

"'He talks more than needed,' I will add a little more and convey it to Mrs. Charulatha.

"'He goes home early,' Mrs. Charulatha will tell Anthrose. She might forget what she heard. But she will remember that it was something negative.

"'He takes bribes for loans,'Anthrose is supposed to add and tell Mr. Dinky. It should go on till APM concludes, 'He is not loyal to Smile Bank.'

"You will also hear some of it, but will be unable to defend yourself because the number of people who believe rumours always exceeds the number of those who know the truth," Velevendran stopped for a few minutes while entering the shop again, and ordered drinks and boiled eggs.

"Smile Bank always wants a manager who cannot sleep just because he did not get any reprimanding from a customer, from his boss, or at least from a subordinate." He laughed heartily, but this time the glass did not spill over.

"Once, I got the rubbing when I was at Hassinara branch," Velevendran continued as soon as the eggs were served. "The APM was a Northern Marcardian. He did not like me for whatever reason. My letters were not answered. My bills were delayed without reason, or they would ask for a dozen clarifications which would drive me nuts. There were frequent visits by officers from the controlling office, looking for faults. All the letters I received from them were unpleasant. Finally, I went to the doorstep of the boss and waited for an appointment. He was too busy to meet me. The Revolutionary Association leader who was sitting near the cabin called me and I got a warm smile from him." Velevendran stopped for a second and pushed a boiled egg into his mouth. He could not speak fluently for some time.

He was struggling like a snake which has swallowed a bigger frog than usual.

"I told him the truth that my wife was ill and so I had to go home early. He offered his sympathy and suggested a good doctor in the area. He even culled out the mobile number of the doctor." Velevendran burped and it smelled of soda, boiled egg and arrack.

"But all that I said reached the busy boss immediately. I wondered at the technological progress made by humans in transmitting information that fast with such precision to a busy man inside the cabin.

"'I have to transfer you from that branch,' the APM played his first card on the table, as soon as I entered his cabin. That was the trump jack in the game of twenty eight, and I was sweating profusely, even though the air-conditioner was set at the coolest temperature.

"'Why Sir?' My blood pressure soared, and my face became as white as the blank papers on his table.

"'There is potential in the area for more business and you are going home early without bothering about the corporate call given by our beloved Principal Manager to open one lakh accounts of the physically challenged.' I understood why he had played the trump jack.

"'Sir, I will open one lakh accounts of the physically challenged,' I begged.

"'Who wants it?' the APM laughed. 'That's for publicity. We want business,' APM taught me business.

It was my turn to run from pillar to post to please the boss and get an assurance for my continuing there. Nothing moved for some time, until tears rolled down my cheeks, and I started hitting the wall with my forehead.

"'We will consider your retention as recommended by our Revolutionary Association leader,' the boss said finally. He collected back all the cards from the table and kept them in a secret pocket for later use, maybe with another manager.

"All were happy in this small game. I was happy that I could attend to my wife's health for some more time. The Bank was happy that I would be going to work like a donkey hereafter. The Revolutionary leader was happy that he could pass the necessary input to the boss at the right time, and his name was mentioned in the final pact."

"The boss was happy to know that I'd responded to rumours and it could be further used at any time. He even asked, "How is your branch working?" That is a big luxury in Smile Bank, since nobody likes to hear the problems of the branch. He issued an internal circular too, praising my work, since I stood politely for some time before sitting in the chair in front of him."

"Luckily, I went to meet him. Had I not, his conclusion would have been finalised and stick therapy would have started. 'Your branch has been selected for manpower study,' a young officer will turn up one fine morning. After a bit of paper work, he will recommend the reduction of two clerks and one officer. That will be the first stick."

"You will get annoyed at the injustice and may utter a few unpalatable words against the boss. You may even call up the Revolutionary leader and repeat them. Now, they have valid proof about your blatant arrogance. Even your wife will not sympathise with you."

"You know the transfer route of loyalists?" Velevendran asked, crushing the burnt stub of his cigarette on the rim of the ash tray.

"There is a normal transfer route for the loyal officers in our Bank. On joining, all will be posted in remote places where words like electricity or telephone will be far removed from the imagination of the common people. If the officer is loyal and doubles his own workload, he is eligible for a place closer to his home. It will have electricity, and there will be a single line manually operated telephone line. Water will also be available three days a week, and there will be a mini bus to carry him to the nearest railway station once a day. The officer is happy now, as his standard of life has gone up considerably. He is expected to increase his workload further." He stopped and lighted another cigarette.

"If he works there to the satisfaction of all Tom, Dick and Harrys, he is posted at his native place, where his family receives him as if he has returned from the dead. They will all be happy for a short time, till the next promotion is announced. Having suffered a lot, why leave it? It is fun to be one cadre up than earlier. He packs up to go to another remote area of Marcardia, but it will be a better place than the first posting. If he works well there, he can return closer to his home. He repeats this process till his retirement."

"We will push off. It's getting late," Thobias was much disturbed after knowing the darker side of his beloved bank, and he did not want to hear further at that time.

Velevendran stood up, folded his *lungi* midway and tied it on his hips. Thobias also followed suit and enjoyed the air that came in when the *lungi* was lifted half way on that humid day.

"I tell you, Thobias, the system cannot work without these small tricks. We are in the service industry, and growth is possible only if one works from one's heart. There is no effective system to know whether you are working with your full mind. Ours is an old bank and time has proved that these are the best tricks, far better than modern, what you call 'scientific' systems."

"Confine what I said to yourself only. Even pillars have ears here," Velevendran told Thobias before parting near the Maruthoth Bridge.

16

RAJAN ACCOMPANIED THOBIAS to the headquarters of Smile Bank in the morning.

"Sign here," the security guard ordered. "Get down at the eighth floor. The Legal Department is on the left side when you enter."

"Many big bosses ruled here with an iron fist, playing big games and funny tricks, and most of them have gone underneath the soil," Thobias told Rajan while ascending the lift.

"Here most of the staff are from Northern Marcardia," Rajan made a discovery.

"Southern Marcardians had started going for better jobs at the time I left the Bank. New entrants were from northern backward areas of Marcardia. They were not having many job options there at that time," Thobias explained the reason.

"Can I meet somebody looking after court cases?" Thobias asked the aged woman sitting in the counter.

"Meet the Deputy Principal Manager," she pointed towards a cabin with a small glass window.

"Can I meet somebody at the lower level?" Thobias was a Manager when he resigned from the bank, and never dared to sit before a Deputy Principal Manager.

"There are only two persons in that department, one Assistant Principal Manager and one Deputy Principal

Manager. Assistant Principal Manager is on leave today," she smiled and Thobias understood the job of APM and DPM.

Thobias entered the cabin after knocking twice, and gently opening the door.

"Yes," the DPM raised his head from the paper he was busy reading.

"Who said there is a case?" he asked Thobias, when he presented the case before him.

"Marcardia State Investigation Bureau," Thobias said.

"Then why don't you ask them?" The question was genuine, but the suggestion was not practical.

"I thought this route will be easier, as I am an ex-employee."

"See, I came here only six months ago. So far, I have not seen a case against any Thobias Mathai," he said the name correctly in spite of his north Marcardian accent.

"The account must be written off and the case may be pending with MSIB," the DPM guessed.

"When did you leave the job?" the DPM asked in a hurry.

"Twenty years back," Thobias too replied fast so as to save the valuable time of the executive.

"Then," he paused for a moment and said, "you had better check up with our Old Records Department. You give an application in writing, and I will recommend it to the Assistant Principal Manager, Old Records."

The Old Records Department was situated two kilometres away from the headquarters. It was an old building in the old city area where rental rates were cheap. It was established on the ground floor to avoid lifting of big bundles of old records upstairs.

"You had better come tomorrow," the Assistant Principal Manager was not customer conscious, and was not prepared to negotiate further.

"We will go to the Head Office again and look for a familiar face." Rajan followed Thobias again to the Head Office.

"We will go to the eighteenth floor. That was where I sat when I was here," Thobias always liked going to his past.

"Hey, look at this photo." Thobias had not seen the photo near the third pillar on the ground floor when he came in the morning. "This is Mr. Mehman," he pointed to the picture of a dark, tall man showing most of his white teeth outside. "He was the Principal Manager at the time of my resignation. He knew me personally."

Mehman was closely known to Thobias from the days when he was a Manager. He took big risks, but was very lucky to escape from pitfalls without bruises.

In those days, Smile Bank used to conduct business campaigns at periodic intervals. It also gave feedback on managers and helped to portray a few performers as role models.

Mehman was an active participant in all of these campaigns. He used to open thousands of savings accounts in a single stroke. The critics used to say that it was all for the records and that the accounts were not real. There wouldn't be any money in them, and these harmless accounts would be closed during the next campaign for closing zero balance accounts.

A few accounts left without closing would be converted as Recurring Deposit accounts when the campaign was announced. Thus, he would always be in the limelight and climbed the ladder faster than anybody else.

Only one major error occurred in his entire service period; he withheld a few cheques for big amounts, for a small period of one month, when they came for collection, to prevent the deposit figures of the branch from falling down. It became a case against Smile Bank and the bank was forced to pay one million Lians as penalty. Luckily, Mehman became an executive that year and the heavenly halo appeared behind his head.

In Smile Bank, people seldom spoke badly about their superiors. It was not due to love for the teachings of the great saints of Marcardia, but due to the fear that the origin of the truth might be traced in due course, and they would experience the fire of hell while on earth. So, if someone wanted to say that the king was naked, they would write it and circulate anonymous letters, with a copy to the Banking Authority of Marcardia.

It was sheer luck that Mehman was there, at that spot at that point of time, to stop one such letter war which could have caused much damage to the image of the Bank.

There was one Mr. Kamodayan, who was the Principal Manager at Trivania for a short period. He exhibited certain weaknesses. He would visit only those branches where more ladies were employed or where there was at least one beautiful lady.

Thobias saw him once when he visited the Cohiana office. Thobias was there to submit a loan proposal to the Assistant Principal Manager and was waiting at the visitors' lobby. Suddenly, a lean man entered the office and the entire office stood up with respect. Those who were not in their seats rushed back in panic and occupied their respective seats. It was Mr. Kamodayan, on a visit to the Cohiana office. He went inside the APM's cabin and sat on the big chair.

"Where is Rosapushpam?" he asked. There was relief among the staff at that request. A reasonably pretty lady entered his cabin and the APM came out for a visit to the sections.

A few days after this visit, Thobias saw an anonymous letter in circulation detailing the private life of Kamodayan in public office. Mehman's name was also mentioned in that letter, but it was about corruption which was not a big issue in Marcardia.

When such letters started appearing, Smile Bank normally came out with a solution to lift its reputation. This time, the task was entrusted to Mehman. It was Pannaverse, the leader of the Revolutionary Association, who came running to assist Mehman.

"We will print and circulate an array of anonymous letters depicting all good executives as bad. That can bring a doubt in the minds of all, about the truth contained in the original letter," Pannaverse made a valid remedy to uplift the image of his beloved organisation.

"Your brain is smarter than I thought," Mehman said. "You can count on me for a return favour before I retire."

"But we have to lift the image of those whom we are tarnishing," Pannaverse was God-fearing.

"Sure. At a later time," Mehman was not sure about God.

There was one more occasion that came Mehman's way to prove his ability. This was while he was the DPM at Trivania. The business growth of the city branches was negative and all employees were complaining about the workload. There came a compact disc to all branches from Mr. Mehman with instructions to play the same in the morning, just before the start of business, each employee holding another employee's hand. The time allotted for singing was three minutes.

It was a simple prayer,

Oh, Almighty in heaven,
Let me see you in truth,
Let me see you in love,
Let me see you in justice,
Let me see you in my mother,
Let me see you in my father,
Let me see you in my bread-giver,
Give me faith in my Smile,
Don't make me lazy.

After the introduction of the prayer, business growth went up by thirteen percent. It also led to a very lively interaction among the staff as it gave some people an opportunity to hold the soft hands of the good looking ladies, which was otherwise not possible. The holding of hands was later done away with because one naughty male employee in the Vazhala branch used his middle finger to scratch the palm of an innocent female colleague. She complained to Mehman and he issued a circular to stop holding hands while at prayer and also reduced prayer time to two minutes. After that, the prayer lost its charm but it did not affect Mehman, as he was promoted and had gone to another chair in another cabin which was three feet wider than the earlier one.

It was the era of computerisation. There was no recruitment of fresh staff in banks in Marcardia for years together and vertical mobility was affected.

Even after the promotions one would find oneself doing the same job. Smile Bank tried its best to give the feeling of forward momentum by bifurcating sections and changing the nomenclature of departments.

Mr. Mehman was dealing with staff matters at the HO as Assistant Principal Manager. When he was promoted, he moved to a bigger cabin, which had a fax machine and an additional dining area. He got an increment of four hundred Lians per month and an additional five litres of petrol for conveyance.

Mehman was not so fortunate when he was promoted the next time. He was transferred to Doncity to the head bank's Controlling Office there. The normal term of three years was reduced for him as a special case because his talents were urgently required at the Head Office. He came back in six months and occupied the large cabin on the seventh floor.

Mehman always liked the cacophony associated with the promotion process; the mock interviews, group discussions, pulling and pushing and the restless days and nights till the final displacement order comes along with the promotion.

"See, Thobias. You've got a very good service record and capacity to go upto the level of Vice Principal Manager before you retire," Mehman said when Thobias was to leave to pack his frugal luggage at the time of his transfer to

Doncity. It was not clear why Mehman limited the scope of Thobias' vertical mobility only upto VPM level.

"Maybe possible, but this is okay for me," Thobias had already decided.

"You will come to know the difficulty when a junior sits above your head and orders you," Mehman cautioned.

"Even now, I am obeying inferior ones. I can easily manage the junior too," Thobias replied.

"We do not want somebody to start a new culture here. All should aspire for promotion, work hard for it and show resilience at normal displacements. That is the accepted norm of Smile Bank. Any deviation can cause serious damage to your career." It was a warning from Mehman.

"You couldn't locate any known face so far?" Rajan brought a touch of reality to the otherwise dull regurgitation of memories.

"No, I couldn't," Thobias replied after searching the eighteenth floor. They returned to the hotel.

17

"YOU'RE BROODING TOO MUCH. Whatever is going to happen will happen," it was Rajan's turn to become philosophical, while lying comfortably in bed at the hotel room.

"I was not thinking about the case at all. I was thinking of locating Velevendran. He must have retired by now," Thobias took the impending case very lightly.

"So planning to stretch the journey?" Rajan was not amused.

"No such plans yet. He was a very helpful friend, who taught me lessons on administration from the day I joined HO. Many a time he tried to lift me up in his department so that I could be in touch with the executives and go up in my career. But most of the time it misfired."

"How?" Rajan became interested.

"Once he took me to the APM who gave me an assignment to investigate a complaint.

"'Here's a complaint about our Nisara branch. Go today itself and submit the report tomorrow,' the APM ordered and I was afraid to ask anything further.

"The complainant was a lady whose husband was working in another bank. She was aggrieved that an agricultural loan was not sanctioned to her within the time frame fixed by the Banking Authority of Marcardia.

"I reached Nisara branch by noon. An aged Manager was sitting in his cabin and there was a long queue of customers to meet him. One officer was sitting outside the cabin assisted by two clerks. The peon stood near the counter and was helping the officer to dispose of the crowd as fast as they could.

"'I am from the Head Office. There is a complaint against you,' I introduced myself to the Manager.

"'Just go to hell and do what you want. I am expecting worse than that. You know that APM who directed you to investigate? We both joined the bank on the same day. He became big because of his caste, and now he is finding it fun to fire me on a daily basis. I am working here like a donkey,' his eyes became red. 'Last month, he removed one of my officers and I am struggling to answer the customers,' he continued.

"'Tell me your comments about the complaint?' I exerted my authority and did not wish his versions to overtake me.

"'You investigate and report. Whatever be the punishment, I don't mind. There is only one year for me to retire,' he revealed his age and started attending to the next customer.

"I went in search of the complainant based on the address given and located the house in an interior village, around fifteen miles away from the branch."

"'I signed it, but you ask my husband who wrote the complaint. He will come in the evening,' the lady was not cooperating with me. She also closed the door of the house without letting me inside. I waited in a tea shop till her husband arrived.

"'Loan to agriculture is a national priority, but I was forced to go to Smile Bank twice and that Manager was insisting that he would not give the loan without visiting the farm,' he was angry about the delay in getting the loan.

"'Why didn't you take a loan from your bank?' I had this doubt from the very start.

"'Ours is a busy branch, and our manager says he needs one month's time,' he revealed the truth.

"I wrote up a mild report and submitted it in time to the APM. In the evening Velevendran came running to me.

"'What's this, Thobias? You are saying that the complainant is not aware of the complaint? You have totally reduced the scope of action on the complaint. Don't get upset if you get a transfer tomorrow,' Velevendran said.

"'See, Thobias. You stand exposed; you are not with the management. If you kick self-goals what can I do? Do you think that the APM is not aware of the frivolous nature of the complaint?'

"'If there was no error with him, you could have gone to the procedures; whether he has accepted the loan application with dated seal, whether he acknowledged it, whether he issued the token of service, whether he entered it in the register, whether he gave the date for visit and all. Our procedures are so cumbersome that nobody on earth can comply with all of them and you can get enough reasons to charge sheet even the most meticulous fellow at any time. That is the beauty of Smile Bank.'

"'Velevendran come here,' the APM called over the intercom.

"'As expected,' Velevendran said, while rushing to the sixth floor.

"'I solved it this time. I could make him believe that you are a very soft person except for the tongue.' Velevendran too was happy while returning since he did not want to miss an officer who was subservient to him fully.

"'I will introduce you to more people here so that you will get a better idea about surviving here,' Velevendran suggested one day.

"That was how I first met Mr. Pannaverse. He was sitting in his small cabin at an empty table. At that time, an option scheme was in force. An officer could opt for either Pension or Provident Fund as retirement benefit.

"'Welcome! Mr. Thobias Mathai,' Pannaverse stood up and extended a warm handshake.

"He was a tall fellow with a broad forehead, which seemed to indicate that nothing was impossible. He bent forward to extend his hand, but his body did not go back to its original position immediately. The most prominent parts of his face were his teeth and the most insignificant ones were the lips. Since the teeth were always available for public display, the lips had lost their significance and were nearing extinction in tune with the theory of evolution without waiting for the future generations.

"'All say you've done well. Now, it's your turn to study administration, and grow big to lead our beloved bank to newer heights.' Thobias could read the hollowness of the words easily.

"'What did you opt for as retirement benefit, Mr. Thobias? Pension or Provident Fund?' Pannaverse entered into a serious subject straightaway.

"'Pension,' I said. It was the better option because one could get income during his entire life.

"'Ha, ha! Why?' Pannaverse laughed as if the choice was too bad. 'Can you tell me why you opted for it?'

"'It helps you to pull on in life after retirement,' I wanted to end that subject there because I was sure about my option.

"'Did you calculate the Provident Fund benefit?' Pannaverse was not leaving the topic.

"'Mr. Velevendran, what did you opt for?' Pannaverse turned to Velevendran this time.

"'I'm for Provident Fund,' Velevendran said, without any hesitation.

"'You heard it? Now try to rethink, Mr. Thobias,' Pannaverse came back to me but the entry of another officer to his cabin stopped the discussion abruptly.

"While coming back I asked Velevendran why he opted for Provident Fund.

"'Do you think I have opted for it? That answer was for him. He is propagating the Provident Fund for somebody.'

"'Why?' I was naive.

"'Health standards are going up, and each month a pensioner survives will be adding to the loss in the balance sheet of Smile Bank.'

"'I also came to know about the conversation that took place in the board room. Revolutionary leaders were expected to encourage Provident Fund option, dumping Pension scheme. In return, Pannaverse would be the secretary of the Association till his retirement. Even if he was not re-elected, he would be retained at Trivania without any work. Pannaverse could also opt for pension and it would be kept a secret. That was the pact.'

"'He kept his word and the work out made on the advantages of Provident Fund was an instant hit. Many who had initially opted for pension withdrew the option in favour of Provident Fund and Pannaverse continued as leader without any work at Trivania.' Velevendran continued.

"'But an itch started developing in his heart and he met Mehman many times in this regard. The Big Boss assured Pannaverse that the Bank would give another option afterwards, say after five to six years. The Smile Bank wanted to assess the outgo first, then rework on it, without affecting its health. They would be a few occasions to go on strike, without any penal action. But the strikes should be friendly; one day at a time, then two days after a gap and finally withdrawing at the last moment when the strike started making an impact. That much was agreed upon at that time.' Velevendran knew the inside story.

"'But, Pannaverse was persistent for a pension option to those who had been duped by him. That infuriated Mehman.' Velevendran continued.

"'Those who are wiser and able to understand the issues would have taken the better option. Those who do not have the brain to understand the difference between the options, and those who are gullible enough to believe you, let them suffer. They are not eligible for a better life than what they are having now,' Mehman was categorical. Pannaverse cried and repented, but he did not hang himself as he did not want to go to hell early." Thobias was unable to forget the penetrating sarcasm in Velevendran's words while narrating the incident to Rajan.

18

"LOOK," Rajan pointed to a thatched shed on the ground through the window. "It looks like a chicken farm. I will visit it and come back."

Thobias appreciated the intuition of the chicken farmer and decided to join him.

It was a medium sized layer unit. Shabby white hens were packed in small cages with provision to eat and drink in the sitting posture. The chest feathers of most of the hens had vanished due to their constant rubbing with the bottom iron wires of the cage, exposing the pink skin.

"This is an advanced model of a chicken farm. Hens are made unable to move, preserving their energy. They will give bigger eggs," Rajan educated Thobias enthusiastically.

Thobias went back to his childhood. Amma's hen flock came to his mind. They enjoyed walking around the farm, eating from the paddy spread for drying, and running en masse when angry Amma came running after them. They even had a romantic life, where the hero was a tall cock with a red tail from neighbour Thoma's flock.

"Good! Good, as long as it does not know the thrill of standing up or the fun of roaming around," Thobias agreed conditionally.

"When we improve efficiency, that is but natural," Rajan said, while examining the cages thoroughly.

"We in Smile Bank had such a system," the tone was far from appreciative.

The advanced system reminded Thobias of what Velevendran had told him three decades ago, which was still fresh in his mind.

It was the first Sunday after pay day. It was a practice to celebrate Sundays over a bottle of rum. Velevendran was the guest that day and Thobias, the junior in office, the host.

Velevendran gulped down the first peg without saying cheers and closed his eyes for a second to adjust to the taste left on the tongue. He put the glass back on the centre table and caught hold of a fried chicken leg.

"I am worried about my leave. It is yet to be sanctioned," Thobias started with an official subject in the unofficial meeting.

Velevendran put back the chicken piece and sat silently for a second.

"It will be delayed and, sometimes, may not even come through," he revealed an official secret.

"Don't think that I'm a miser in granting leave to good workers. The APM told me not to recommend your leave application."

"What?" Thobias raised his eyebrows. Velevendran ignored the question and took the chicken piece again.

"Thobias," Velevendran called affectionately. "Suppose we permit your long leave, it can give you the luxury of being with your family and enjoying life more than needed. You will slowly begin to forget about the pending work. The pleasure of life should be sparingly given to you to keep the desire for it alive throughout your career. If you taste it too much, you may think about the meaning of life and the meaning of work."

"I don't think you are serious," Thobias believed so.

The chicken roast was very spicy and Velevendran drew a strong current of air to his mouth to reduce its intensity. Thobias was aware that chicken fry from pubs would be spicier to make the customer drink more and pay more. Thobias waited till the end of that mouth exercise.

"I have to ensure the availability of carrots for you. I have to do my part in asinisation. I have to turn you into the sandwiched hens in the rearing farm," Velevendran stopped and studied the face of Thobias.

Thobias tried to believe that Velevendran was joking. Still, he feared in some corners of his mind that he was being tricked for no reason.

"The problem is that the APM is not sure whether you are running behind the carrot or before the stick. You are showing the symptoms of both. But he knows that you work sincerely."

"If you are a carrot chaser," he continued, "you will be very close to the APM. You can't imagine a junior sitting in the posh cabin and ordering you. You will fear the errors and rumours that can affect you. You will fear the customers, auditors, VIPs, the dons of the area and even the peon of the head office. You will even fear a situation where there is nothing to fear. This fear should come to you even after you work perfectly."

Velevendran stopped the talk for a minute and gulped the thick brown liquid.

"In that process, you will be running faster and the results will be better. There will be fire in your abdomen.

The Big Boss will ensure that no junior overtakes you, so that the carrot of promotion is available around the season. Imagine your happiness when the first carrot lands in your lap in the form of a promotion!"

"That is temporary. I will see another big cabin." Thobias became a good student.

"That's it. You are getting time to think. We have to feed you with more work. I suggest you don't reveal yourself too much," Velevendran also showed his gratitude for the drinks.

"The APM says that you are yet to become a carrot chaser. You want to be treated as a horse. It's a good animal, energetic and working hard. But the cost of maintenance is high and the animal rebels easily. It is not needed in routine work like going round and round with the milling stone. Donkeys will be happy with what they get. They will suffer adverse situations silently and will not avoid them further. They can be moved faster if the carrot is also made to move faster, permitting the smell to reach them continuously. In between, give the carrot to another donkey which is about to fall, or at random, but never to a donkey that has got the stamina to continue moving," he paused.

"Horse power is measured in HP," he started again. "Donkey's power is never standardised. The owner can add to the load till the donkey stretches its legs, leading its belly to kiss the dust."

"I am obedient and hard working. Still, why do you want to push me to what you call asinisation?"

"Something is missing there. You are not always thinking about Smile Bank. I think about pending work even when

I am in bed with my wife. Ha, ha," he tried to crack a joke about a serious issue.

"I believe in working for the institution. I am not a carrot chaser because I know that Smile Bank has got a 'chosen race' for decorating the cabins."

"That's what the APM also said. He predicted your early exit from the carrot phase. They will deskill and de-capitalise you before long."

"What?"

"If you are intelligent," Velevendran continued his class, "you will be first trained in foreign exchange portfolio, and will be posted to a branch for agricultural lending. You will have to devote much energy to grasp the new work. Once you pick up the nuances of these rural uplift schemes, it is time to learn the legal side of banking in an administrative office, then to general section dealing with demand drafts, and then to the currency chest. It ensures that you never become a master anywhere, except in obeying the boss. An expert can bring in disobedience and can jump out. Jack of all trades will be exhibiting sufficient inferiority complex and after one or two rejections in promotion, he will be absolutely sure about his ignorance level, so that he will not try for another job. Then he is easily manageable," Velevendran stopped for a moment to gulp down the next glass of rum.

"Ridiculous," Thobias tried to present a brave face for no reason.

"Thobias, watch now. The *crab* in the HR department will spot you. He will focus his lens on you. He will watch your steps, your posture, your smiles, your respiration and your perspiration."

"'Sir, look at this guy,' he will tell the APM of HRD. The APM will take his big lens and start watching you.

"'You are right,' he will pat the *crab* on his back.

"'Is he forty? I think he is becoming wiser. Is he rich? Is his wife employed? What are his kids doing? Are his parents alive? How is his health?' the APM will ask many questions mixing it with funny comments.

"The *crab* will do research on your personal life. He will identify the maximum inconveniences and inform the APM about the best time to strike at the hot iron. An order will come at the appropriate time, transferring you to the hillocks of northern Marcardia. You will experience how your hard earned money goes towards train fares, keeping the family in a more civilised place, getting school admissions for kids and taking care of parents in absentia. These are the essentials of de-capitalisation.

"You're frightening me."

"Why to get frightened? Get asinised. They are the happiest people, as long as asinisation is complete."

"The stick-phase starts after ensuring that your roots are sufficiently cut through frequent transfers. You won't have anybody to share your sorrows with or to defend you. You will enter a new world where you are the villain responsible for all ills, surrounded by a group of saints without any productive work, but trying to save the institution. This system is evolved over a period, much researched and improved by the best brains, so that it goes undetected during your entire service period," Velevendran said and left.

That night Thobias prayed to God, "Oh God, make me fully asinised."

But, God was having more serious preoccupations.

19

"WHICH WAS YOUR LAST BRANCH?" The Assistant Principal Manager at the Old Records Department looked at the early morning nuisance.

"Milky Station, Doncity," Thobias replied, fully realising the extent of the APM's irritation. "But the case seems to have been filed by the Head Office," he indicated to help him locate the file easily.

"You have to wait. After the introduction of the Right to Know Act, we have to keep the files for long, about twenty-five years. The scope of searching is very high. At the same time, you are lucky to get information about a case which is twenty years old. I have got only one Manager in my department. He is from North Marcardia and he will be available only for a few days in a month." Thobias understood that things are more or less the same in Smile Bank even after twenty years.

"Please come in the evening. I will locate it for you," the APM offered his help.

"Here is it," the APM stretched a yellow file as soon as he stepped into the cabin in the evening.

The case file read:

Thobias Mathai S/o Pappu was employed by Smile Bank in 1972 as an officer. He offered his resignation on 05-07-89 while working as Manager at Milky Station Branch, Doncity, without sufficient reasons and the bank has not accepted it in view of various irregularities of very serious nature committed by him, which have resulted in pecuniary loss to the Bank, roughly estimated as under:

Milky Station Branch, Doncity:

Mr. Thobias Mathai was working as Manager for the period 1987-89 under the branch-in-charge, Mr. Kusagran. Mr. Kusagran had sanctioned loans to the tune of 5 crore Lians during the above period, all of which were detected as fraudulent subsequently. Thobias Mathai, being the second in command, did not inform the higher authorities in advance or during the release of these loans, indicating his collusion with Mr. Kusagran in cheating the Bank. This is blatant violation of clause 11.2 under section 134 of Smile Bank Officers Service Rules.

It was the responsibility of the above officer to follow up the loans meticulously for recovery. But, no follow up was done and no recovery has been effected and the bank has suffered huge monetary loss. This dereliction of duty is punishable under Marcardia Employment Contract Rules, Section 130, Sub-section 22a.

In the case of loan No. 12035 for Lians 35,00,000/- sanctioned by APM Mr. Perfecta based on the recommendation of Kusagran, the above officer has signed the demand draft favouring Siraj Perverse, the seller of the property. The draft was directly handed over to the loan department instead of giving to the seller of the property. Had the Manager searched and identified the seller, the fraud could have been prevented. This indicates collusion between Kusagran and Thobias Mathai.

Loan No: 120001 Cohiana Branch:

The above loan for Lians 14,00,000/- was sanctioned by the above officer in the capacity of branch-in-charge for a cine projection unit on 12-11-82.

The party has stopped repayment in 1989 and the present liability is Lians 43,700/-. The scrutiny of the account revealed that the stamped receipt from the seller of the projector is not available with the documents, and it indicates that no purchase of the projector has taken place. The ledger sheets also do not show the post sanction inspection dates, indicating that Mr. Thobias Mathai has never visited the unit financed by the Bank.

Loan No: 98710 Kallar Branch:

The above officer has audited the Kallar branch from 11-1-85 to 16-3-85. The above account was showing signs of weakness and the account became unrecoverable in 1988, with a liability of Lians 3,22,000/-. All the securities pledged to the bank turned out to be fraudulent. The manager who sanctioned the loans retired on 11-11-1988. While inspecting the branch as an auditor, Thobias Mathai could not locate the fraud in time, causing the branch in charge to retire without penalty. This is negligence of duty.

The Bank could not get any response to various letters, memos and charge sheets issued to Thobias Mathai at his last known address.

Absence of explanations leads to the conclusion that the charges are true, and the Bank has dismissed the above officer on 13-4-1992 in absentia. Bank could reliably learn that Mr. Thobias Mathai has absconded after committing the wilful crimes listed above, resulting in a total loss of 5,43,12,750 Lians, including investigation charges.

This letter is to elicit investigation by the Marcardia State Investigation Bureau to bring out the role of the above officer in these crimes and to punish him as per the rules of the Bank and the rules of the great nation of Marcardia.

Yours faithfully
Panaloshan
Deputy Principal Manager,
Smile Bank.

"Something serious?" Rajan was watching Thobias reading the charge sheet.

"Yes, serious on paper," Thobias did not elaborate.

20

"YOU COULD HAVE REMAINED in the administration throughout, so that such type of charges would've never come to you," Rajan became wiser.

"You're right. Actually I took a long time to understand this," Thobias confessed.

"You've not changed much from the schooldays, when you were a good student but a poor amateur in life."

"True," he could not avoid admitting it. "But it is also true that I was not suited to administration."

Thobias flew back to his Smile Bank days. One day, the Principal Manager was lecturing on the importance of smiling in customer service, though nobody had seen him smiling except when facing the camera.

Thobias carried his doubt to the department. "How can he direct us to smile when he is not smiling?" he asked his immediate boss.

"Power is to make others do things which one does not like to do," the boss was frank and to the point. "You too can try this down the line."

"Also control your tongue if you want to remain in the administration set up," the APM summed up the discussion.

Thobias made a similar error a few weeks later. It was customary on the part of all Principal Managers to give yearly self-appraisal speeches at the end of March, narrating the achievements made during the year.

"Refer my circular dated twenty-fifth of this month. We have evolved a new promotional policy. Hereafter, merit, and only merit of the individual will be considered for promotion," he thumped on the podium and the front benchers clapped their hands as usual.

"How was my speech?" the Principal Manager asked the Vice Principal Manager as he placed himself comfortably on the chair.

It was overheard in the entire auditorium as the loudspeaker had not been switched off and the total environment in the hall became casual.

"I want piercing questions from you youngsters," Principal Manager, Mr. Rameshan Rao unnecessarily turned to the place where Thobias was sitting. "Ask me for any clarifications. I'm here to guide you." It was still silence all around, as all were very serious about their future in Smile Bank.

"Yes, come on. Don't feel shy in asking your doubts about the policies we are evolving to make our bank the number one in Marcardia. Divergent opinions make decisions richer in content," the Principal Manager repeated.

"Sir, I've got a doubt," Thobias stood up.

"Go ahead, young man," the Principal Manager was in a good mood. It was the duty of the subordinates to find out the moods of their bosses in Smile Bank.

"We are considering merit for promotion from this year onwards. Sir, what was the criterion for promotion till now?"

The hall became silent instantly.

"Merit is being considered for promotion even now, but . . . but . . . what I was telling was that I am giving more emphasis . . . ," he struggled for a proper reply. His capacity to evade questions which he exhibited throughout his journey to the top did not come to his rescue this time.

"What's your name?" There was an air of authority in those words. "You can come to my cabin afterwards. We will discuss about it in detail." The discussion ended there.

Thobias got his transfer to Cohiana the next day.

"Why is this transfer for me now?" he asked the APM, HRD.

"This is as per request. You had requested for a transfer to Cohiana before coming here and we are acceding to that request now. Since this is a request transfer, you are not eligible for reimbursement of transfer expenses. Also, remember one thing. Never put unpleasant questions to big people, especially when it does not concern you." He switched off the air conditioner of his cabin indicating his intention to stop the discussion and move out.

"But my question was genuine," Thobias persisted.

"Who said it was not," APM smiled. "Do you think that others do not know the truth? Just because a truth is truth, it need not become a truth until it is announced by the concerned authority."

"But the problem is that the power to tell the truth is vested with people who always tell lies," Thobias wanted to say that, but did not.

Cohiana branch was twenty years old and within one year he could double the business. It was selected as the best branch of the northern region. Congratulations poured in and he became a little more important. The old carrot reappeared in front of him at the same distance.

"Your branch is closing at seven o'clock?" It was a normal question from the APM during a meeting. "All others are sitting up to 9 o'clock. Why? Your work load is less?"

"We never waste time, Sir," Thobias confidently replied.

"That means others are wasting time?"

He did not have an immediate answer and reserved the reply for a suitable point of time. "Sir, we have overtaken all business targets by very good margins," he said with all humbleness.

"Maybe. That indicates the huge potential in the area and you have scope for increasing the business further," APM made an invention but did not jump out from the chair in that thrill.

"Sir, this is a twenty-year-old branch and I have already doubled the business within a year," he repeated his plus point.

"I'd heard that statement earlier. Now you also heard me, right?" APM acted as if he was angry. "I am increasing your business targets. You achieve it and take promotion."

The carrot made the difference. Nothing is impossible if one tries. The old poem read out by Pappu came to his mind. It was correct. Anything is possible but, of course, at a cost.

Here the cost was a few years of his life.

"Good! Very good! You are a man who can produce results. The sky is the limit for you," the APM patted him on his back many a time till the area started paining.

Their next meeting was in Thobias' cabin at Cohiana branch.

"You worked in Money Bank for additional seniority? Still, you missed promotion this year too?" the APM's face turned sad. "It's fate. You believe in God?"

"It's okay for me," Thobias replied. He deliberately avoided answering the second part as it was too personal.

"You continue your performance. The sky is the limit for you," he repeated his sentences as if a tape recorder was kept inside his mouth.

Thobias' pace of running came down. Salary became his only motivation. It was the same whether one achieved results or not. Things happen based on the whims and fancies of the boss, or based on the views of the coterie around him, or even based on the fine managerial decisions of the Smile Bank.

"You missed the additional targets this time?" the APM pretended to be angry, though he knew that it was an impossible target set to humble him.

"Just missed it, Sir," Thobias had decided not to confront him.

"Why? I want a proper answer." The additional target itself was for knowing the attitude of the manager properly.

"Maybe the fate of the branch. I believe in God, Sir," he wanted to tell but did not.

"I am concerned about you. Your talents are being wasted and the bank is not benefited by it."

"I too am not benefited by it, Sir," the answer did not impress the APM.

"I had asked you to go in for door-to-door canvassing for deposits to achieve the additional targets. Why did you ignore my instructions?" the APM decided to pin him. Thobias did not have any answer.

"I want an answer," APM thumped on the table. But thumping could not produce a reply from him.

"I want a convincing answer," he was not ready to leave the matter.

"Begging is banned in Cohiana." That was true. The APM exited the cabin without responding.

Velevendran called him that night from H.O.

"I heard some rumours here. You are getting a transfer to the audit department," he cautioned. "Go and beg the APM. If you patch up, you will get a very good branch in Cohiana because he liked your capability and performance. If not, life can be tougher."

Thobias listened, but did not reply.

"It will be very costly for you," he cautioned again. "Your father is on his deathbed and your wife is pregnant," Velevendran was concerned.

"Wow! How did you know about my wife's pregnancy?" he was astonished at Velevendran's knowledge about his personal affairs. Even Theresa had come to know about it only two days ago!

"Our Revolutionary Association representative at Cohiana has already conveyed this news here. That's why they are planning sticks on you immediately. Your vertebral column will be replaced by a plastic one," he laughed. The displacement order took one week to reach him.

The money for admission of children to a new school was a big problem for him.

"Sir, will you return half of the donation I have paid? We had been here for just one year," he pleaded with the school principal.

"Money is like time, my son. Once spent, it will not come back," the Principal revealed his philosophical prudence.

"You are in service?" the philosopher asked further.

"Yeah," the materialist replied.

"You mistook us. We are in business," the philosopher smiled.

It was the worst ever transfer for him. Pappu was terminally ill in his home town, and Theresa was pregnant for the third time.

One day he had taken her to the hospital for abortion and got her admitted to the operation room. But she came out running after a few minutes. She had seen a six-inch long little baby, soaked in blood, freshly plucked from an unfortunate womb, still kept on the tray for disposal. His younger son was that fertilised egg which he had thought of sending to heaven prematurely.

"What should happen will happen," Pappu was worried about Thobias' displacement. "I am sure that you did your job well. When things are designed to teach you lessons, better learn them. Don't worry about me. Take care of Theresa."

As usual, Thobias started his journey with his luggage at midnight to avoid official head-load workers and reached Kallania the following midnight, skipping head-load workers there too.

The audit work involved travelling to far-off places covering the beautiful landscape of the Wadia region of Marcardia. Majestic mountains almost touched the clouds. The tea gardens in between the mountains appeared like a thick green velvet coating. The blue sky, white clouds and enchanting greenery of the Wadia region gave him a few relaxed moments.

The work was simple and he managed to completely satisfy his boss very soon.

"You seem to be a good worker. But why are so many people after you? I've got instructions to show you the boundaries of Marcardia and to be very strict with your travelling bills," the APM was unable to hide the official secrets.

"Can you favour me with a few days of leave? My father is on his deathbed," Thobias requested in return.

"It is your duty to be near him now." He granted him leave.

Theresa's delivery was expected any time in those days. If it happened during the day, she could manage it alone. But in the night, Thobias had to be there to call a taxi and to take her to the hospital. So he was with Pappu at their home town during the day and travelled back over the next six hours to reach Kallania by near midnight, only to resume the process the next morning. This went on for a few days.

"I am troubling you a lot," Pappu said one day when he was about to leave in the evening.

"This is a small game and I will manage it," Thobias assured him.

That night Pappu made his final journey, with nobody near his bedside, except the duty nurse, who administered injections on him left and right.

"Who is Thobias?" the duty nurse asked in the morning. "Pappu was trying to tell something like 'Thobias' just before dying. He could not complete it but was signalling to me at the end like this." She tried to emulate the gestures before going to the next patient, seeing the doctor coming. Thobias could not understand them.

"Sorry, friend, we will meet in the golden shore of Heaven some time," Thobias said while kissing his feet.

He returned from Pappu's deathbed to the birth bed at All Saints Hospital Room No. 404. He watched the lucky fellow who had taken birth in this wonderful world. But his breathing was not regular and he was gasping for life.

"Did Theresa make any journey lately?" the doctor asked while studying the scan report of the baby.

"Yeah, she had gone to our native place. My father was critical," he replied.

"The child's abdominal membrane is damaged and the viscera are in the thoracic region. It suppressed the lungs from developing. The chance of survival is very less," the doctor explained. "You have to take the kid to a speciality hospital for an urgent surgery to stitch together the remains of the membrane. I suggest Lourdes Hospital if you can afford it, or try your luck with the Government Medical College Hospital, where one ventilator is available at nominal charges."

"Our ventilator is not free now. You better go to Lourdes Hospital," the reply was prompt from the Medical College.

While crossing the beautifully maintained lawn and walking down the granite corridor leading to the enquiry counter of the Lourdes hospital, Thobias made an initial assessment about the possible bill.

"Where is the mother of the baby?" the nurse asked while taking the kid from his hand.

"She is at the All Saints Hospital and the bleeding is yet to stop," he replied.

"Baby's blood is O negative," she said on coming back. "It's a rare group. Who is negative? You or your wife?"

"Wife. I'm thoroughly negative, except for the blood," he said.

"Arrange a blood donor and keep him ready for matching immediately," she ordered and vanished.

He ran to familiar faces. They were all positive, except for the blood.

"You can try with Red Cross," the nurse suggested, when she spotted him sitting in the corridor chair, tired.

"Baby Theresa," the nurse called through the small window of the operation theatre. "Get these medicines urgently," she pushed out a long paper as soon as Thobias returned from the Red Cross after a failed search for O negative blood. "I called you many times. Keep somebody here when you go out," she was a bit angry.

He was to go to the jewellery shop to sell off the remaining gold which Theresa got from her mother. While inspecting the ornaments, the salesman returned a small piece of gold back to him.

"This should be your wife's *thali*. You must have mistakenly brought it."

"Yes, thank you," he replied soberly.

He took it back and returned with a few bundles of hundred denomination Lians to the payment counter of Lourdes Hospital.

"Did you get the blood?" the nurse was standing near the door of the operation theatre.

He did not reply. She must know that money is more important than blood.

"Get some milk too from the mother. I can try giving it when the baby regains consciousness after the operation."

"You're running too much," a bystander near the operation theatre sympathised.

"Yeah, it has got a long history and now I am used to it," he impressed him with a smile and ran towards Room No. 404 of All Saints Hospital.

"Has the operation started?" Theresa detected even the slightest movement around, even when she is asleep.

"How do you know about the operation?" he was surprised.

"I'm his mother and I haven't seen him so far. I can guess. Is it a major one? You can tell me." He was forced to tell her about the operation.

"What's his blood group? Yours or mine?" She was not aware of the other permutations.

"Yours," he whispered.

"Don't run around for blood. I can give." She was familiar with the problem of this rare blood group.

"Your bleeding is yet to stop. Moreover, the doctor won't allow you to move out at this stage," Thobias was hesitant to accept that offer.

"Let the nurse go out. I will try to stand up. We will get out without their knowledge. At Lourdes, they won't know my condition," she tried to smile.

"Baby wants your milk too."

"Look there," she pointed towards a small steel vessel kept covered by another similar vessel. "It's for him."

"Go and be with the kid and come back if blood is needed. Bring one shawl to cover me to go out undetected," she planned things well and Thobias obeyed.

"Baby Theresa," a call came again through the small window of the operation theatre. "Bring the blood donor for cross matching."

He ran to Room No. 404 of All Saints Hospital, with the bed sheet of Room No. 705 of Lourdes Hospital neatly covered with Marcardia Express newspaper.

Back at Lourdes Hospital, he introduced the blood donor to the impatient nurse and withdrew to a vacant bench of the corridor. Theresa slowly moved to the side room of the operation theatre and occupied the small stool to give the sample blood.

"You come here," he nurse shouted at Thobias after a few minutes. Her words were without any respect that was usually shown to an adult male in that part of Marcardia.

"Are you an animal? Bringing a bleeding mother for blood donation?" she was trying to control her anger.

There was no error in her question. Humans are part of the big animal kingdom and such a question is generally asked when humans do things which are more realistic and in tune with general animal behaviour.

"You take rest. I will take care of the blood," the nurse advised Theresa and thus solved a big problem for him. Had she solved it earlier, he could have concealed his animal nature without detection for some more time.

The doctor was all smiles when he came out from the operation theatre.

"We have done our job well. I can tell you the result only tomorrow. You have to make arrangements for a long stay supported by the ventilator; I mean, make sure that you can afford it."

"Can I get the Bible?" Theresa asked while returning from Lourdes Hospital.

"Right now? No, dear. We are in heavy traffic and it is raining outside. I have to make a bigger search for the Bible than I did for blood," Thobias was practical.

"Which part do you want to read?" he asked her casually.

"Something reassuring."

"I shall quote for you from memory.

Can a woman forget her nursing child?
Or no compassion for the child of her womb
Even these may forget,
Yet I will not forget you,
See, I have inscribed you,
On the palms of my hands."

"Hey, you," she stopped him. "You know the Bible that much?" She was surprised at his recitation.

"I used to read it daily in my childhood. It left a deep imprint on me, and I could not become a crook and go up in life."

"I am happy today," Theresa remarked while re-entering Room No. 404 stealthily.

"Happy?" He could not believe it as their child was still in the Operation Theatre.

"We became husband and wife today," she whispered after a few moments of silence.

"What's your definition for the relationship we were having till today?"

Thobias thought of getting things clarified immediately.

"Partners in life," she replied promptly.

He kissed her on her cheeks. It was wet with rolling tears.

21

HAVING COMPLETED THE MISSION, Thobias decided to leave Trivania early in the morning.

"You seem to have had a tough time in Smile Bank," Rajan commented.

"Not always. I was happy when I was asinised and I could live in that blissful ignorance for half of my period. I would have been happier, had I been fully asinised or had become a lunatic."

"How will you deal with the charges now? They can put you behind bars for them," Rajan was still brooding over the charges.

That may not happen," Thobias was firm. "I may go before the trial starts."

"You said you are not going back to USA," Rajan looked at him doubtfully.

"Not to USA, but to a place where nobody can touch me," Thobias did not reveal the destination and Rajan did not ask further because he knew his ignorance level and he was sure that there are many places in the world other than the USA.

"The incidents at Doncity are the gravest. How did you get transferred there?" Rajan asked curiously.

"It was Mehman's decision to pull me out of the Audit Department when he found that I had well adjusted with the job and even started enjoying it."

"Most of the Doncity branches were managed by South Marcardians, because they were sufficiently asinised to receive additional workload with a smile as in the emblem, without bothering about the working hours or the salary. The best results were obtained when South Marcardians went there without their family, so that they were not disturbed at work."

"After receiving the transfer order, I climbed the HO staircase many times and waited in front of Mehman's cabin for an appointment, like I did before at the operation theatre at Lourdes Hospital.

"'Let me see. You give your request,' Mehman said at the first meeting.

"'It's not in my hand. You go and meet the APM,' he said during my second visit.

"'Take your seat,' he was magnanimous during the third visit. 'Tell me, why can't you go to Doncity?'

"'My son is in the tenth standard. I cannot shift my family this year. Please give me a posting near here for a year,' I pleaded with him.

"'Okay. If we give this favour to you, what will you give in return?' Mehman put it straight.

"'I will meet the business targets, as I have proved earlier,' I was confident.

"'Okay, okay. I know those things. Everybody does it, and there is nothing special in it. Business growth is based on economic growth and individuals do not matter there.' I had heard a similar statement from Mehman at the time of my first promotion interview, where he was a member. At that time, I could not believe it fully, but now I believed it fully because it was a must.

"'What I need from you is . . . ,' he paused for a second, 'is your full cooperation in implementing the corporate strategies. Can you join me in that?' He stopped, looking at my pale face.

"I understood the meaning. *Be part of the system; promote asinisation further.*

"'I know you cannot decide easily,' he continued. 'You've got the reputation as an upright performing Manager and your comments are very catchy and true, though highly irritating to us. So the deal is clear. If you are on this side, take the modification right now and if you decide to be on the other side, you will be one of the fifty thousand staff and I don't know you at all. In such cases, transfers are routine and we are not modifying them.'

"I sat silently.

"'Once you decide, it should be firm. Yeah, I know that you are a man of words. Still, I have to say that. I am also going to forgive the few comments made by you during your audit period. You remember them?'

"'No, Sir,' I became humble.

"'You said promotion and transfers in Smile Bank are based on religious proximity with the boss, indicating me.' His look was piercing.

"'Not exactly, Sir. I only said that objective decisions are possible only by computers and religion is a good base to establish a rapport with the boss, if he too is from the same religion. It has been proved by sociologists and I stand by it.'

"'Then what did you say about our Kids Deposit Scheme?'

"'It's a good one, Sir,' I readily agreed.

"'But you made some comments somewhere, and I want to confirm it,' Mehman insisted.

"'I don't remember, Sir,' I thought I would take a chance there.

"'If you don't remember, I can tell you. You said canvassing in schools is difficult, as parents are not there to take an immediate decision. But if one went to maternity hospitals, we could get all of them together and we would be the first bank to welcome the kids to planet earth with a smile. That was too much. I am pardoning it because I know that will happen in the days to come,' Mehman was candid on that point.

"I sat silently appreciating the management information system of Smile Bank.

"'You did not tell me your decision so far,' Mehman was getting serious, and for a moment, he seemed to doubt whether he had talked more than needed.

"I was in two minds and could not say anything for some more time. Meanwhile Mehman seemed to have taken his decision on my transfer.

"'I am busy. You may go and discuss with the DPM further,' he pointed towards the next cabin and I entered there hesitantly.

"'Yes?' An aged, angry looking, lean man raised his head from the financial newspaper, obviously indicating his dislike for the intrusion.

"'I am Thobias Mathai. I came to request a transfer modification,' I was hesitant to continue, seeing the apathy of the DPM.

"'What?' He did not even apply his mind. 'Where do you work?'

"'In Smile Bank, now at Kallania,' I acknowledged his belittling.

"'Why did you come to me for that? You talk at lower levels.' He looked at the newspaper again."

"Why did Mehman send you to him?" Rajan asked.

"Just to show me the insignificance of the Manager called Thobias Mathai in Smile Bank. It was a cat-and-mouse game. Those hapless high-fliers do not have any other avenues for fun and they largely depend on request-seekers to kill time."

"The feeling that Amma too may suffer like Pappu made me meet Revolutionary Association leader Pannaverse, in a last ditch effort for a modification.

"'Who is there to look after your aged mother?' he joined my sadness by stretching the corner of his already insignificant lips leftwards. 'Go, meet Mehman again.'

"'I prefer cats eating the mouse than playing with it,' I told Pannaverse and rushed back to my quarters to pack my frugal luggage.

"Doncity is the financial capital of Marcardia. It is a peaceful city because the people fear each other and generally keep a distance between them. Law and order is maintained by the police during the day and the early part of night, till the vast middle-class majority slips into deep sleep after a hectic day at the workplace. Dons take charge of the city thereafter, dispensing justice to the lower and upper strata of society. The biggest advantage of Doncity is the availability of two agencies for getting justice, charging more or less the same for their services.

"However, the middle class generally keep a distance from both these friendly law dispensers. It does not mean that both these agencies have a perfect working relationship. Occasional skirmishes cannot be ruled out when dons go beyond the permitted unwritten clauses of the Special Penal Code in their enthusiasm to dispense justice to a larger section of the population. Any of their actions, which can affect the peace-loving middle class, are sternly dealt with since they are largely unattached in politics and they create opinions which can cause en masse shifting of loyalties and change of rulers.

"Both these agencies have good management information systems, and nothing happens in Doncity without their knowledge and permission.

"Still, it was a far better place than the rest of Marcardia because the people there meant business. They learned better survival skills, and the best learner naturally became unbeatable in business in all of Marcardia.

"The suburban train is the lifeline of Doncity, carrying millions and millions of commuters to their workplaces and back. Railway stations and roads leading to them are crowded like a honeycomb. Fast life is really made slow here, as you wait for the one in front to lift his feet and leave a few inches of valuable space for you to accommodate your ready-to-move legs.

"But, at times, the space can come to your way liberally when you are helpfully pushed down from the moving train during your attempt to disembark at the station. At that time, you will be assured of space on the platform for a four-leg fall, permitting even a full width roll, before you stand up trying to collect baggage parts.

"My dislike for train commuting was not exactly owing to the hostile energy of the commuters who seemed to seek to throw me on the platform. I had intelligently avoided it by travelling in the early morning, when most others would be still asleep. But, the morning scene visible through the train window was capable of spoiling my mood for the entire day; herds of people would be sitting on the unused steel rails, evacuating their stomachs," Thobias said.

"We will stop here for breakfast. I like *idli* and *sambar*. What about you?" Rajan intervened to stop the story telling for a while.

"Anything will do for me," Thobias too agreed to have breakfast, though the old pictures were coming up again, ruining his appetite as in his early days at Doncity.

22

THOBIAS CONTINUED HIS STORY immediately after the car revved up after breakfast.

"The Milky Station branch of Smile Bank at Doncity presented a shabby look from the outside. The inside was elegant with a curved granite-top counter. There was a centrally placed glass cabin to house the boss of the branch who could watch the entire proceedings in the banking hall without coming out of it. I put my suitcase down and knocked at the cabin door. There was no response. So I pushed in and confronted the stout man who was sitting like a statue without any expression. He was Mr. Kusagran, the boss, and I was to work under him as Manager.

"'Where is your relieving letter?' he asked, firmly determined not to smile at the new subordinate who had come to his cabin after making a two thousand-kilometre journey, even skipping breakfast to be on time.

"'I was asked to report here and the relieving letter would follow,' I showed him my Smile Bank identity card and the transfer order.

"He took his time to read the order signed by Mehman, as if there was no other work for him for the entire day, occasionally looking at the photo in the identity card and at my face.

"'That's your seat,' he pointed at a half cabin near the entrance. 'You have to manage the branch. Don't come to me with your problems. I am an executive; knock at the door and get permission before you enter the cabin. Don't send any customer to me unless I ask you to. I will give you your BRA tomorrow.' BRA meant *Basic Responsibility Areas* in Smile Bank.

"I sat on the push-back chair comfortably, a few seconds before the opening of the branch without knowing the heat under it. At 8.30 am sharp, the front door was opened and a big crowd crashed in like fish coming out of the fishing net, some silent, some flopping and some in frantic search of water to sustain life. A long queue was formed in front of me in a few seconds, and all were miserably restless and trying to save a few seconds of their time.

"'What is this entry?' the first in the queue stretched his pass book close to my eyes.

"'Give me a few seconds. Let me get a password and get into the computer system,' I humbly requested the first angry man.

"'That's your headache. You just reverse it now, or I will take you to court for the mental agony caused by your bank,' he thumped on my table and a few papers took leave of it thanks to his brute force.

"'Hey gentleman, you are taking too much time," the second in the queue came forward and pushed the first man behind. "What happened to the clearing yesterday? My account is not credited. This is a horrible bank.'Thobias was also sure about it, but in another way.

"'What's this? See how your staff spelled my name in the pass book,' the third one in the queue wanted immediate rectification.

"'How many times should I come to you for my credit card?' said the next one.

"'You are slow in settling death claims. I have to take up with your Principal Manager at Trivania,' the one next said.

"'You're not taking the phone and attending to our valuable customers. It is coming to me,' Kusagran came in between, pushing the crowd sideways, and expressed his first displeasure. 'I am going out for business canvassing and will be back before closing. Reply to the phone calls from the controlling office promptly.'

"My computer is not working, Sir. The customers are shouting. Please call the vendor,' a lady staff came from the other end of the hall, ordered and vanished into the dining room.

"'You are in charge of the premises and the computer systems. This is the key to the LAN room. Please acknowledge.' It was the turn of the good looking Advances Manager to push the crowd and come forward.

"'Please sign here, Sir.' It was an employee.

"'Please sign here, Sir.' It was another employee.

"'Please sign here, Sir.' It was yet another employee. It went on.

"'You are in charge of cash. Please come and check it, Sir. I have to catch the train at 5.30.' The cashier gave a gentle smile.

"'5.30?' I could not believe it. 'Yes, Sir. It is 5.30 now. Our business hours were over one hour back and now we are doing extended service. The people you see now are our customers who entered the bank before closure of the front door and some are our high value customers. They come after business hours, so that things will be faster.'

"'Welcome to our Region.' It was a call from the APM of the Doncity Region. 'Yours is a good branch. Try to keep that reputation intact. Today, I was told that your branch has not submitted many important statements to our office. Why is that happening in your branch? I am a mild man, but I cannot tolerate delay.'

"'I joined today only, Sir. I will look into it.' I thought I will not reveal my original stuff to him in the new place that fast.

"'That's okay. But, how much time do you require to verify with the staff about the pending statements?' It was an angry tone made for the situation and he was doing his duty of pestering the south Marcardians for better output from the start.

"'You want it in seconds or minutes?' I sought a small clarification. He never expected such a prompt and specific question and the phone went off, maybe to take time to plan how to deal with a non-asinised subordinate.

"'I missed breakfast. Where can I get lunch?' I asked the part time employee who had come in late under the staggered working arrangement. Actually, I had not noticed the exit of the earlier staff and the fact that their place had been occupied by another set.

"'Lunch? At this time? Sir, you can take dinner in another half an hour.' It was true.

"While finishing the balance work in the early night, the part-time employee gave a few tips about Doncity life.

"'Here life moves in seconds, both for the staff and for the customer. Only in the night shift one can talk in between.'

"'Where are you put up?' he asked again.

"'That's what I am thinking now.'

"'Hotels are costly. Anyhow, it is very late now. There are only a few more hours to open the branch again.'

"I caught his idea. Why close the branch? I changed my attire into a comfortable *lungi* and lay down on the posh sofa in the visitors' lounge. I understood why forced bachelors from South Marcardia give better output at Doncity. I slipped into a kind of sleep, occasionally brushing aside the mosquitoes which made single string music near my ears.

"'Why so many newspapers?' I asked the peon who entered the bank first in the morning.

"'For the boss. He reads Marcardia Express in the morning, Marcardia Business Journal after that and Stock Journal after lunch if he hasn't gone out.'

"'Where is he from?' I asked.

"'From Doncity only. He is working in Doncity for the last thirty years.'

"It was a middle-aged and short lady officer who was sitting near me who first showed some unofficial touch. 'Work as per rules only,' she advised. 'Here customers are more intelligent than you. In Doncity, only the fittest will survive. And don't underestimate anybody in business dealings. They can play any game, any time.' I wondered how she measured my intelligence objectively in the short span of twenty-four hours. Still, it was a welcome piece of advice in a place where no one talked anything personal.

"She was Mrs. Jaykar, working in the loan department under another middle-aged lady manager whose body language hinted that she wanted to keep a distance from me, even though I was superior to her in the official hierarchy. I recollected the old proverb, '*Child quarrels with the father and joins the grandfather.'* That must be the reason why Jaykar told me in the early morning hours of the second day, 'Here only small things are discussed in the open. Big things are done in whispers.'

"'I did not get it. Can you elaborate?' I asked.

"'Watch, you can detect it. Watch my boss Mrs. Smylitha closely.' I left it there without much exploration.

"The second day was also not very different from the first day except for the shift in accommodation.

"'You can stay in our Pinnakkaval transit quarters. It is very close to your branch. There are more than sixty flats in that building and you can select any of them. The key for Flat No. 21 is available at the shop just opposite the building. The keys of all other flats are available in Flat No. 21. Try to go early and if late, take a torch or candle. The main electric switch is close to Flat No. 27 on the first floor. Don't worry about the loneliness; it can be real fun to be away from the crowded Doncity streets.' It was the instruction from the Quarters Section of the controlling office.

"'Why the question of loneliness? All are vacant?' I was aware of the accommodation problem at Doncity.

"'It is marked for demolition and is fully vacant. But don't worry; it won't fall as fast as you think,' the officer was very optimistic.

"It was a big relief when I located the main switch and put on the lights. I selected the dusty sofa of Flat No. 21 to sleep because the other flats resembled centuries old ghost dens seen in horror films. I understood one thing; the most important requirement for sound sleep is a tired body. In the morning, I felt that the blanket had become a bit heavy. While peeping over it, I saw a joint family of rats sitting on it over my chest and eating the balance bread of my raw dinner.

"'Good morning,' I wished the eldest member. Although it did not wish me back, I could see myself developing a relation with the big rat family there. You know how? The sofa I was sleeping on had big holes underneath and the inside was fully occupied by rats. They did not allow me to sleep when they were having their midnight parties and dances in their house. When I thumped on the side of the sofa in half sleep, all of them understood me, obeyed me and kept quiet.

"'This is your BRA,' Mr. Kusagran stood before me next day and stretched a few pages of neatly typed papers at my eye level. 'Sign on all pages and return one copy to me.' I obeyed without reading it, as I knew the boss is always right.

"While glancing through the pages, I understood the depth of knowledge Kusagran possessed in understanding the various Smile Bank functions. He had covered the entire gamut of banking functions as duties of his subordinate; meeting business targets, keeping internal control of the branch perfect, granting quality advances, recovering the loans granted, practising the best HRD concepts, submitting statements promptly to controlling offices, control over hardware and software, extending the best customer services, managing cash and security items, enforcing staff punctuality, controlling expenditure, increasing income, answering phone calls, building branch image, uplifting the poor, preventing frauds . . . ; it went on.

"Each task carried marks and the total was eighty.

"'Twenty marks will be earmarked for your additional achievements over and above the basic responsibility areas.

Your performance will be objectively evaluated by me and your future placements will be based on the marks you secure from me.' He took a threatening posture.

"'I have included sanctioning of loans under your BRA. But I will help you there by identifying good parties,' he offered his help without smiling.

"'Your BRA is small,' Mrs. Jaykar said. 'It has not included settling border disputes of Marcardia or preventing global terrorism. But, granting of loans could have been avoided. It was the duty of my dear madam, Mrs. Smylitha. She wanted to escape from it and Kusagran agreed to that. She only typed the entire eight pages of your BRA, sitting late.'

"The fourth day gave me an opportunity to meet almost all the staff, though the context was not that great. There was no water supply and all got agitated over it. A few took leave and went home and the rest gathered in my cabin seeking immediate redressal of their grievance. Then only I observed them; most were ladies and some were very beautiful and a few were dressed to kill. I enjoyed the gathering very much. Some were very angry and their faces became red, adding to their beauty. I wished the water would never come.

"But, I was forced to solve the water problem the next day. The Water Authority Supervisor came by noon and sat on the chair in front of me quite authoritatively.

"'Acknowledge this,' he extended a letter in duplicate.

"I scanned it before acknowledging. It said that our water meter was not functioning for the last fifteen days and we have to replace it immediately along with remitting approximate water consumption charges and penalties amounting to Lians . . . . I left the figures and concentrated on the spirit of the letter.

"'It was not working because there was no water,' I told the supervisor.

"'I do not want to know it,' he was sure about the boundaries of his work and was not prepared to cross it. 'You have to change the meter immediately, or else we will be stopping the supply.' Though it was a threat, it did not say anything new.

"'Sir,' the all knowing sweeper came forward and winked his eyes, 'I will manage it. You just sign this,' he extended a bill of two hundred Lians and I signed it, solving a big problem.

"'But, I want the water meter running,' the supervisor was duty conscious even while accepting the small gift.

"I became the ring master for three dozen busy people. The junior Manager was feared by all, as her husband was working in the Banking Authority of Marcardia, which controlled all the banks in that country.

"It was easy for me to recognise the normal customer of our branch. They would be old people like the staff behind the counter. They were still dealing with us due to their laziness in complying with the account opening formalities of new-generation banks. Some people like to keep those accounts to issue accommodation cheques or to get attestations or to deposit small dividend warrants or just because they can command here like kings after retirement from service, when nobody calls them *Sir* any more."

"As days passed, I found a new set of customers opening accounts to the surprise of all. They were young, energetic, well dressed and impatient. They used to refer the name of Kusagran whenever there was any delay," Thobias continued.

"It was Mrs. Jaykar who first brought this to my notice. She observed the new customers coming out of the cabin and opening accounts without proper introductions.

"'Keep a watch on those accounts,' I cautioned her.

"'I did. All are ending with big loans,' she was sharp. 'Unfortunately, I have to recommend these loans. I am unable to find any fault in them, though I smell something bad.' No officer dares to question an executive in the Smile Bank.

"'Are you analysing the loans carefully?' I asked Mrs. Smylitha when I got her alone in one evening.

"'Please don't doubt an honest man. You know the experience of Kusagran? He is an expert in credit portfolio. He is helping me in visiting the parties and preparing the inspection reports. He even sanctions the loans on behalf of you. He has reduced my workload as well as yours very much.'

"'I wish you don't get back the reduced workload sometime later,' I ended the topic there.

"'Good work, Thobias,' the APM from controlling office called one day. 'You are extending full cooperation to Kusagran, so that he is doing a good job in Advances. Continue supporting him.'

"'I will, Sir,' I showed courtesy.

"'Smile Bank always rewards performers and supporters,' the APM added.

"It was not news to me. It was stated by a lot of people left and right but was forced to be repeated because nobody believed it.

"'I want to take promotion and want to be an APM,' Kusagran told me a few days later. 'I hate sitting idle and taking salary.'

"It was natural to wish for bigger cabins and lesser work. Entering the executive level had an additional charm. A heavenly halo develops behind their heads as soon as the promotion list is sent for typing. They get colours immediately after the list is published. And everybody can see it when the order is received by a new executive. It is a symbol that the executive is a Saint and that he never does anything against the bank. No executive was ever punished in the long history of Smile Bank. This kept the post of executive attractive and the entire asinisation process worked upon it.

"If an employee is fully asinised and chasesthe carrot of promotion, the boss can give out a sigh of relief. Kusagran was sending the signals to me about his motive for working, so that I could retransmit them to the people who mattered.

"Even without my efforts, the APM Mr. Marayonthan found it out. 'He wants promotion.' He smiled at getting a fully asinised branch-in-charge at Milky Station.

"I was sure that Kusagran was not the one for promotions and sacrifices. But, there were no takers.

"'You want leave?' Kusagran surprised me one evening.

"'Sure. I will be happy if I get it. I was going on postponing certain medical consultations of my elder son's thoracic problem.'

"'I will recommend that to the APM,' he was very kind.

"I was unable to understand his increased love for me.

"'Did you watch Mrs. Jaykar closely,' he asked again a few days later. 'You can have a better side view of her, if you push your chair a bit leftwards.' He was measuring me and I became more alert. Something is happening here, or is going to happen. I went to the controlling office after settling the branch chores and met Mr. Marayonthan, the APM, a South Marcardian.

"'I have got some doubts about the loans Mr. Kusagran is giving.'

"'Ha, ha. What else is expected from a guy who is fresh from the Audit Department?' he laughed. 'See, you are a manager in a branch. Use your words carefully. There are big customers and big loans in Doncity unlike in South Marcardia. Don't peep too much and you will be taken to task for false allegations.'

I sat silent.

"'There is a system here. Don't try to move against it. Come with solid proof, if you want to make a point,' he advised.

"'It is a perfect branch. Don't spoil it,' he advised me again, while I was moving out from his cabin towards the lift.

"*Perfect branch* has got a meaning in Smile Bank. It will be like a family. There will be a grandfather without much work, always peeping into others' work and giving suggestions without actually knowing it. His nuisance value has to be accepted by all. Below him, are a few productive people, majority of them South Marcardians, who run the show by absorbing the tension and getting scolded by the higher-ups and occasionally experiencing the thrills of getting leave sanctioned by the grandfather to go to the native place for quarterly sex. Below them there will be a few supporters, mostly females who are sincere to the job but often bothered by family chaos and well-earning husbands. Then come a few who are not at all bothered about the bank and they make their presence unnoticed when they occasionally come to office. The next layer consists of a few who will always create a feeling that their absence from the branch is more appealing than their presence. One will be too happy to send the salary as money order to their houses. The extreme outer layer consists of a few sincere people who are handicapped, a few alcoholics and a few perverts whose psyche is not understandable even by the best psychologists.

"All in the same cadre get equal salary but those who work better can get more work. They can also create more mistakes and get more punishments than others.

"All will be in the same queue for transfer and promotion. Those who work well will be indispensable and their transfer request will be held back, giving others a better chance. Same will be the case in granting leave.

"But, the news was not that perfect when I reached the office next day. 'Kusagran wants to talk to you,' the peon informed me even before a formal 'good morning'. I entered the cabin after knocking twice. His face was red hot.

"'How many letters are pending for despatch?'

"'None.' I could understand his efforts for finding something faulty.

"'I am getting complaints from our valued customers. You are not finding time to deal with them nicely. I will be forced to report,' he extended a threat and sat silently for some time.

"'You can report it,' I agreed with him. He did not like my fearlessness.

"'Thobias,' he called again when I was about to withdraw from his cabin. 'I am having only a few years to retire from service. I want to take promotion and become an APM before that. I never rule out errors in Advances portfolio completely, and I also know that there won't be any errors if I sit idle.'

"'You know our great Assistant Vice Principal Manager Mr. Baldorin at Head Office? You know how many bad loans he had given when he was here at Doncity? Smile Bank appreciated his risk taking capacity, and where is he now? Please don't spread rumours about me.'

"Kusagran also knew things about Mr. Baldorin. Never allow a subordinate to suspect anything. Entrust the subordinate to do the lengthy and cumbersome documentation. If they are not falling in line, just remind them about the 'waiting customer' and the 'BRA'.

"The Bank always retains the advantage with it to catch the manager at a later stage, citing some documentation error. The executive can escape the ordeal as he need not sign anywhere and is not responsible for the loan documentation.

"There were only two options for me; either become another Smylitha or find out the exact nature of the dealings with proof and knock on the door of Mr. Marayonthan. I arranged a person as proxy and sent to Kusagran for a loan of 2,00,000 Lians. Kusagran talked to him politely and went through the submitted balance sheet carefully.

"'Come with the projected balance sheet,' he said.

"It was done in two days, and he again approached Kusagran just after the business hours. 'You did not say who the guarantor is,' Kusagran was very polite there too. 'Get me the proof of his assets too.'

"During the next trip, he sought the clarifications about the debtors and creditors and politely requested for statement of the same certified by a chartered accountant.

"At the time of the fourth visit, he discussed the valuation of the assets by an approved valuer.

"During the fifth visit, Kusagran promised to visit his unit at a later date. But, it was postponed and another date was fixed. It was postponed again. Finally, my proxy got tired and left the scene.

"'Surely there must be an easy route,' he said while quitting the assigned work."

"We have reached Panamkara. I did not feel that we spent that much time talking," Thobias told Rajan and he was looking cheerful for having got a chance to open his heart.

23

"THERE WERE CALLS FOR YOU every half an hour, during the entire day," Teena said as soon as Thobias reached home. "The caller did not say who he was, but went on repeating the call. It may come again any time now."

"I am from Marcardia State Investigation Bureau. Can I talk to Thobias Mathai?" the call came as expected within minutes.

"Speaking," Thobias did not show any anxiety.

"You have to appear before Mr. Tejaram at this office tomorrow at 8 a.m. sharp. Our office is at Kiloor, four kilometres from Cohiana airport." The line went dead before Thobias could respond. He had wanted to postpone the meeting by a day as he was very much tired, but the caller did not give him a chance.

Disobedience can hurt the ego. Hence Thobias made up his mind to undertake another journey early the next day. There was some discomfort in his chest and Thobias took considerable time to slip into sleep. Around midnight, the phone rang again.

"Sorry to disturb you again, somebody wants to talk to you urgently," Teena came upstairs and knocked on the door. She was apologetic.

"I am from Marcardia State Investigation Bureau. Am I talking to Mr. Thobias Mathai?" The tone was not to the liking of Thobias.

"Yes."

"You will be coming tomorrow morning itself?"

"Yes."

"I called to confirm it." The phone was disconnected. Thobias felt irritated for having his sleep disturbed, especially when it was becoming a rare commodity. He could not get sleep afterwards and departed to Cohiana early next morning.

The guard at the entrance directed Thobias to the third floor. Tejaram was looking seriously at Thobias when he entered his room after knocking. It was a dead sharp look capable of instilling fear in anybody. Tejaram was tall and well built with medium complexion, and his body language indicated that he meant business. He was sitting upright on the chair, with his arms placed on the arms of the chair, reminiscent of the portrait of a majestic Nazi general except for the colour.

"You can sit," Tejaram tried to ease the tension in Thobias but continued reading his face.

"You feel sleepy?"

"Yeah, very much. I was travelling for the last two days to find out the charges made by my previous employer."

"Did you find them out?" Tejaram asked.

"Yes, I got a copy of the charge sheet."

"Then I can go straight to the subject. Where are you keeping the funds?"

"I have an account in USA, a regular salary account."

"See, you said you know the charges. I have got information that you have amassed wealth and escaped to USA. I am asking about those funds."

"I don't have any other account," Thobias insisted.

"Are you sure?" he paused for a moment. "Okay, then see this pass sheet," Tejaram showed him an old pass sheet from Solacian Bank of Marcardia.

"Yeah, I admit. It was opened just to discount a cheque," Thobias apologised.

"So, you told a lie to start with?"

"But, that was a nominal account."

"I did not say otherwise," Tejaram used only calculated words. "I am also not after your nominal accounts. I was asking about the fatty accounts you are having in foreign banks. How much did you make at Doncity?"

"I did not make anything there. I was very much in debt in those days."

"Who is going to believe you?" It was a genuine question because Thobias knew that truth has only a few takers. "Tell me truth only. I am not a fool to believe all your words. I've got detailed reports about you."

"How much did you send home monthly?"

"Around 10,000 Lians."

"No. You have sent 12,000 Lians in four months when your net take-home salary was just around 13,000 Lians. Where did you get money to live in Doncity?"

"I just managed a hand-to-mouth existence for three years." It was a hand-to-mouth life for twenty years, but Thobias did not tell that far.

"You are not opening out. I can easily make you do that." Tejaram made a move for the first time in the chair by tilting a little to the left side. It was not exactly a threatening posture but was very near to it.

"Why should you collude with Kusagran to defraud the bank without any benefit to you?"

"I did not collude. In fact, I only blew the whistle in time, to prevent further frauds."

"How did you forewarn?"

"I informed the DPM and stopped further loans."

"Is there any proof for that?"

"No."

"Then, how can I believe it? Even if it is true, why didn't you warn earlier? You warned when Kusagran stopped sharing the booty with you?"

"Did Kusagran say that?" Thobias had a doubt.

"You need not question me. Here I'm the boss and I am questioning you.

Is that clear to you?" Thobias was not sure whether the anger shown by Tejaram was real or created for the situation.

"Yes. Yes, Sir." Thobias addressed him as 'Sir' for the first time.

"You have not answered me yet."

"I did not warn earlier because there were many people who audited the branch and certified that they were all good loans."

"Who were they?" "Concurrent auditors, regular auditors, external auditors and the executives who visited the branch."

"Does that absolve you from your duties?" Thobias did not reply.

"How was your relationship with Kusagran?"

"Satisfactory. He determind when I could take leave and go home. It implies that he decided when I could take my kid to the hospital, which festival I could celebrate and when I could meet my relatives. So, he was everything to me and I obeyed his orders."

"So, you colluded with him for those favours?"

"I said I obeyed, not colluded."

"Who detected the frauds?"

"It's a story."

"You tell it. But, be brief."

"Once, I went to a pub at Doncity along with Mr. Sasian, a friend of mine, who was working with Doncity police. We received VIP treatment and were seated in the front row, and were served with a pint of brandy and a small packet of peanuts."

"Oh! So, that was the way your money went? You visited bars regularly?"

"I visited only once."

"Why? You did not like it?"

"My purse was thin," I replied.

"So, money was a constraint for you?"

"Yeah, sure."

"Money was a constraint for you," he repeated the sentence emphatically as if he got a big lead in a complex case and wrote something on his notepad.

"Go ahead," he gave the green signal.

"A well dressed lady was singing a film song and the orchestra was trying its best to cover up the croaking. Another group of ladies, dressed to expose more, were standing in the middle and gently twisting their bodies to suit the music. 'Earlier, they used to dance with us. But it is banned now,' Sasian said. 'How is the music?'

"'Nice,' I was not sure when I said it.

"'I used to come here,' Sasian said, 'to see who all are coming here. Most of the clients of this pub are criminals in our records. Some are innocent too, like you.'

"As time passed, the rhythm of the music changed to suit the mood of the crowd, and a person stood up and threw a bundle of new notes into the middle of the dancers. The girls competed with each other to collect the falling notes, like kids in a competition. He again threw another bundle and those who got less in the first attempt put more effort to collect the maximum this time. This went on and he became their darling.

"'You know him?' Sasian asked in my ears, pointing at the man. I shook my shoulders.

"'He is a don of this area. An extortionist and a dangerous crook, who can do anything for or against you for money.'

"I looked at him again to watch his face but he was surrounded by girls and they were writing something, maybe phone numbers. We exited from there.

"At the door, a neatly dressed man was waiting for Sasian with a readymade smile devoid of any warmth. He extended an envelope to Sasian which he put into his trouser pocket without opening.

"Sasian shirked his shoulders as if to say, 'don't ask me about it.' I could understand that it was his weekly *hafta*. 'An equal sum will be paid to the local *dada* too on a weekly basis,' Sasian knew the system well.

"A few days later, Mrs. Smylitha sat in front of me, showing an interest in talking."

"Smylitha? Who was she?" Tejaram asked in between.

"The manager-in-charge of the loan department," Thobias replied.

"I have not seen that name in any of the investigation reports," Tejaram raised his eyebrows. There was silence and Tejaram scratched his forehead for some time trying to locate the name. "You can continue," Tejaram was rewinding his memory, but he did not want Thobias to sit idle.

"'There is a problem in one of our accounts, M/s Classic Innocents and Co,' Mrs. Smylitha told me. 'We have discounted their export bills and the foreign bank has rejected them saying they have already forwarded the payment. There seems to be some problem.' She was not smiling this time.

"'It seems that there was no Form 92 of the Customs Department at the time of discounting the bill. That form is the proof that export has taken place. Kusagran asked me to discount the bill without it.' She placed the entire loan documents in front of me for no reason. I opened the loan file casually and looked at the photograph of the borrower.

"'Wow!' It was the same man I saw at the pub, throwing notes at the dancers.

"'You know him?' Mrs. Smylitha read the changes that took place on my face.

"'Yeah. Some say that he is a criminal.'

"'Really?' She became pale, as if blood circulation avoided her face.

"'He is the guarantor for two other big loans too. We are going to release those loans day after tomorrow.' She was about to burst.

"'I will stop it,' I told her.

"One phone call was enough to get a fax from the APM stopping all new loans because I could collect evidence from my police friend.

"'You have saved millions and millions of Lians. We will take care of you,' the APM told me over the phone."

"Did you get any record for it? Say, an appreciation letter?" asked Tejaram.

"Ha, ha. No," Thobias said.

"There was a call from the DPM the next day," Thobias said.

"'What is happening there in the loan portfolio?' the DPM asked.

"'An export bill has gone bad. You can get the details from Kusagran and even Mrs. Smylitha. They are dealing with that account.'

"'You do not know anything?'

"'Only very little. They know much more than me.'

"'What do you do in the branch?'

"'I handle everything other than loans.'

"'What is that everything?'

"'Deposits, staff matters, cash, computer, clearing, *tapal*, customer complaints . . . . ' It was an endless list.

"'Employees are given to you for doing that. Give me a report as to what you were doing during the last three months towards deposit growth. It should reach me tomorrow,' he ordered.

"'Are you not happy there?' the DPM continued.

"'It is a relative term, Sir.'

"'Can you define it?'

"'Happiness is inversely proportional to the difference between reality and expectations,' I repeated my old definition.

"'Are you a banker or a lazy thinker frustrated in life?'

"'Both. I am working in Smile Bank, Sir,' I informed the reason for my frustration too.

"'Your family is here?' He was not ready to believe my version because he too was in Smile Bank and was still happy.

"'No, Sir.' Thobias expected a word of sympathy in the next sentence.

"'Then you can devote more time for the Bank,' he identified a business point there.

"'But there's a small problem,' I could not agree with him immediately.

'They are still alive and their problems come to me only.'

"Surprisingly, the DPM did not tell me to eliminate them to increase my productivity. He only asked a very simple question. 'You know whom you are talking to?'

"'Yes Sir, to the DPM.' My answer was correct but he was not happy with that correct reply. He cut off the phone. I could not understand the reason for cutting the phone when the discussion was progressing well. Maybe, he could not adjust to true answers, which were not in conformity with the accepted norms of replying to an executive in Smile Bank."

Tejaram was not keenly listening to the regurgitations. He was just watching the lip movements of the culprit, and later went out from the cabin without saying anything.

Thobias sat watching the blank white-washed wall and the neatly kept table without anything on it except a notepad on which Tejaram had scribbled something in a shabby handwriting. The previous night's sleeplessness started catching up with him. Some discomfort was also brewing up near the lung region. Thobias came close to the table and placed the elbow of his right arm over the table supporting the head and welcomed the goddess of sleep. Suddenly, a short man appeared before him and shook him up.

"This is not a place to sleep," he said politely.

"Sorry."

Time was ticking away without any meaning. Otherwise too, is there any meaning to it? He thought for a while. He had to spend the balance time and was getting serious situations to pass it, rather than monotonous eventless minutes. Still, these crucial seconds in this universe could have been better utilized. No, not that way. Here, he was spending the time very effectively trying to prove his innocence. Had he not been there to defend this case now, a bad reputation would have befallen on the family.

"Can I go for some rest?" Thobias asked the man who entered the room.

"Who brought you here?"

"I was talking to Mr. Tejaram. He went out without a word. Now more than five hours have elapsed."

"Ha, ha," the visitor laughed. "He has left for home many hours back."

"Can I go home then?"

"Tejaram is my superior officer. You disobey him at your risk."

"But he's already gone."

"Maybe. But that is no excuse. You have to talk to his superior to know his itinerary. He is available upstairs." The man withdrew from the room hastily.

Thobias sat on the same chair for a few more minutes before slowly moving out and climbing the stairs. He found all the cabins empty. It was already night and nobody was expected to be there right then. Thobias took a decision to move out and go home. Night driving was never a pleasure for Thobias due to the piercing lights from vehicles coming from the opposite side. However, he was used to doing a lot of things without pleasure.

It took more than three hours to reach home. The phone was ringing when he entered the drawing room after parking the car.

"Mr. Thobias Mathai?"

"Yes."

"I am from MSIB. Mr. Tejaram wants to talk to you."

Tejaram at this hour? Thobias could not believe it.

"How did you go without my permission? Who permitted you to go?" he was shouting in anger. "Come back just now or we will send a team to arrest you. It won't be a pleasure trip," he threatened and put the phone down.

It was midnight. Thobias weighed the pros and cons of going at such an odd time and finally decided in favour of going.

Thobias took a pain killer and swallowed it without water as he always did and reversed the car to follow the same route. The roads were deserted this time and there were not many lights to penetrate his eyes.

The security guard at MSIB directed Thobias to the very same cabin where he had spent the whole day before. But, the cabin was empty. There was nobody on the entire floor. Further investigation proved that there was nobody in the entire building, except the guard.

Thobias returned to the cabin and got seated after a few rounds of walking in the building. He put the elbow of the right arm over the table and held his head with the palm and slipped into a sleep like situation. The pain killer did its duty of taking away the thoracic pain he felt earlier.

"Hello," life entered the building and shook the sleep off him.

"Yes," Thobias woke up from his doze and looked at the tall stout man in uniform.

"Mr. Tejaram told me to permit you to go tonight, if you can report at 8 a.m. sharp."

"Otherwise you can wait here. But, we will not permit sleeping here," he said politely.

"Then, why did he ask me to come back at night?"

"This is MSIB and you are a fraudster. Our duty is to prove your crime and we will do it."

Thobias decided to wait till 8 a.m. in the cabin itself and sat erect on the chair. But, soon his eyelids started drooping and he again put his elbow on the table to support his head which was coming downwards against his wish.

"I told you not to sleep here," the same tall man in uniform appeared again in front of him. This time, his sound was very harsh.

Thobias decided to move out and sleep for the next three hours in a hotel. He crossed the road and walked to his left, seeing a few lights glowing brightly. A four-storeyed shabby lodge with a small reception was the nearest. Thobias knocked forcefully on the main door to wake up the receptionist. He was not happy at being woken up from his sleep, but came forward and switched on the light at the counter.

He led Thobias to a small room, just sufficient to accommodate a cot and a table. He changed the bed sheet and the cover of the hard pillow and exited.

It was a great feeling when he stretched the legs on the bed, as if he had not slept for years together. Slipping to sleep was very much enjoyable. The intercom rang with a loud sound as soon as Thobias drifted into deep sleep.

"Is it Thobias Mathai? I am calling from MSIB office. This is to remind you about tomorrow's timing. Be here at 8 a.m. sharp."

"Wow . . . !!" This time Thobias lost his cool and was about to tell something harsh. But, the phone went dead before that. He could not believe that somebody from the MSIB was following him up to the hotel.

Thobias could not sleep again. It was already 5.30 a.m. He had to keep to the time fixed by Tejaram. His eyelids were not closing as fast as earlier; probably some messages might have gone from his heart in the rush of anger.

It was ill luck again. The door bell rang exactly at 6 a.m. Thobias jumped out of bed as if something grave was happening but realised that it was just the door bell. Thobias waited for a second on the bed analysing what exactly was happening around him and where he was. He opened the door without concealing his anger for being disturbed.

"Tea, Sir." It was the room boy.

"I did not ask for tea. You should have the basic decency not to disturb a late sleeper." This time Thobias' face was literally red.

"Sorry, Sir. The man standing there asked me to give tea to you now itself," he pointed his fingers towards the reception counter. Nobody was there at that time.

Thobias did not attempt to sleep after that. He got refreshed and moved towards the MSIB Office.

24

TEJARAM WAS IN TIME, sitting in his usual upright position with hands resting on the arms of the chair. He was wearing a light coloured shirt, but his face wore the same seriousness.

"Did you meet Kusagran after leaving Doncity?"

"No."

"I was told that you were in the Audit and you smelled out things better than dogs. How can I believe that you did not detect anything unusual during the siphoning out of 5 crore Lians?" He seemed to know the entire background of Thobias Mathai.

"Yeah, I did not get any evidence in the initial days though I developed some doubts when a new set of customers started coming to the branch with introductions from remote branches. I had informed it to the higher-ups in time."

"Why didn't they take any action?"

"I can't say why. They might not have believed me. Kusagran was not a small man."

"How much did Kusagran make?"

"I do not know," Thobias said.

"See, I cannot adjust to ignorance." But, Thobias could do it easily when he was in service.

"What was the exact nature of the frauds?"

"Availing loans using forged documents. All documents would be forged including tax returns, property documents, identification records, agreements and address proofs."

"Didn't the Bank complain to the Doncity police?"

"Yes. They came and took photocopies of all documents. I do not have any idea whether they tracked the main person behind it. Or they might have reached him and stopped there."

"Main person means?"

"All the frauds followed a common pattern. The original borrower appeared knowing nothing about the backward chain. They were supplied with a set of documents and a portion of the loan amount, with instructions to avail of loans from identified branches. Repayments would come for some period and the loans would look fine as long as new loans were sanctioned. Meanwhile, the borrower would escape from the area and remain undetected. The onus of repayment would rest with the big man who was at the extreme end."

"Who was dealing with the loans?"

"Kusagran."

"You never got involved with any loans?"

"In a very marginal way. Loans were usually released in a hurry. All documents were prepared by Kusagran and it would come to the section for release. Kusagran would follow it up for immediate release through the intercom. In one case, he fixed the date of the loan on a day when Mrs. Smylitha was on leave. Naturally, the papers were to come to me for signing."

"When other staff were on leave, the pressure would come to me. I had to run the branch and it was difficult to detect anything suspicious in a short time. In this particular case, the loan was sanctioned by the APM Mr. Perfecta on the recommendation of Kusagran. I was very confident that such cases cannot be fraud. Delaying the release can antagonise the borrower, and by chance if he is a VIP, the complaint can go up to the Principal Manager. I signed the account payee demand draft for 35,00,000 Lians and handed it over to the party. The rule says that it should have been handed over to the seller of the house. It was a lapse."

"How did such an error come about?"

"I did not know who the borrower was, and who the seller was. It was not possible to go and meet the seller and hand over the demand draft when I had to attend to the routine work."

"Where was Kusagran?"

"He went out for business development as usual."

"Smile Bank punished you for that?"

"Yes."

"What was the punishment?" He was interested in knowing the punishment systems of Smile Bank.

"They cut two increments from my salary. They marked lien on my terminal benefits for an equivalent amount to take care of my early resignation and getting out. They recorded the omission in the personal file and informed me about their right to review the punishment at any time with a view to award higher penalties, if it was deemed fit, during the course of my balance service."

"You saved the bank from an incoming fraud of 5 crore Lians. Then why did they move against you too?"

"I had reported the fraud to Mr. Marayonthan, the then APM. He reported to the Head Office that, with his sixth sense, he could locate the incoming frauds and he acted quickly to prevent it. He got a promotion for that."

"Did you see his report to the Head Office?" He brought down the confidence level of Thobias.

"No." That was also a truth.

"I can tell you, Mr. Thobias. They let you off initially, but came to know that you were the advisor to the innocent Kusagran. You colluded with him leaving all evidence against him, while escaping to USA with the booty."

Thobias did not reply. He just smiled at the turn of events.

A call came to Tejaram and he went out as usual without saying anything. He did not return for hours. But this time, a boy in a grey uniform appeared and gave Thobias a glass of water, two pieces of bread along with a small ball like potato mix. Thobias gulped it in two bites and gushed down the water creating the same noise as when water moves half filled in an empty pipe.

"Sir, twenty Lians." The boy stretched a bill.

"Take this. Thobias extended a fifty Lian note. "At this moment, its value is far higher than this." Thobias remembered the law of marginal utility taught by the fat economics professor.

Tejaram returned in a hurry, soon after Thobias finished the food. He occupied the seat in the same posture as earlier.

"Kusagran continued in the branch even after the frauds?"

"Yes."

"Why?" Tejaram was a bit surprised.

"Kusagran was required there as a grandfather. If Kusagran was removed, a few more frauds would have come to light which Smile Bank did not want."

"What?" Tejaram seemed to have taken note of that point seriously. "What was the problem in frauds coming out?"

"Smile Bank was having the maximum number of frauds in Marcardia at that time. It did not want to add to it further during that financial year."

"There was upward percolation of economic benefits?" Tejaram suspected collusion of others too.

"Could be."

"Don't make irresponsible statements. You will be asked to prove them."

"It is based on inferences. After my three-year term at Doncity, I was eligible for a placement of my choice. I gave Cohiana as my option. The DPM at Cohiana was the same Marayonthan, who was promoted to DPM. My posting did not take place.

"'We do not want such Managers at Cohiana,' he wrote on my transfer request with red ink and initialled below it. Nobody could override it, because he knew me at Doncity and his version commanded more respect. I did not do anything wrong in Milky Station branch. I blocked some fraudulent loans and it must have hurt him."

"Was Kusagran charge sheeted?"

"Yes."

"Punished?"

"No."

"Charge-sheeting was for absolving?"

I did not reply.

"You were charge-sheeted?"

"No."

"How can it be? You too deviated from rules to help the loan release. Did you influence at the top like Kusagran did?"

"No. In fact, I got a call from the APM on an afternoon, soon after the crowd vanished. The APM said, 'I heard that you have signed the demand draft in one of the fraud cases. We are not initiating any action against you. We know your integrity and capacity. Errors happen to those who work. It is our duty to protect you, in case an MSIB enquiry is ordered. We want our people to be protected at any cost.' I became *our man*.

"I was not sure whether it was a carrot or stick. It must have been something in between; neither a carrot nor a stick, but both in one.

"I found the effect the very next day. There was a letter from the APM.

Dear Thobias Mathai,

I am really impressed by the deep knowledge you have gained so far in the branch. In the light of certain developments, all future loans will have to be handled by you and you will be responsible for achieving the Advances targets, recovery targets and perfecting the documentation. I am sure this will not constrain you in completing the already allotted BRA. We are sure that you will rise to the occasion and will take the branch to new heights.

Yours faithfully
Assistant Principal Manager. Region Doncity

"I found my workload going up and absence of anything other than bank work helped me to complete the work. It took a few months to adjust to the new routine. I found that anything is possible when there is a will and you don't have any wishes of your own. But, the next letter made me really sick.

Dear Thobias Mathai,

You are hereby posted as the Management Representative for securing certification from Standards Organisation. This gives you an opportunity to evaluate the systems and procedures of our beloved bank from the angle of Certification. You can collect feedback from the customers on a daily basis, in small lots as per their convenience. Tabulation should be done on a monthly basis. As a special case, you need only maintain less than a dozen relevant registers. The list is enclosed.

While updating registers on a daily basis, you can get immense insight into the customer expectations and your deficiencies.

I am confident of your ability. Non-compliance, if any, will be viewed seriously.

I am extremely pleased to permit you to pay a fee of Lians 20000/- to the certifying agency.

The details of the certification procedure is available in our circular numbers 172,181, 134b, 176c, 876, 456, 890, 342, 321, 45b, 567c and related manual of instructions. You can also collect the information from the Banking Authority of Marcardia and the certifying agency M/s Kudorerkers.

Wish you all the best.
Assistant Principal Manager Region Doncity.

"You can judge what my influence was."

Thobias watched Tejaram for a moment and stopped his story.

"I was watching the ease with which you are describing it. It has got a good flow, but behind the flow there must be hatred," Tejaram said.

"I don't have love. That's for sure."

"You have got hatred too and such fellows make frauds. That is a universal truth." He was pointing the finger at Thobias.

"It is enough for today. I don't think you are going to tell me the truth with gentlemanly treatments. You have to undergo medical tests too next time. It's a precaution," he revealed his future method of questioning.

25

"A LETTER FOR YOU," Teena stretched an envelope to the tired Thobias as soon as he was back from the MSIB office.

Thobias did not open it as he was tired after the terrible grilling, but just looked at the sender's name. It was one Mr. Sahaloshan, 7/4142, Mount Road, Trivania. He kept the letter on the table and collapsed on the bed like a felled tree. He opened it the next day only. It was not a lengthy one:

Dear Thobias,

Hope you remember me. We were together in Smile Bank at Trivania.

I came to know that you have arrived from USA. I want to talk to you urgently on a very important matter. Please come at the earliest. My phone number is 20241103 and address is available on the envelope.

I am looking forward to meeting you early.

Yours sincerely,
Sahaloshan.

Thobias could not recollect the person immediately from the name. Maybe his popular name was different, or age must have caught up with Thobias. Many of the memories of his friends had gone into oblivion. It is natural that only a few make imprints on the memory.

Thobias was sure that this letter could be related to the case and he decided to phone him immediately. It was ringing but there was no response. He tried again after breakfast but the result was the same. Thobias was not prepared to make another journey immediately and he left the matter to rest for a while.

Memory fades fast, especially in old age. Thobias too was no exception. He nearly forgot about the letter the next day and did not attempt to call further.

"Again a letter from Trivania," Teena said the next day, lifting up a post card from the letter box.

It was again from Sahaloshan, but this time the message was in a post card, readable to anybody. He seemed to be ensuring that somebody read the message and conveyed it to Thobias.

Thobias tried to call him over the phone many times without success. He decided to make another trip to Trivania. It was a lonely trip this time as Rajan preferred to stay at home to assist Sivan in chicken vaccination. Anyhow, Thobias was lucky in getting issues that took away his attention from his lung cancer and the cut off date for his eternal journey.

He could easily locate the house of Sahaloshan. It was a double storied building; painted sky blue, overlooking Mount Road, near the Institute of Orwell Studies.

"Yes?" A lean lady opened the door and made a customary look at the unknown.

"Can I meet Mr. Sahaloshan? My name is Thobias Mathai."

"One minute." She went inside casually, but returned in haste. "Please take your seat. He will be here in a few minutes."

Thobias sat watching the neatly arranged showcase and the rotating fan for some time. A thick photo album kept at the bottom of the centre table attracted his attention. It was a handy tool in identifying Sahaloshan. Thobias could recognise the 'crab' from the first picture itself. He was working in the HR department on the eighth floor. His nickname was so popular that the real name was quite unfamiliar to many. He was considerably older than Thobias and always contributed much to the office noise pollution through his silence. All feared him because he was very close to the power centre and generally nothing favourable happens from it except for the chosen few.

Velevendran was a close friend of the *crab* since both were from the same village of Palveria District. Thobias met the *crab* at a family get-together on New Year's day.

"You know crab?" Velevendran asked him after two pegs of rum.

"Very delicious, if cooked well," Thobias was in his usual innocence. "Pappu knew how to cook it with pepper powder."

"I am talking about human crabs." Velevendran laughed heartily and could not speak for some time. "They pull down others so that nobody escapes from the ditch. Come with me, I will introduce you to one."

"Don't open your mouth carelessly. This is a dangerous *crab*." Velevendran cautioned Thobias while moving to the hall. "We are from the same village and I can take some liberties with him."

"Our duty is to adapt the new generation to the Smile Bank culture, so that it can take up higher responsibilities in future. We believe in the capabilities of ordinary people and our efforts will be in bringing out those capabilities for the benefit of the Bank," the *crab* explained the role of the HR Section briefly. The first meeting ended there.

"Talk to him at your own risk," Velevendran said after the fellowship was over and all were waiting for the New Year to arrive. "All words will reach the power centre very fast because he is coordinating the management, Revolutionary Association and the staff."

"I was not sure about the culture he was talking about," Thobias said.

"How many meals are you getting today?"

"Three, for sure."

"How many meals were you getting before joining Smile Bank? It must be two only," Velevendran asked and inferred the answer too. "The essence of the culture is the way you think. Are you sufficiently loyal to Smile Bank for the three meals they give you?"

"I was getting two meals from Pappu free before joining Smile Bank. Am I not to be more loyal to him than to the one who gives me three meals for my work?"

"You are not fully acclimatised. You have got a long way to go. It is not the question of truth here. It is the way of thinking. We want people who think like that, just think like that, not necessarily loyal or hard working. Those who think that they can get three meals outside Smile Bank don't have any place here." Velevendran stopped there, as the New Year had just arrived and all went to greet each other.

Thobias could not comprehend Velevendran's words. Still, he decided not to ask about it at that time.

Thobias met the *crab* in the cabin of APM Ritish Sahanoy a few days later. Thobias was already there to submit a loan proposal for sanction. He even lifted his buttocks from the chair in an attempt to move out as soon as the *crab* entered the cabin. But the APM signalled that he could continue there.

"Sir, this is the revised promotion list," the *crab* told Sahanoy.

The APM went through the file for a minute or two and kept it on the table.

"Did you see the business growth?" Sahanoy asked the *crab* and continued without waiting for the reply. "Low cost deposits are coming down. The Principal Manager is very concerned about it."

"Yes, Sir. It's coming down." It was a norm to agree and he would have agreed even if the APM said just the opposite.

"We should start a campaign to increase low cost deposits," Sahanoy suggested a way out.

"Yes, Sir," the *crab* agreed there too, because it never affected him.

"This time, we will make it a serious one." The APM was aware that some campaigns were meant for fun. "An executive will visit the branches to supervise the campaign. Let them do it on Sundays. We will give lunch to all the staff. Give a T-shirt and a cap also to them and drive them out to nearby flats for canvassing accounts." He had a clear cut idea copied from the Sunday Business Mail to which he was a subscriber for two years, since Smile Bank made it compulsory for the executives to subscribe a business magazine.

"How can an executive visit all branches?" The *crab* knew the lethargy of a pedigreed executive.

"You do not know business." The *crab* did not subscribe to the Sunday Business Mail. "I'll explain it later," the APM continued. "First, you do it in ten branches. Arrange for caps and T-shirts with our emblem of the Smiling Donkey prominently displayed. You tell the executive when he should make the visits. Follow it up for account opening on a daily basis. Let them open the maximum number of accounts. Give me feedback on the number of accounts they are going to open on the day of the executive's visit." Sahanoy did not reveal his mind fully to the *crab*.

The *crab* stood there for a second looking at the file containing the promotion list, anticipating that the APM would talk further.

"Have you understood?" the APM asked. *Crab* shook his head.

"Start the campaign in right earnest. The news about the seriousness should be spread. Catch hold of one or two branches which stand on the road like donkeys thinking about their life. Send them to the gallows. Let them see the boundaries of Marcardia on transfer. Then the campaign will get the required seriousness." The *crab* nodded in agreement.

"The branches will be running behind easy accounts. They won't leave out any shops, slums, dance bars or brothels. Then do it," Sahanoy was looking elsewhere.

"What?" The *crab* could not guess the business logic.

"Postpone the visit of the executive," Sahanoy could not hide the secret for long. "The people behind whom the branch people ran earlier will be coming to open the accounts. The branch will be compelled to open them and the bank will get new accounts."

"Give a new date for the visit of the executive and see that the branch is again on the run. They will be running again on those very roads, but covering byroads this time. Tell them the canvassing is not sufficient and . . ."

"Postpone it again?" The *crab* was now caught up with the imagination of the APM.

"Exactly," Sahanoy gave a smile. He also winked his left eye before taking the file submitted by the *crab* from the table.

"You have not included the specified persons," Sahanoy found out the faults very fast. There cannot be faults in the HR Section and the *crab* might have left out the names purposefully, to get the views of the APM.

Mr. Salien had reached the business targets. So had Mr. Marvends. Mr. Pannaverse was also eligible for promotion that year. Mr. Memenna was a very sincere and hard working fellow, but he had missed the targets because a big business group shifted away from his branch for its own convenience.

"First, you issue an internal circular about them and make them ripe for promotion. Let everybody know that we are only promoting performers," the APM instructed.

"Okay, Sir. We can issue publicity circulars for Salien and Marvends easily. But, what about Pannaverse and Memenna?

"Which section is Pannaverse attached to now? Tell him to give a performance highlight if he wants promotion. Or just connect me to him."

"About Memenna?" The *crab* asked, but the APM had something else in his mind.

"What about Mr. Pavira? He is an intelligent officer." The APM looked at the statue of judgment, a half naked blind-folded lady carrying a weighing balance. It was given to him the previous year as a birthday gift by Pavira.

"Issue a good circular about him too," the APM directed.

"But . . ." The *crab* hesitated.

"He is very practical. Smile Bank can depend on him. Issue one circular for Mrs. Rechanaji too. She is very much after me for promotion." The APM returned the files back to the *crab*.

"But Sir, there are only three vacancies from Trivania," the *crab* reminded him.

"We will see that later. You find out some plus points and issue the circulars first. We will look into the promotion later." He too was practical.

"Sir, Pannaverse is on the line," the *crab* said.

"Yes, Pannaverse, your department is not in the limelight. How can I promote you?" It was a true concern.

"I am trying." It was a lie from Pannaverse.

"What trying?" Sahanoy knew that it was a lie.

"Actually, I do not have any work. Then, how can I come into the limelight?" Pannaverse revealed the business secret of a Revolutionary Association leader.

"I know. I can suggest a way out." Sahanoy held the phone for a second and looked at Thobias and the *crab*. It was an instruction to go out and Thobias obeyed instantly. The *Crab* also obeyed, but after a while.

"I do not know what is meant by limelight," Thobias said just to make the *crab* talk, while in the lift together.

"There is a method for coming into the limelight." The *Crab* fell into his trap. He did not like the way the APM had forced his exit from the cabin. "Keep everything pending. Sit idle for a few days. Don't try to tally the Government subsidy account, the only work in the department of Mr. Pannaverse. Then, it will go to the top management as a complaint. All will be concerned about the difference in the government subsidy account."

"Everyone in the Head Office will notice it. There is a difference in the government subsidy account and Smile Bank is unable to reconcile it. Pannaverse will now start acting. He will tell his clerk to do her duty. She will reconcile it because she knew how to do it and she was doing it earlier too. Then he will call the DPM at ten o'clock at night from the office to tell him that the subsidy account has been tallied. He has to call the Vice Principal Manager too. All are happy now. An internal circular will follow. But, I cannot support the APM in this. Those who work sincerely and efficiently are just left out and treated as fools. What can we do? I think it happens in every institution." The *Crab* also showed that he was not a crab.

The *Crab*'s concern made Thobias interact further. "I have a doubt. Srini is a very good officer and gives very good business results every year. Why are you denying him promotion?"

"Yeah, he is a good worker. When somebody is working nicely without any expectations, why should we promote him? After all, our aim is to get the work done perfectly. Isn't it? How can we get a suitable replacement for Srini at Veliora branch? We have to work out a lot of practical issues before finalising the promotion list."

"Those who work better are needed there to work further. Those who are not in the habit of working hard can be effectively used further to make others work. So they should be given promotion and should be placed appropriately," the *crab* said something which he was not supposed to say.

Thobias could read a lot of beautiful circulars thereafter. All drafted in beautiful language, punched with vibrant words, illustrated with pictures and printed on colourful paper.

'Pannaverse Shows the Way,' one circular said, with a picture of the founder of Marcardia leading the people, extending a stick to a kid.

'Pavira is heading to the moon. No one to challenge. He issued the maximum number of letters in the official language.' It was printed in haste and showed two spelling errors for 'language' and 'challenge.'

In the case of Marvends and Salien, it was two simple lines. 'They could humble business targets in time.' Nothing more was required because everybody was aware that they did it.

"Hello," the *crab* came out to the drawing room, probably after a bath. Sahaloshan had not changed much. The same serious look was seen in his eyes, presenting a mood that he had to do something to make the earth move correctly on its axis. Thobias stood up from the sofa. The instruction to stand up came from the subconscious mind and all the body organs obeyed it automatically.

"I was trying to contact you for long."

"I was away."

"I knew it."

"There was a reason," he continued. "You resigned and went to the USA. I was there in the HR Section at that time. I accepted it and put the note before the DPM. It never came back to me. Once I asked the DPM as to why your case is pending.

"'Why are you in a hurry, Mr. Sahaloshan?' the DPM asked me. 'After all, he has resigned from a branch which made frauds of millions and millions.'

"'But, he only caught the thief at the end,' I made my comment.

"'Yes. You said it correctly. *Only at the end*. Why did he take that much time? How do you know that he was not associated with it?'

"'I know him personally. His integrity too.'

"'When did you know him? That must be long back. People change over a period. There is nobody in the world who won't lick when honey falls on the palm.'

"'No, Sir. Our inquiry has revealed as to who the culprits are. It was Mr. Kusagran who did it and the credit manager Mrs. Smylitha just overlooked things. It has been recorded by the inquiry officers. Thobias had also informed about the possible bad loans. Nobody heeded him at that time.'

"'Don't get emotional, Mr. Sahaloshan. Ours is a commercial organisation and not a theological seminary to preach gospels. There is a reason to hold it back as I know, and there can be more reasons to hold it back that I too do not know.' The DPM was firm.

"Thereafter, we never discussed your resignation, except a few days prior to the retirement of the DPM.

"'Sorry Sahaloshan, I have to tell you some bad news about your old friend. You know the entire history of Doncity branch. But, you do not know one thing. You do not know who Kusagran was.'

"'No, I do not know him.'

"'There was a big shot behind him, a very influential man. A single phone call from him can stop the entire city of Doncity.'

"I was silent.

"'He has got great connections. The bigger the man, the bigger the connections are. I can't reveal the details to you. He had instructed us to dilute the cases against Kusagran. Moreover, Kusagran was an executive and all instructions were oral. All the written papers were missing from the files. Logically, he has to win the case if a case is filed against him. Then there was no point in antagonising an influential man.'

"'This is too much, Sir,' I protested.

"'Why too much? We are in business. There can be losses at times. Do you think that I was happy when Kusagran moved out with retirement benefits? No, never. But, I had to think about Smile Bank's future.'

"'But why Thobias?' I asked him.

"'Who else is there? Mrs. Smylitha? You know her? Her husband is in the Banking Authority of Marcardia. She got elevated only because of that. Mehman was expecting a second term as Principal Manager. He won't displease anybody in the Banking Authority of Marcardia. Now tell me who is left out? Without framing somebody and punishing him, do you think the directors of the bank will permit the writing off of such a big amount? Will the general public tolerate such inaction?'

"'Thobias has resigned and gone out of the country for good and we could reliably learn that he is well settled there and may not return to Marcardia again. Nobody can ask for his deportation, as there is no proof of his involvement in anything. Naturally, Mehman gave his green signal.'

"'What are the charges?' I asked him.

"'We know the charges won't stick. Mr. Pannaverse researched his track record, and with much difficulty he could cull out certain observations of auditors. They all added together to become a good case,' the DPM said.

"'Is it morally right, Sir?'

"'Did you do only morally correct things so far in service?'

"I could not answer that. Still I said, 'Sir, this is not a small case, but a serious sin.'

"'You feel old; that is why you talk about sins. I am still young like Mehman, though I have to retire now.'

"Thus, I was forced to file the case with the MSIB. I felt bad for you and tried frantically to alert you. I did not get any response from your home either," Sahaloshan said.

"I was not in touch with Amma too in those days," Thobias regretted.

"Your case was pending for more than fifteen years and Smile Bank has already written off the loans from its books, though we were occasionally alerting the MSIB about our pending case," he paused for a moment. "You are not saying anything."

"I was not expecting any virtues from Bethlehem," Thobias was brief.

"My purpose of calling you is different. I want to tell you something else." Sahaloshan moved closer to Thobias and literally came close to his ears. Thobias too developed a sort of curiosity as to what was in store for him next. From the way things were happening after his return, this news too could not be good.

"The DPM who filed the case retired and passed away a few years ago. Soon after his retirement, I was acting in his place as the DPM on staff matters. I found your resignation letter and my recommendations in a red file lying at the bottom of his drawer. I accepted my own recommendation to accept your resignation with full retirement benefits. I copied your signature at a few places to complete the formalities. I did not consider it wrong. It is a good sum. The amount is kept in an account with the Bank of Paradise where my son works, with registered instructions."

Sahaloshan stopped and came face to face with Thobias, probably to observe his facial expressions. Thobias looked detached, though he was happy that the present news was not a bad one.

"Your son is in a bank?" Other things were not of much interest to Thobias. It was a bit surprising for Thobias, as children of bankers in Marcardia never went for bank jobs, except in the case of compassionate appointment on death.

"Frequent transfers spoiled his studies. Hence, it was the last resort. Again, I believe children are to suffer for the wrongs of their parents. I did a lot of sins. As you know, I was a *crab*, as you people called me once, pulling down performers to ditches and spoiling those who were shining with pinbrush." He laughed and the laughter hid his pain. Sahaloshan extended him a pass book and cheque book of the Bank of Paradise and a paper with a sample signature which had been put for the account.

"Your photo is available with the bank," he said while leading Thobias out of the house to the parked car.

"Thank you very much for the pain taken. But frankly, this may not do any good for me; I mean I may not require this money at all. There was an age when I wanted it."

"Don't say that. This is what you have toiled for all your life and now you are being chased by the MSIB. Who knows how that will end?"

"I know," Thobias commented softly while starting the car and Sahaloshan did not hear it.

Thobias stopped the car after starting and came out.

"Sahaloshan," Thobias called the old friend who was walking back to the house, "why did you take this much pain for me?"

"I admired you in those days for your frank and fearless way of communicating things. I too wished I could do that. But, at that time my parents were ill and were dependant on me. I had to stay at Trivania at any cost," he stopped.

"So I became a crab. A *Crab*," Sahaloshan repeated the word as if it had made deep imprints in his heart. However, he was not interested to reveal his emotions to Thobias. He walked back to his house hurriedly.

26

WHILE DRIVING BACK, Thobias was brooding over the magnitude of distortions and deceptions that had happened to a straight-line event; how innocents were intelligently trapped and how the fittest survived. If such an evolution process was allowed to continue, the world would be full of crooks in a short time and the others would be pushed to the wayside. Thobias' mind was disturbed after knowing the background of the case. The disturbed mind made its impact on his driving. He did not notice the warning sign at Maruthoth Bridge in the suburb of Trivania. It was a narrow bridge.

The car had to be stopped to avoid a collision with the oncoming bus, which was in no mood to pardon a lawbreaker. Everything happened in seconds. Thobias made an attempt to steer clear but it went off too far. The car hit the concrete structure on the left side of the bridge. It made a somersault and landed upside down into the stream. While falling, Thobias could see the bridge going up. It was an error in perception and Thobias had perpetual perceptional difference with the majority, and at times with reality.

When he came to his senses, there was a large crowd around the car trying to turn it up to extricate the driver whose head was drenched in the black, polluted water of the stream.

"He seems to be alright," the leader of the crowd said. Thobias too realised that his time was yet to come for the big journey. Their generosity took him back to Trivania and to the casualty department of Merdeck Hospital.

"Nothing is visible outside. Any pain?" The casualty doctor was cheerful at the fact that he was being relieved from further follow up of an accident victim.

"No pain." Thobias suffered more from mental pain.

"Your heart beats are not normal. That must be due to the shock. Take rest and meet me again before you decide to go," the doctor moved to the next bed.

"Please admit me," Thobias made a request and the doctor did not have any hesitation in admitting one, as each admission gave 500 Lians as incentive to the referring doctor at Merdeck Hospital.

Thobias visited the accident site in the morning the next day. The body of the car was damaged at a few places. The mechanic he contacted assured him that he would lift it and complete the official formalities in a day.

Coming down the hospital staircase in the morning was an easy trip. Nobody asked Thobias who he was and why he was going down. But, going up was a tough job as in the Smile Bank service. He was asked many times who he was and why he wanted to go up, because he did not have the inpatient pass with him. Even the lift operator refused to admit him for the same reason.

"You meet the Public Relation Officer for the pass," the lift operator suggested. "He will come at 10 o'clock sharp."

Thobias was in no mood to wait and searched for the possible security lapses of the hospital. He was sure that lapses are human. It was true, and he found that the security man at gate number three was absent. It led to the staircase. The only problem was that he had to climb the stairs.

Thobias started his slow walk reading the boards and watching the arrows to the left and right at each floor. A big board at the entry point of each floor showed the list of in-patients. It was readable from a distance. Thobias started reading it from the fourth floor onwards because he got tired by then and wanted rest at each floor.

It was on the sixth floor that he decided to rest more because his chest was causing a little more pain than required to teach him a lesson. Breathing was becoming difficult. To spend his time, Thobias started reading the names of the in-patients who were going to contribute to the kitty of the hospital during the week.

"Wow!" There was a familiar name. Mr. Mehman, House No. 708, Dheeraj Road, Trivania, Room No. 606. Thobias remembered Amma's words that everything happens for a purpose and understood why his car made a somersault at Maruthoth Bridge. But, was it necessary to push him down that dirty stream to serye a small purpose of meeting Mehman? Mehman was available at his house too in those days and Thobias could have met him without this fall, had he searched for him.

Thobias was in two minds initially, whether to meet him or not. Finally he decided to meet him, because both were to meet on the golden shores of heaven shortly, may be smiling at each other as if nothing had happened on earth between them.

"You've got a visitor. Can I take leave for one hour?" The lady bystander was eager to exit. Soon Thobias entered the room.

The wrinkles on the face of Mehman were more conspicuous and the eyes had sunk into the sockets considerably. The teeth remained prominent, though they had lost the shine and developed spaces in between. The dark muscles on the hands were loose and the hair was as white as that of Thobias' pet Pomeranian.

"My name is Thobias Mathai. I was in Smile Bank twenty years ago when you were the Principal Manager." Thobias bent over the reclining man.

He gazed at the face of Thobias for some time, trying to recollect his bygone days of glory, taking his own time like an old computer loaded with large amounts of data. A smile-like expression came on his face for a second but it faded immediately. Thobias found his face paling further and eyes lowering, just to avoid the holier-thanthou look from a former subordinate.

"Take your seat," he said dryly. "I can sit up." He got up from the bed and pushed his weight on to the white pillow on the slanting wooden support attached to the hospital bed.

"You were in USA? Now came back?" He recognised Thobias for sure.

"I came last week and am unable to go back due to a case against me," Thobias added a little spice to the truth.

"Isn't it over now?" He expressed his sympathy.

"No."

Silence filled the room for a while. They looked at each other as if both knew the culprits and the action taken. Both were not sure as to how and where to start.

"The MSIB is after me now. You know, I am innocent in this case and the culprit is somebody else. Will you please use your influence and get me out?" Thobias broke the silence.

"What influence does a banker have after retirement? All relations that we get are for a purpose, just like we make with others while in Smile Bank. When the purpose is served or when you are unable to deliver, the relation ends and the contact shifts its loyalty to the next one who occupies the chair and can do things for him."

"What is the position of the case now?"

"I am on the run. The MSIB says that they can prove that I am the culprit and they may do it anytime now."

"Nobody on earth can make you admit a falsehood. I know you very well, Mr. Thobias. Be firm like earlier." The praise was unexpected.

"But, why did you do this to an innocent man like me?" Thobias persisted.

"Smile Bank was in business. There is no right or wrong in business as long as it gives profit. The decisions can be ad hoc and they may not be applicable in the long run because the situation changes, the people change, the economic situation changes, the law changes, politics changes and virtually everything changes. It was not easy to manage a bank with half-a-lakh employees. In that process, individuals might be left out because they are not very important in an institution. If the institution is healthy, it can hire better persons. I only looked from that angle as to what was good for Smile Bank and I was not worried as to who gained or who lost in that process."

"You mean you're convinced about the case against me?"

"Yes, it was the best option at that time. You do not know the condition of that lady manager. What was her name?"

"Smylitha," Thobias said.

"I knew her condition very well. You were away and well placed to meet any eventualities. I had to instil confidence in those who worked well. Smile Bank had come up due to the toiling of thousands of men and women who lived and spent their life in frugality, preserving everything for the coming generation. I'd to see their sacrifices and bow to them. One or two individuals are not important to Smile Bank. It is the system and the values that had to be kept in mind. There can be false promises, bogus promotions, false victimisations, undeserved extension of benefits. But, one thing was there. All were done for the benefit of Smile Bank."

"You mean to say that all these things were there?" Thobias queried.

"Those who want to pursue life away from theses can go elsewhere. Smile Bank is not the place for them."

"You had spoken about de-capitalisation of the officers. It is true. Capital makes an individual disobedient. Only if you are dependant on the bank, can you be trusted fully. You were transferred out to Doncity just to make you shell out what you made in your audit period through travelling and halting allowances. I was paid to take care of Smile Bank and not to take care of the employees."

"Definitely. But, I'm yet to adjust to the fact that a big institution like Smile Bank filed a case against an innocent individual, fully knowing so."

"What about that credit manager? Wasn't she innocent? She signed the papers as directed by her boss. Suppose you were in that seat. It would have been you who would be signing it on the direction of Kusagran. So, as far as the Bank is concerned, it was only a minor change of person and not a big matter."

"But I only blew the whistle," Thobias said respectfully.

Mehman said nothing for some time.

"You're a US citizen right now. You cannot be harassed without proof. Think about us Marcardians. If the investigating agency decides to prove a case against one, they will prove it. There's no proof against you and you can simply escape it, unlike Mrs. Smylitha who had all evidences against her."

"Still, I cannot digest falsehood," Thobias said.

"I told you already. We are in business for profit. Profit will not come without exploitation somewhere. We are in the service industry and the only thing to be exploited is manpower. We give big concessions to big parties, charging the small ones heavily. I am sure you did it too. It's business. Don't dig deep. Scratching can give pleasure," he said visibly happy, but stopped for a moment.

"I ordered for the continuance of Kusagran in the Milky Station branch even after the frauds came out. Once discovered, he wouldn't attempt more frauds. He came to the Head Office and cried before a lot of executives. He was trying to impress upon us that he was innocent. I gave the order that his version be accepted. He was to retire in two years. He could be effectively utilised for marketing our products. He would run like a leopard at our orders, because he wanted to re-enter the good books to escape punishments. I reserved the punishment for the last day after his two-year running. But, he was clever. He escaped at that moment with outside help.

"I appreciated you a lot as long as you were in the team with us. But, once you opted out from the team, we were forced to deal with you accordingly. Institutions grow not because of a few brilliant officers, but because of the loyalty and hard work of the less-than-averages.

"There can be crooks and fools with higher loyalty than you. We prefer them to the top posts. You also know that vertical mobility is just an ego satisfaction to extract better, paying peanuts.

"Do you think that everything happens on merit outside Smile Bank? What is the definition of merit? Who evaluates it? You have seen people going up in politics. You mean to say that only the honest and the sincere are going to the top there? Or can you point out anybody from that group ever going up?

"This is *Kaliyuga*. Things will happen upside down. The crooks, the corrupt and the *chamchas,* all will get an upper hand over those who are innocent and hard working. You should not have taken birth at this point of time; of course I know you're not responsible for that."

"All systems have got a portion reserved for errors. Our aim is to limit it. It cannot be eliminated at all. You were a good worker, but never came forward and apprised your boss. There were people who worked less, but they came forward and presented themselves better. We want that culture. This type of voluntarism helps the institution to grow even if the boss is useless.

"No great country is ever saved by a good man. The best results may come out under a big crook who is interested in making money. He will produce good results to cover up his corruption and that in turn benefits the institution. I prefer such a man over someone with high integrity doing nothing for growth."

Mehman stopped and looked through the window to the open sea and the vacant beach that were not far away from the hospital.

"How do you spend your time?" Mehman asked a personal question. Thobias did not reply. He just looked at Mehman without any expression and then looked through the window to the deserted beach as Mehman was doing.

"I might have treated you badly while in service. It was purposeful. Treating donkeys as horses can create a feeling that they are better creatures. Treating horses like donkeys, in the long run, can instil certain qualities of donkeys in horses. So, as a matter of policy, Smile Bank always treats all officers as donkeys. There is nothing personal in it. Nothing personal."

"I saw the potential in you. Giving tougher targets and harder conditions were to bring out the full potential in you. Once you suffer the hardships and go up the ladder, you expect your colleagues and juniors to go through the same type of hardships and bring in results like you. This benefits the institution."

"You should know the story of the vineyard worker in the Bible. Labourers came in different times and got the contracted rates but those who came early and worked more were unhappy. This unhappiness was there even at that time.

"You do not have the discretion to decide as to who is good and who is bad. The system decides who is the best. Once he is placed on the throne, he is the best and you will be forced to bow and obey him. If the relations are bad, life will be made tougher for you and if you are on the good side, you can enjoy the sad part of Smile banking even better." The answer made Thobias analyse its meaning.

"You mean to say that the carrot and stick are one and the same?" Thobias had a doubt.

"You are willingly running in the first case. In the other case, we are making you run."

"Motivation is required to get you started. Once you make it a habit, the stick is better than the carrot. It takes time for an officer to understand that he is just an ordinary mortal.

"We want people who work happily. Their brain should be just sufficient to understand the banking rules. They should not peep much into the managerial systems.

"It's all a game. I played the game for my stomach and to bring up my family. You too played the game for that. Unfortunately, we were in opposite teams. I was in the administration to make you work maximum with minimum expenses and you were on the other side to take the maximum benefit with minimum effort. I do not know as to who won at the end. It is not important at all. We both were living while playing the game. There was only one difference, I was enjoying my game and had a good life and you were not enjoying the game and had a bitter life. I'm not responsible for it," Mehman stopped.

Both sat for some time without any words in between. Thobias could not appreciate his justifications for not drawing the line between ethics and business profit. Smile Bank norms were deeply embedded in him and nothing else mattered. Thobias wished him to have that blissful state of mind for his last few more sunsets. He offered a formal smile and exited.

27

AFTER HIS TRIP to Trivania and the accident, Thobias was confined to bed for a week. The shoulder muscles bore the brunt, as much force was used while holding on to the steering wheel when the car tumbled into the stream. Eventually, pain gets to those who work.

There was no call from the MSIB either, to keep him on his toes. The lone visitor he had in the entire week was Rajan. He came one Sunday evening.

"Did they harass you physically during questioning?" Rajan asked.

"No. Not so far. But Tejaram plans to, it seems," Thobias said.

"Try some way out. Don't you have any connections in Marcardia? I mean political connections?" Rajan asked.

"My connections were limited to Smile Bank. The long stay outside Marcardia destroyed those tender roots too," Thobias expressed his inability.

"What about Kusagran?" Rajan was optimistic and was searching for the alternatives.

"If I go to him, it will affirm the collusion theory further," Thobias replied.

"Let them infer that. What difference does it make? Now you are the culprit. Collusion is a lesser crime than that." It made sense.

"Yeah, I can try that. Now he must be retired and devoid of tendencies that are normally exhibited by Marcardians when they are in a position of power." Thobias agreed to make a trip to Doncity in search of Kusagran.

"You can join me this time?"

"How'll you locate him?" Rajan did not say whether he was coming or not. That was his nature. He often shifted the subject if he agreed to something.

"We can go and enquire with the Smile Bank office there. They must know where he stays, over the soil or under it decayed." There was a smell of hatred in those words.

"I'm flying for the first time," Rajan said while tightening the seat belt in flight number 165 of Orient Airways. "I thought I would disappear from the earth without going inside a plane, like most of the farmers. You are all fortunate than us enjoying the frequent flights." Rajan was a little jealous.

"Ha. Enjoying the flight? Definitely not now." Thobias too enjoyed it when he made his first flight. "There are a lot of risks with high-fliers."

"You always talk with double meaning. I think your mind is highly disturbed and you're hiding something from me too. You cannot crack jokes as earlier. You are unable to smile like earlier. Some fear is chasing you. The old Thobias has gone somewhere. I love him more than you." Thobias could not understand what made Rajan speak the truth.

He sat silently for some time, thinking how Rajan evaluated him within a few days of association and wondering how much far Theresa might have analysed him during their thirty years of living together, but never revealing it to him, avoiding damage to their bond.

"I did not change. For me, the world has changed a lot. Previously, it used to smile at me. It used to dance with me. It permitted me to roll over its green grasses, bask under its moonlit nights and the deep blue sky used to embrace me. The valleys were greener and it always whispered to me, 'Come to us Thobias.' But now I am not getting any smile. No one calls me to dance. The sky has become grey. The greenery has disappeared."

Rajan looked at Thobias for some time, as if he were seeing a lunatic.

It was late night when the plane landed at Doncity. Thobias could not locate the exit point easily, as the area had undergone tremendous changes. He just followed the crowd.

"We can try locating him even now," Thobias said while moving to a low budget hotel at the crowded Sanam Road.

"At this late hour?" Rajan did not believe him.

"Yeah, this city never sleeps. Smile Bank officers will be available in their quarters now. I know one of those nearby."

"That will be a disturbance for them now," Rajan was hesitant.

"I assure you that they will be awake now. Majority are without their families here. They will be simply restless and will be moving around, braying like donkeys. Ha, ha," Thobias laughed heartily.

"You too did the same?" Rajan had a doubt.

"Sure. The salary won't be sufficient to have good sex. Naturally one had to bray it out." Thobias was not sure about what he said.

"You can have sex without love?" Rajan was surprised. "I believe in the purity of life."

"Maybe. I can't tell a lie, dear friend. So, don't ask me much. I am sure one can see a lot of wonders if the sun reappears at midnight," Thobias gave a tickling. "It is just fear that makes us gentlemen."

Rajan was smiling. "You are too blunt. How did that bank tolerate you for twenty years?"

"Not twenty. Only fifteen years," Thobias corrected him. "You know something? Before I started to Doncity, Theresa said something interesting which I cannot forget even now."

"Like?"

"'This is an important age for you,' she said. 'You are away from home and going to be alone. All males leave a space between them and their wives. Maybe, it is a precaution to take care of the balance life in case of some unfortunate eventualities. But if somebody gets into that vacant space at Doncity, just think about our kids. You may not have time to think about me.'

"It was a genuine fear which she was trying to conceal."

"'Why don't you too leave a bit of space like that?' I asked her as I always believed in equality.

"'We never do it,' she talked on behalf of her entire community.

"I found her fears real. When sitting alone in the flat watching the attractive ones walking through the street, you feel that you are missing something. Then, the subconscious mind will start searching for that missing item, sufficiently prevented by the conscious mind in the initial stages but accepting defeat later."

"The Red Street was the sex outlet for the average man and it was a licensed area in Doncity. After the advent of

AIDS, the rush to the Red Street came down and it increased elsewhere seeking safer partners, paying handsomely. The police conduct occasional raids in those new areas catching the breakers of the sixth commandment of God because they did not have licences issued by the Corporation.

"It was risky and costly," Thobias said. "So I confined myself to my flat."

"But, what about the ordinary low income group?" Rajan was concerned about the low income group because he always considered himself one among them.

"They go to massage parlours," Thobias said.

Rajan did not speak. He only raised his eyebrows.

"My legs pulled me there once," Thobias started narrating his experience. "There was a queue in the corridor. There were four rooms, and a hefty man was directing the customers to the rooms as and when a bell rang.

"'Next,' the hefty man called me. I looked around and entered the room.

"'Remove your pants and shirt and lie on this bed,' a young lady invited me to a bed, smeared by a dirty rexin-smelling oil. She was in a hurry.

"'Our charges are 500 Lians; additional 300 Lians for personal service if you want.' I was watching her tired face.

"'What is personal service?' I asked her softly, as I was unable to distinguish between *official* and *personal*, which were one and the same in the Smile Bank.

"'You do not know?' She winked her right eye and put her hand on my private part, as if unintentionally. 'Tell me fast, this will be counted in your total time.' She stood there expecting an answer.

"'How many customers do you get a day?' Basically I was an economist, half developed.

"'Can't you see the queue?' She was taken by surprise at my lack of common sense.

"'Still?' I persisted.

"'Ten minutes per person,' she said softly.

"That meant six persons in an hour, minimum fifty persons in a day and around 25000 tax free Lians a day. I looked at her with awe.

"'Why are you looking at me like that?' she asked me.

"'Admiration,' I said.

"'You are not normal,' she discovered.

"'Are you a reporter?' she asked me.

"'What?'

"'I am asking you. Are you from the press? Or from the police? You are not the type who normally queue up here for treatment.' She felt scared and I could see the insecurity behind her well-earning job.

"'Please get dressed. I can't do any personal service to you and I am too tired to give you a massage. Please move out. This is my bread. I have got a handicapped husband and two daughters.' I could read the expressions on her face clearly. It was half fear and half fatigue.

"She rang the bell.

"'Take the backdoor for going out,' the hefty man commanded and I obeyed. I didn't make another attempt after that."

Rajan had shown more interest in listening to Thobias this time.

While withdrawing into the thick blanket, Rajan remarked, "You could have gone for promotions and become

an executive, so that this journey could have been avoided."
He seemed to have grasped the entire functioning of Smile
Bank. "Why didn't you opt for promotion?"

"It did not happen. I exposed myself too much."

"Exposed?" Rajan did not get the meaning.

"Yeah, I worked well and made outstanding results."

"It's good. Isn't it?" Rajan looked innocently.

"It is not good. They knew that intelligent people do
not take much effort. They make others work. They exhibit
better business sense and are the best to go up the ladder.
My first rejection was due to a bacterium." Thobias could
not hide a smile.

"Bacterium?" Rajan could not believe it.

"Yeah. The second time it was due to a virus. The third
time it was due to a bifocal glass. By that time, I had reached
the Audit Department. It required a lot of travelling from
one end of Marcardia to the other, giving me a lot of time
to think. I recognised my asinised life. I did not wish to be
a part of it and I quit the race."

"I am not getting anywhere near the possible role of
bacteria and virus in the promotion process of a big bank
like Smile Bank." Rajan always respected things which were
big.

"Bacteria play an important role in the life of a banker.
We stay away from the family for the greater part of our lives
and depend on budget hotels or *dhabas* to suit our purse.
We can't avoid bacteria entering our stomach. It upsets the
stomach for some days till we familiarise ourselves with it.
Unfortunately, we will be forced to shift the hotel as we get
fed up with the same stuff. There, another species will be
waiting to enter the stomach. This is an ongoing process, till

one familiarises oneself with almost all species of it in the city. In the next city, we start the game again."

"On the day of the promotion interview, the venue was shifted from hotel Garden View at Trivania to Hotel Slum View at Cohiana to save expenses. The DPM in charge of it had to travel to Cohiana in the Intercity Express and eat breakfast at the Slum View hotel. The bacteria at Slum View were very virulent. I saw the DPM going to the toilet more than four times before my turn came for the interview. He again went outside, as soon as I entered the interview room. There were two APMs to assess me. One was Mehman, who was feeling sleepy after the travel. The other was reading a newspaper. We sat there for some time looking at each other like a fresh group of train passengers waiting for an opportunity to start talking."

"The DPM returned after some time and extended his hand warmly and said, 'Best of luck.' His hand smelled of bathroom soap. I said 'Thank you,' and the interview ended. It was the same story for almost all candidates. He was to fax the marks immediately after the interview to avoid influencing by outsiders. He was an innocent man and gave the same mark to all, but to be on the safer side gave '*satisfactory*' rating only. When it was amalgamated at the Head Office, '*excellent*' ones all over Marcardia overtook the '*satisfactory*' ones from Cohiana."

"Smile Bank took care of the bacteria next year. The DPM was given packed mineral water and clean lunch from Trinity Hotel. But, a virus entered the data floppy and it deleted a few names at the time of amalgamation."

"Smile Bank took care of bacteria and virus again the next year. The APM sitting on the left of the DPM was restless from the beginning itself. From the marks on his nose and side of the head, I could guess that he normally wore glasses. The glasses were missing that day and his restlessness was due to the difficulty he faced in reading the prepared questions to be shot at the candidates. He had to sit straight seriously while asking the questions, so that the candidate should feel that all the questions were coming directly from his grey matter. He was struggling to hide his glancing through the piece of paper, each time he tested my knowledge. I felt sympathy for him and gave a gentle smile, as if there was no problem for me even if he read directly from the paper."

"The DPM who was sitting at the centre understood the meaning of my smile. He was familiar with all types of smiles in Smile Bank. 'This fellow is not fully asinised. He is unable to see the holy halo behind our head,' he whispered in the ears of the APM who sat on his right side.

"'I too was observing it. He is just enjoying the difficulty of an executive, not to speak about the absence of fear,' the APM replied after gently feeling the invisible holy halo behind his head with his right hand. He too was developing a doubt about its existence.

"'Best of luck,' the DPM said that year also. But, his face was like a red hot iron and the result was on the expected lines. Smile Bank evaluated me fully by this time. They knew that I may not be loyal enough to bark loudly for the master."

28

BOTH OF THEM STAYED INDOORS for the rest of the night, talking about the other side of life away from Smile Bank.

In the morning, Rajan made an optimistic remark just before leaving the room in search of Kusagran. "I am sure Kusagran can suggest a way out."

"Why do you think so?" Thobias was always a doubting Thomas.

"He was there in the middle of it and has escaped. No theoretician can teach better lessons than one who experienced it."

"But I cannot rely on him. He included me too in his designs. He's a cheap crook," Thobias was apprehensive.

"You are judging things too fast. Your involvement was just rudimentary. He included Mrs. Smylitha only, who had got connections to escape unpunished." Thobias did not say anything, though he could not digest Rajan's view.

Collecting the residential address of Kusagran was not difficult. The petty shop just opposite the Milky Station branch was owned by one Ramesh Chokra, who was in touch with the staff of Smile Bank who came to him for cigarette and pan. Kusagran was asked by Smile Bank to work without any powers, and he had become a frequent visitor to the petty shop.

"He stays at Vasora. It is only an hour's journey from here if you go by the suburban train till Borvalo. From there, take a taxi and it will take thirty minutes to reach Sullana. You should reach the east side of the Sullana Bridge and then ask for Parpur junction. There, ask for Redstone Gardens and Flat No. F 704," Chokra missed no detail.

It was Kusagran who opened the door to the visitors. The old statue-like structure seemed improved to a moving one, aided by a walking stick. Some facial expressions suited to humans had appeared on him, though the muscles were still able to fully accommodate the changes that happened during the transition from official to unofficial life. He had become bald, leaving the periphery decorated with grey hairs. The moustache was still pointed to impart seriousness, but the eyes had lost their piercing look and had become sober as if he had wound up playing serious games.

"Wow! It's you?" He seemed to have forgotten the name of the visitor.

"Please come in." The invitation was emphatic and was with a smile which Thobias never saw when Kusagran was his boss in Smile Bank.

The room was cool inside.

"You had left Marcardia long back? It's nice to see you again, Thobias," he recollected the name by this time. "Who is he?" He looked at Rajan.

"A friend," Thobias did not elaborate.

It was silence thereafter for some time. Both were searching for appropriate words to continue the conversation. Silence was broken by the host.

"What will you take? Tea or coffee?" He was reducing the scope of selection while moving towards the kitchen.

"Don't bother about us," Thobias did not want his former boss to make tea for him.

The flat was an average one; far below the standard for a big fraudster. It was a two-room apartment with a medium sized drawing-cum-dining area. The drawing room was neatly kept with a showcase on the left side, decorated with many exhibits. They must have been received from Smile Bank customers during his long service. The wall on the right side was decorated with big pictures of his favourite gods garlanded with fresh flowers. There was a red carpet on the marble floor welcoming all, unlike in his service days.

"What made you come to Doncity again? I know you won't come without a reason," he started the ineviable topic.

"My passport has been impounded and the MSIB is after me for the frauds that have happened in Milky Station branch. Smile Bank's case file shows me as the culprit." Thobias stopped there as more details were not needed.

Kusagran did not make any immediate response. He closed his eyes for a few seconds and then hung his head down and stared at the red carpet for some time. When he raised his head, his eyes were red and there were tears in them though not sufficient to overflow. He took a deep breath and crossed his hands over his bulky stomach. Nobody talked for some time and the only action made by Kusagran was to liberate the crossed hands to scratch his forehead very gently. This went on for some time. Probably he was working out something within the scratched area.

"Please come inside." It was a hesitant invitation. Still, Thobias followed Kusagran to the bed room on the left side. The room was spacious, with a wooden cot at the centre with a spring mattress on it, a small writing table on its left near the window, and two chairs on each side of the writing table. Kusagran took the liberty to sit first and invited Thobias to join him on the chair opposite.

Kusagran opened the bottom drawer of the table, stooped slightly and took out a brass key from the extreme end of the drawer. He kept it in his hand for some time and looked at the wall. The wall was decorated with three framed paintings. The one at the middle showed a few coconut trees, one of them bending to the unending sea. To the left to it was an incomprehensible modern art work and the other one showed a few penguins walking over ice. Kusagran stood up, closed the door, came back and removed the modern art from the wall. There was a keyhole behind it and the brass key could open a small door on the wall. Thobias did not get a full view of the inside of the hidden cupboard from his chair. But, two boxes, one green and the other maroon, were easily visible. He slowly lifted the boxes and took out a file from underneath them. Putting the file in front of Thobias, Kusagran occupied his chair.

"We will take a drink," he stood up again and moved towards a small shelf with another set of keys. Thobias kept looking at the unopened file, and waited till Kusagran returned with a bottle of Scotch and two glasses. His hands were shivering while pouring the brown liquid into the glasses.

"It should not have come to your doorstep. It was my cross." Kusagran did not go further than those sentences for a few moments. Thobias understood his hesitation to open up and decided to wait till the alcohol relaxed his brain and loosened his tongue muscles.

"In fact, I wanted to talk to you when you submitted your resignation. But, I did not have the permission to talk," Kusagran said.

"Permission? From whom?" Thobias always liked to settle his doubts immediately.

"I too do not know who that man was. But, there was somebody from whom I was to take permission. It is true." Thobias was also sure that Kusagran need not tell a lie now.

"I told them that an upright and hard working officer is resigning because of me. But, they asked me to shut my mouth and sit there." Thobias sat listening to him expecting the storyteller to reach the climax fast.

Kusagran opened the file and took out a white cover with his shivering hand. There were three photos inside.

Wow! It was the middle aged Kusagran, fully naked, holding a pretty lady close to his chest. She too was fully naked, revealing her pretty curves and buxom bulges. It was a side view where the face of the man was clearly visible whereas the woman was looking to the other side, making it difficult to distinguish her face. The second photo was also similar in content, but the woman was different. The method of holding her was also different and the scene of action was the bed. The third one did not show the face of Kusagran fully. The face of the lady was also out of the picture but other body parts were clearly visible as they were not covered at all.

"Her name was Abinita, as I know it," Kusagran pointed towards the second picture, and Thobias had a second look at the medium-built, fair and well maintained body of the lady with shoulder cut hair.

"I was at Sooryajit branch immediately after my promotion as executive and I was staying there alone. It was a big branch with a lot of big customers. It was normal to mingle with them and attend parties and fellowships. I met Abinita at one such party. She was very attractive and very pleasing to talk to. So, I met her again and again."

"In a few months, we became very close. Once, she invited me to her flat. She was staying alone. We took drinks together and, you can guess, slept together. Once again we met in the same flat in the same way. I tried for a third time and she did not refuse. But, it was a different lady who opened the door of her flat at that time. Look at the first photo. It was she. She once called me to recommend a loan for her relative. It was not a big loan. Just 100,000 Lians, and I gave it."

"It was a male voice who recommended the next loan at Sooryajit. He introduced himself as a friend of Abinita and asked me for a loan of 500,000 Lians. The loan proposal did not appeal to me much and the amount involved was bigger. I took my time and refused the loan."

"That night Abinita invited me to her flat. But, it was not she who opened the door. It was a fierce looking stout man with many scars on his face. The tip of his left ear was missing as if cut off with a sharp weapon. He looked me in my eyes and uttered only two words."

"'Sit down,' he pointed towards a chair. While obeying him instantly, he handed over a cover to me. It was full of photographs. Even the first photograph was sufficient to understand as to what it was about. All my actions in that flat were photographed.

"'We have got the videotape too. Would you like to see it?' he asked me. My blood pressure ran high and I started sweating profusely. I found the room revolving more or less in the same way as in those days when I was alone with Abinita in that very same room, except for the direction.

"'Do you want these to be sent to Smile Bank?'

"'Do you want these to be sent to your daughter, Shari?'

"'Do you want these to be sent to your wife, Neemarose?' The voice of the stout man was very low, like a whisper. I sat silently without any response.

"I sanctioned that loan of 500,000 Lians. I also managed a transfer to Milky Station very fast, thanks to my connection with the APM, Mr. Perfecta. It was a great relief when I escaped from the clutches of that scar-faced man and the sweet witch, Abinita."

"I joined Milky Station branch on a Monday. I entered the cabin and sat on the revolving chair after making a formal introduction with the staff. There was a lean man with an unshaven face and informal dress already sitting in one of the visitors' chairs in front of my table. He was cool, silent and was in no hurry to say anything. I did not like the appearance of the first visitor and it was reflected on my face."

"But, he was not bothered about my facial expressions. He stretched a white envelope towards me and sat there as if nothing had happened. It contained copies of the same photographs which made me run from Sooryajit branch. The man extended his mobile to me.

"'Do you think you can escape from us?' a deep voice shouted through the mobile. I did not reply. This time, the cabin was revolving around me and my revolving chair was static. I felt a pain in my chest and uttered some frantic shouts. The lean man too helped me to reach hospital."

"I thought of resigning the job. But, my unofficial boss even read my mind well in advance. The lean man came again with the cell phone."

"'You cannot escape by resigning too. I assure you that if you cooperate with us, you too will benefit. I am offering you the best percentage of commission that has been offered to anybody else so far. Again, you need not fear anybody. All consequences will be my responsibility. Just cooperate with us and enjoy life. You would like to meet Abinita again?'

"I did not reply. But it was a silent permission."

"Did you meet Abinita again?" Thobias could not resist the temptation of asking.

Kusagran did not respond for some time.

"Yeah, I asked her why she spoiled my life like this." Kusagran knew what Thobias wanted to hear.

"'All are in the game of living.' It was a short reply from her and there was no fun in meeting her again."

"They decided the loans, they decided the security, they decided as to when I should take leave, when I should give leave for you or Mrs. Smylitha. It was they who suggested that I should feed you with the maximum work, so that you wouldn't get time to peep into the loans which I had been giving. I did that perfectly, but you were more efficient than I imagined. You came over it. I think it was you who informed the DPM about the happenings in the branch and blocked further loans."

They did not say anything for some time. Kusagran emptied one more glass of the brown liquid and looked into the eyes of Thobias, as if he was expecting some questions or comments from him. That silence was boring for Thobias too.

"Did they compensate you sufficiently?"

"Not bad." In Marcardia, it was the way of saying that something was good.

"I am more interested to know as to how you escaped it. I too want to try that route."

"Success in life depends on finding out escape routes. Nobody will show you that without any motive. All escape routes have got a darker side too. Some innocent ones have to bear the brunt. Here, you have to move against Mrs. Smylitha in the court, seeking inquiry against her. If you can do that, there is a chance of transferring the onus from you. My unofficial boss did that for me, transferring the responsibility of the fraud to you. I do not know how exactly he scuttled the enquiry against me, whom he contacted for that and what benefit he extended for it. He may have had more white envelopes in his cupboard and he must have selected the appropriate envelope for the occasion. There is a system for it and only those who are in that job can tell you how exactly it is being done. I do not know who the real boss is. I can only answer him when the call comes to me and never vice versa. He never called me after Smile Bank withdrew my loan sanctioning powers."

"I am suffering for your wrong-doings." Thobias did not like the way Kusagran was evading his request.

"It is common that somebody suffers due to the fault of others. Children suffer due to the faults of their parents. Citizens suffer due to the faults of their leaders. Companies suffer due to the faults of their directors. Naturally, the subordinates have to suffer for the faults of their boss. You too can make those faults, and let others suffer it, if luck smiles at you some time."

It was a dry ending, in spite of the wet table between them. Rajan was relieved when Thobias came out of the closed room. And he felt more relieved when he reached Panamkara next day and sat on the easy chair in the veranda looking at the road watching the youngsters strolling without much purpose.

29

"THERE WERE FREQUENT CALLS from the MSIB for the last two days. However, now they have come down," Teena conveyed as soon as Thobias reached home.

It came again in half an hour. Thobias should reach the MSIB office at Cohiana in the early morning.

"Keep the phone in engaged mode so that they won't disturb my sleep," Thobias directed Tina. However, she did not follow that instruction because his younger brother would be calling Amma late in the night on all Saturdays on the very same phone. Surprisingly, there was no call from MSIB during the entire night.

Thobias reached the MSIB office sufficiently early and waited for Tejaram at the first floor corridor.

"I am yet to confirm the date of questioning you. Today I have got another case to investigate," Tejaram announced the reason for not disturbing him at night. "We will inform you the date later." Thobias took leave of Tejaram.

The telephone was ringing when Thobias reached home. It was Tejaram at the other end. "Mr. Thobias, I changed my plans. You be here before one o' clock. I have got instructions to finish this case immediately." The car took the same route back for another three hours to reach the MSIB office. This time Thobias took the medical reports too, just as a precaution against the MSIB using brutal ways to disprove his innocence.

Tejaram was sitting straight as usual, with hands firmly on the arms of the chair and with a look that could pierce anybody like x-rays. He was in his uniform, black trousers and blue shirt with an emblem of a lion stitched over the pocket.

Thobias stood near the chair as an accused used to do till proved innocent. Tejaram did not ask him to sit and instead went straight to the subject.

"I am not convinced about the reasons for your resignation. All fraudsters resign immediately after committing frauds. That is the universal practice. Look here, Kusagran was still working in the same branch in the same position when you resigned. You were resigning after a long period of service without any apparent reason and without getting the Bank's approval. You did not even collect your retirement benefits because it must be a paltry sum compared to the huge amount you have made. With my twenty-five years of experience in financial crime investigation, I can easily arrive at the logical conclusion. You are the main culprit and the Manager dealing with loans was taking instructions from you. You have spoken earlier about your dislike for Smile Bank. You also spoke about the de-skilling process initiated by Smile Bank to prevent exiting. That means, as an obsolete individual, you were not expecting a better job than you had then. Hence, your intentions were to escape from Smile Bank to a country where you must have transferred the booty, or must have arranged swaps here to get a fortune abroad intact." Thobias could measure the depth of the doubt Tejaram had about him.

"You have to undergo medical tests today. It is better you tell the truth. I won't leave you alive if an iota of lie is detected in your statements. Henceforth, all your statements will be recorded on tape. Before starting, you will have to make a statement that you have not been coerced, threatened or physically tortured to make the statements." Thobias uttered the statutory lines as soon as Tejaram switched on the recording system.

"I wanted to quit the job as soon as I discovered the asinisation process, but it was always postponed. In the first week of an August, I was forced to take a bold decision and call it a day. The first week is a busy time in the branch, with long queues at every counter. All those who attend the branch in those days struggle to complete the work. The others conveniently take leave on those days fearing the crowd and enjoy life at home. As usual, I was struggling to manage the crowd and Kusagran was on leave that day. A tall man with a full sleeves shirt, and with his Smile Bank identity card prominently displayed on it, came forward pushing the customer kings sideways.

"'I am an investigating officer. There is a complaint against you,' his tone was very serious.

"'Complaint?' It was a normal thing in Smile Bank, but still there was no warning about it unlike in other cases where the customers would be shouting and threatening before making the complaint.

"'You insisted on a tax clearance declaration before handing over the deposit receipt,' he took out the chargesheet.

"'Yes. It is as per directive.' I was sure about it.

"'Maybe. But, there is a way of introducing a directive. You have made a man angry. That is not permitted in the directive. You could not provide the copy of the directive from the Banking Authority of Marcardia to the customer and settle the issue. Our Principal Manager has directed that all complaints be taken very seriously and asked me to investigate. I suggest you to go and meet the complainant and apologise to him.'

"'Apologize for what?' I was not sure about the complaint settling mechanism of Smile Bank even after fifteen years of service.

"'You invent some reason and apologise profusely till the heart of the complainant melts and he withdraws the complaint in writing. This is beneficial for all.' The enquiry officer knew how to reduce his workload and I did not have any objection to that.

"The autorickshaw driver was very helpful in locating the complainant's small clinic thanks to the arrow like direction board hanging from a medium sized casuarina tree, immediately after crossing P.S. Road, but he was not kind enough to return anything when a 100 Lian note was given to him. The balance seemed to have been accounted towards the service charges for locating the person.

"'I am from Milky Station branch of Smile Bank,' I made the self introduction after waiting for my turn in the not-so-busy clinic.

"'So? How's the learning process?' The doctor was all smiles like us in Smile Bank.

"'Learning process?' I could not understand.

"'You forgot your statements, Manager! I had told you that I will teach you a lesson if the deposit receipt was not handed over to me instantly. You told me that it's very difficult to teach you a lesson because you're a slow learner.

I knew your demand was right. But, I love teaching slow learners bitter lessons. Having come and apologised, I am permitting you to go in peace.' I did not wish him peace but wished him more patients so that his time is fully engaged and a lot of slow learners could escape without learning.

"The investigator was not happy like me when I returned back to the branch. 'There is another complaint. Somebody has telephoned the Principal Manager that you were not available in the seat for the last 32 minutes and he has asked me to investigate it and report.'

"'I went outside as per your instructions only,' I was furious.

"'I never told you to go now. Moreover, it was your duty to place somebody there on your seat, so as not to inconvenience the customers. Again, I am just an officer and you are a Manager and senior to me. You should not have obeyed me. Now, I have to report this and there will be some punishment for sure.'

"'Punishment? Like?' I was curious.

"'Maybe just one increment cut.' He had already made the enquiry report in his mind.

"'That's okay.' I understood the reason behind the negligible increments the Smile Bank gave to its officers; cutting should not affect them financially.

"My complacency was shattered by a phone call from the DPM in charge of customer service. 'Why are there are a lot of complaints against you? Why are customers forced to wait for more than ten minutes for a demand draft?'

"'Today there is a rush at all counters, Sir.' I was not sure about why there were no complaints against others.

"'As Manager, you have to manage the rush. I am also not happy with the business growth. You are not disbursing sufficient loans. You are also not going out to canvass deposits. Just sitting idle,' he paused for a second to imagine the next possible weakness of the branch.

"'Growth of deposits and advances is followed up by Mr. Kusagran,' I humbly tried to escape.

"'I am talking to you now. What I want to talk to Kusagran, I will talk to him at my discretion. By the way, what is your work there?' In the Smile Bank hierarchy, the superiors could ask anything and they also followed the same level of ignorance. The earlier DPM had also asked me as to what my work in the branch was.

"'I am here in the branch working from 7 am to 9 pm.'

"'What do you do in the balance time?' he did not ask what I do there during these hours.

"'I go home, Sir.' There was no other way out at Doncity.

"'What do you do there?'

"'Sleep.' Luckily, Theresa was not there in those days with me. Otherwise, I would have been forced to tell a lie to the DPM.

"'You want to sleep at 9 pm?'

"'No Sir, at 10 pm.'

"'How many hours of sleep do you require? What's your age now?' the DPM was too lazy even to look at my biodata and I had decided not to tell him the age.

"'Did you finish the data entry for core banking?'

"'No, Sir.' I knew that was not a good answer. Anyhow, the answer was not important for him. It was just for the sake of asking and just to pin me on the defence.

"'NOOO?' It was a shout from the other end and the phone flopped from my hand though I could grab it back easily.

"'Just complete it in three days and confirm to me in writing. This is an order.' I understood that some of the earlier statements were not orders.

"'What happened yesterday? Your computer system went off for half an hour?' He was in a fault-finding mood.

"'Yes, Sir.'Agreeing avoids a lot of arguments. "It was a computer problem," I washed off my hands.

"'That I know. I was asking what that computer problem was.' Actually, it was a perennial problem in Smile Bank and one with a bit of brain could take a doctorate in computer problems easily than elsewhere.

"'It was a hardware problem.'

"'What hardware problem? You do not know?'The DPM was taking my time.

"'No, Sir.'

"'How dare you say that? For how many years are you dealing with computers?'

"'I was in the Audit Department, Sir.'

"'I don't want to hear about what you did earlier. Tell me about the present. Did you feed all the customer data?'

"'Not fully, Sir.'

"'Why?'

"'Staff shortage, Sir.'

"'What shortage? Who is deciding the shortage? You? Or we here?'

"'You, Sir.'

"'Just complete it and report.'

"'Yes, Sir. I will complete it as soon as the staff on leave join back.'

"'What? Who is on leave? Who permitted it?'

"'Genuine reasons, Sir.'

"'Who decides genuineness? Is our pending work not genuine?'

"'Can we pay for overtime?'

"'WWWHHHATTT???'

"I held the phone away from me to avoid sudden malfunctioning of my ears.

"'How dare you talk about overtime with a DPM? Have you ever heard about overtime in Smile Bank? I do not like your attitude. I can be very bad. You won't be going back to Cohiana or anywhere near it in your lifetime.' He was showing his trump card.

"I wanted to go back to Cohiana on the next transfer. So, I came very early to the branch the next day and started data punching for core banking implementation. However, it was interrupted by two VIPs who showed their identity cards.

"'I am from the Banking Authority of Marcardia,' the man in front lifted his identity card slightly upwards from its normal position on the chest. 'I will be inspecting your transactions related to the Government of Marcardia and pension payments. My colleague Lolan will be inspecting other aspects,' he pointed towards the other person who was not making eye-to-eye contact.

"'Who is sitting at the *May I Help You* counter?' he asked. That is a counter where all financial problems are solved and the customer can talk anything as in the *zero hour* of Marcardian Parliament.

"'Nobody, Sir. We are already short of hands and the only available hand has been taken out for data punching.' I stood up with folded hands.

"'I am not here not to hear about your grievances. If you do not have staff, you request for it. I want all the counters to be manned as per the Kooriyan Committee recommendation on customer service. If it is not done immediately, I will be forced to ring up your Principal Manager at Trivania,' he revealed the equations of the protocol.

"'I will sit there, Sir.' He was visibly happy at the obedience shown by me, till he moved to the cash counter.

"'What is this? How long does one has to wait in the queue for encashing a cheque?' He was upset by the big queue in front of both cash cabins.

"'Staff shortage, Sir.' I stood apologetic as if I had the power to recruit staff and had forgotten to do it.

"'I told you already, I am not here to hear your problems.' He was fully enjoying his power without responsibility.

"'You don't sit there. Get me the data of direct taxes and pension paid for the last three years,' Lolan was not permitting me to handle the *May I Help You* counter, where his colleague had directed me to sit.

"'Oh, God!' Yeah, I called his name for the first time after several years and instantly understood his value for a man in distress. I also understood how belief became a part of Marcardian life.

"'This gold is spurious,' the leader of the team used the official language of the branch from inside the strongroom where the gold ornaments pledged by the customers were kept. Shouting with full lung power was the official language of the branch. Both the customers and the staff were well-versed in it. Thobias took time to learn it.

"He was cross-checking the quality of the ornaments, against which the Bank had given loans. Normally, gold is tested by an expert before pledging for loan.

"'One more fraud,' I told myself while going to the police station for filing a complaint against the borrower who had pledged spurious gold.

"Filing a complaint was not a big job, but the time released for it from the routine work caused a few red faces here and there in the branch.

"'We've got a complaint against you. An innocent customer has pledged high quality gold at your branch to avail a loan against it. Now, he has learned that your people have substituted that gold with spurious metal and that you have filed a false complaint against that innocent man. I want to investigate that too. Come here fast.' It was a powerful instruction from the police through the phone, immediately after my return to the branch. I forgot about the auditors and rushed to the police station again.

"'I have got reason to believe him too,' the police officer was demanding that I prove my innocence, for which there was no easy route. 'For me, both cases are equally important and I won't leave both of you till I find out the truth,' he was earnestly pursuing the truth giving the benefit of doubt to both and at the same time suspecting both parties equally.

"'Let both of them be in the cell,' he ordered his subordinate. 'Truth will come out automatically.' I too knew that only truth will survive at the end. But I was not sure that staying in a lock-up along with the real culprit was needed for the fragile truth to survive.

"The cell was a 100-square feet room with an iron grill door; there were a few plastic mats stacked in one corner. There were only four culprits in that cell that day, including me and my customer. He was always moving in front of me with a warm smile and a cool face, as if nothing had happened between us.

"'We can settle it. If we don't settle, he will prove both of us guilty,' the customer pointed his fingers at the man in the uniform, who was busy dealing with another case, sitting on his wooden chair in a shabby room.

"'If you are prepared to share the cost equally, we can prove that both of us are innocent,' the customer told me again. I was not interested in the partnership, as the cell was more comfortable for me than the office and decided to enjoy the fully paid holiday comfortably. But, by late night, somebody at the top who understood my happiness in the cell intervened and the cell door opened for me pushing me to the branch again in the morning.

"Kusagran invited me to his cabin in the early morning. I was sure that it was to ask about my suffering in the police cell. But he did not ask anything about it.

"'The Marcardia Banking Authority people are here. If they ask anything about the big frauds, you do not know anything about it. Tell them to ask me.' He determined my level of ignorance.

"'I know a bit about it. How can I tell a lie?' I raised a doubt for which he just stared at my eyes as if he was going to do something to me. I left the cabin without saying anything further.

"'Thobias Mathai, the APM in charge of Audit follow up wants to talk to you,' the telephone operator of the controlling office was very polite while ensuring my availability.

"'What happened to the data collection as desired by the Banking Authority officials?' the APM asked.

"'I started collecting it, but meanwhile I was in a police cell yesterday,' I made an excuse.

"'Who asked you to go there? Who asked you to accept spurious gold from customers?' The accusation was unexpected.

"'It was appraised by our gold expert and only then accepted by our branch.'

"'Does it absolve you of your responsibility?'

"'No, Sir.'

"'Then why do you talk like that?'

"'Sorry, Sir.'

"'Mr. Thobias, yours is a light branch. Still, things are not getting done. Business is not picking up. I want thirty percent growth this year. As far as internal control goes, it's your headache. You only have to suffer the consequences of bad internal control, like that of the gold loan. You have got sufficient staff and you have to extract work from them.' His words were firm.

"I could visualise the agony of the struggling bullocks pulling the loaded cart uphill, unable to move an inch, when the carter twists its tail, pokes it in the pelvis, beats and shouts to get the final jerk to reach the top.

"'You know the contents of the interim report submitted by the auditors from the Marcardia Banking Authority? *May I Help You* counter is unmanned. Citizen Charter is not displayed in the banking hall prominently. Cut and mutilated notes are not exchanged freely. There is a big queue at the cash counter. These are all very serious and damaging remarks and they are happening again and again. Do you want to go back to Cohiana?'

"'I want to go back to Cohiana, Sir.' That was the main aim of Thobias for the last three years.

"'How can I give that without achieving the business targets?' the APM showed his helplessness. Actually, business growth was not his territory. There was another APM exclusively to take care of it. He called only during the night, just before the manager went to bed. He was practising the psychology degree he was holding. He believed that the topic heard late in the night will be carried over to sleep and to the brain to remain embedded there longer.

"'I will rectify those observations immediately,' I became positive.

"'That you have to. There is no other go. I am concerned with the business growth,' the APM repeated. I understood that the psychologist was on leave and he was holding the concurrent charge of deposit growth.

"'Sir, even now we are struggling to complete the work. Further growth will add to that workload. Our systems are obsolete and the people prefer the high-tech banks. It is difficult to bring new customers without police powers,' I said a truth.

"'What?'

"'Nothing, Sir.' I was hesitant to repeat those words which came at the spur of the moment.

"'Mr. Thobias, I heard what you said. Don't think that you can escape Smile Bank at any time. You remember that ten lakh dollar bill discounting? Your branch missed reporting it on the same day. That currency has depreciated heavily and late reporting has caused loss of lakhs of Lians to us. I can initiate action against you at any time for that.'

"'I was in no way involved in it,' I refused to accept that threat.

"'Who says so? You are in charge of internal control of the branch. You had to take care of it, though permitted by Kusagran. Now, we are counting upon you for business growth as Kusagran is not dependable. You can achieve those targets as done by you in your earlier branches, though it can be a bit taxing. If you achieve the business targets, we will post you back to Cohiana. Otherwise forget about that and even life.'

"That early night was as unsuspecting as any other early night. I closed the branch premises and moved towards the Station Road. Suddenly, a man came from the back through the left side and harshly pushed me sideways with his shoulders. He was very muscular and wore a black and grey check shirt and black trousers. He immediately disappeared into the crowd.

"I started watching all those around me, occasionally looking back. I could see another man watching my movements and coming against me. He was unshaven and had long hair. He came dashing and hit me with his shoulders and moved past, mixing with the crowd. For the first time, fear gripped me and each step I took was very cautious. But, nothing happened for a long time till I entered an overcrowded bus. It was very difficult to move much inside the bus.

"'Go in, man,' a man who entered the bus just after me shouted.

"He was a dark stout man with brown prominent teeth, exhibiting pieces of tobacco in between them. His clothes were soaked in sweat and smelt bad. His eyes were red and he looked threatening.

"'I told you to go inside,' he repeated, singling me out. He pushed the person standing near me and occupied that space. His face was very close to my left ear.

"'This is Doncity,' he whispered in my ears, 'and I have got a licence to kill.' He caught hold of my left hand and took it to his hip and made me feel a gun kept inside his trousers. He got down at the next station through the entry door pushing the commuters sideways, unmindful of their reprimanding and shouting. I regretted the discussion with Kusagran in the morning and understood the meaning he conveyed through his piercing look.

"Getting back to Cohiana was not an easy task for me. The salary was not sufficient to afford the luxury of bringing my family and staying with them. Now, life was under threat from an unknown. I could not imagine further stay there. I wrote my request for transfer on the very same day I completed three years.

"'We have forwarded your request to the Controlling Office, Cohiana. Now you have to ask them where you are going to be posted for the next term.' the lady manager in the Human Resources section showed her disinterest in the affairs of a colleague.

"The reply from Cohiana was more hostile, 'We did not get your request for placement. Ask them to forward it.'

"'Why should we keep it? It has gone the very next day,' the HR manager at Doncity was not interested in continuing the talk.

"'Why should we say a lie to you, Thobias?' the APM in charge of transfers at Cohiana raised a doubt. 'I cannot attend to all individuals. You approach your Revolutionary Association. They are tracking individual cases,' he candidly admitted the role of the Association in detecting the merit of individuals.

"'Yes. Pannaverse here.' The tone was just like the voice of the APM. They could talk like executives, even though there were no holy halos around their heads.

"'I am Thobias Mathai. Can you look into my transfer request?'

"'Ha ha. You remembered me? Where were you these days? What are you doing at Doncity?'

"I did not try to improve his ignorance level. 'Why didn't you participate in our strike call against the bank?' Pannaverse asked. There was no immediate answer from me. I never understood that participation in strike also counted for placement. It was more than a cat and mouse game.

"I submitted my resignation immediately and left Doncity the same day. Kusagran did not give the acknowledged copy, in spite of my waiting for it. I was sure that the bank also will take its own time to accept it."

"So, you liked the police cell better than working in office. There too, you will be forced to work. You can experience it as soon as this enquiry is over," Tejaram was still not convinced.

Tejaram stopped recording when an attendant entered the cabin and informed him about the availability of the lab for medical check up. Thobias followed the attendant to the fourth floor, carrying the red file he had brought. The lab was handled by a short man with a boyish face. A stethoscope decorated his shoulders. He switched on the treadmill, keeping the angle at four in the scale upto sixteen and speed at six in the scale upto twelve. Thobias could not pace more than a few steps before his face started paling. Thobias was gasping for breath and a few drops of blood oozed out from his nose. The doctor stopped the treadmill immediately, helped him disembark and led him to the examination table nearby, holding him on his shoulder.

"You are a patient?" the doctor asked softly.

"Lung cancer," Thobias was brief and stretched the red file towards him.

The doctor took time to go through it, occasionally copying a few sentences down on a recording sheet of the MSIB.

"Take care. It is a wonder that you are alive now," the doctor smiled and handed over the lab report to the attendant, who accompanied him to the cabin of Tejaram.

Tejaram was visibly upset with the lab report and spent considerable time cross-checking the facts with the doctor through intercom.

Tejaram did not ask any question for a long time.

"Why don't you try catching the real culprits?" Thobias asked.

"Who decides the real culprit?" The answer was a return question from Tejaram.

"If you search the flat No. F 704 of Kusagran at Red Stone Garden, you can get a few nude photos from the hidden shelf behind the middle picture of the leftside bedroom. Try to find the details of it," Thobias made a suggestion to Tejaram.

"I am enquiring cases against you. Still, I will try to see his flat some time. Now, your medical reports are just before me. You are not going to lose anything even if you admit those charges, as your days are numbered," Tejaram tried a shortcut to close the case file.

"I will lose me." Thobias did not wait for a formal permission to leave the cabin.

30

I T WAS THE INAUGURATION of the new dining table in Amma's room that made Thobias make a journey to Kurishumala and brought Mr. Pannaverse face to face with him. Thobias' younger brother had ordered a dining table for Amma with a better height and smaller size, so that Amma could have her food by sitting on the bed. While putting it near her bed, Thobias was feeling guilty that he had never done anything to add to her comfort and instead was confined to himself. He worked in Smile Bank and there was a man called Kusagran in it, and he was attracted by a lady called Abinita; all could be reasons. But that was not a valid excuse.

Amma invited Thobias to join her at the new dining table. It was a small one, where one could dine comfortably. Another person could also join if he was prepared to sit face to face, very close to the other. Probably she liked it.

It was not a great dinner, but the talk was.

"Do you think that I cannot read your face?" She started the conversation as Thobias was silent, watching the glass top and curved legs of the new furniture as if he was really interested in buying a similar one.

"I never underestimated you," Thobias replied. After all, she was a mother and she must be able to read the face of her son.

"I can see your anxiety. I can read fear there. You are hiding your helplessness too." She avoided looking into the eyes of Thobias. Instead, she pretended that she was searching seriously for a piece of ginger pickle in the small steel vessel, using her forefinger.

Thobias tried to smile, looking into her eyes. But it did not blossom out as desired.

"I have got a solution for your problems, but you must believe in it. Give all your problems to God. You remember your childhood days? How happy and smiling you were in that abject poverty? You used to pray for hours. Your eyes were sparkling and my sister kept your photo in her Bible, telling me that you would go in God's way and would become a great man. You lost the way somewhere. It's time to start believing in Him again."

Thobias did not reply. He continued stirring the rice to mix it thoroughly with the *dal* curry, making it yellowish.

"You remember going to Kurishumala during the school vacation? You sincerely believed in the Saint and your warts disappeared from both your hands. You were ready to walk the entire distance in that scorching sun to thank God for the favours received. Where did that belief go? And how?"

Kurishumala was thirty kilometres from Panamkara, where a Saint was said to have meditated and prayed for the removal of sins from humanity. The prayers were so powerful that he attained sainthood and his feet got imprinted on the hard rock at the very top of the mountain. Thobias had a lot of black warts on his fair skin, especially on his outer palms, neck and forehead. He prayed to the Saint and promised to visit his footprints at Kurishumala taking wart-like beads made of wheat flour with him.

Thobias woke up to the biggest surprise in his life the next day. All the warts except one between the nail and skin of his left thumb had vanished from his body. Little Thobias jumped in joy and the thrill of experiencing a wonder brought him to tears. He kissed the picture of the Saint and set out to thank him, walking the entire route, which of course, was not included in the original promise.

"But one is left out. Is it because the Saint could not see the one under the nail?" It was an innocent question posed to the all-knowing Amma.

"That is to remind you about the favour he gave you. Don't brood over the one which did not go and think about the ones which have disappeared."

Thobias visited Kurishumala again with the same respect ten years later on the first Sunday after Easter. It was the festival day at Kurishumala. The route to the rock top was covered with believers. Both sides of the route were lined by stalls selling pictures, handicraft, snacks and tea till the road reached the middle of the mountain. After that, there were lines of beggars on both sides of the rocky road, each sitting or lying at a fixed distance. Many of them were immobile; having no legs, having curved legs, or having only one leg and the others were without some vital body part. The smell emanating from them indicated that they had not bathed for days, if not months. All were crying and begging in a language that was slightly different from the local one but understandable.

It was natural to wonder how these immobile and half-mobile living bodies had reached the mountain top and the researcher in Thobias decided to satisfy himself with an answer. He took his place near a small group, where three beggars were lying together instead of the linear pattern of arrangement in general. They were vying among themselves to show their mutilated body parts, intermittently crying and making loud noises to attract the attention of the Kurishumala pilgrims for a coin or two.

As night descended, the rocky route thinned out of people and the path to the rock top became empty except for the shopkeepers packing their stalls and moving downhill. A tea shop remained open in violation of the general rule of closing at night. The light from a kerosene lamp from that shop illuminated the area, though very dimly.

A dark, fat man, with a piece of cloth tied around his head, was standing in the tea shop watching the beggars, who, by this time, had stopped crying and started talking to each other in their language, probably laughing too, as the light could show a few white spots at the centre of their faces, possibly the teeth reflecting the faint light.

The fat man gently moved towards the line of beggars. He untied the cloth piece from his head while starting his walk like an army captain inspecting the guard of honour. He stopped at each beggar and talked to them. The conversation was mild in some cases, but was close to shouting at times and occasionally he was getting mad and doing something physically, which was not clear from a distance in the darkness.

Thobias only understood the conversation when the guard of honour came near him.

"Only this much?" The captain collected the coins that had fallen on the piece of cloth in front of the immobile beggar. "You know how much I spend in bringing you up here? You know how much I have to give to that tea shop to feed you? If you can't get half of it, you will be rotting to death on the wayside and worms will eat you up."

The beggar did not respond.

"If there is no profit, I will just do that," he said it again loudly when he reached the next beggar who was partially mobile.

"Where was your voice all day?" He was not happy with the crying pitch of the beggar who was under constant observation from the tea shop. He raised his voice further and was shouting and cursing in his language. Still, there was no response. The fat man went back a few feet and came dashing towards him and planted a kick on the left side of his body. The beggar did not produce any sound but got tilted to the other side by the force of the kick. He might have cried in silence, or cursed him or he might not have done anything as he was used to it.

The captain moved down the hill, appraising the performance beggar by beggar and the shouting became fainter as he moved away. Luckily, the beggars had only one boss and the appraisal stopped at one kick. The fat man did not come back for long and the beggars continued their stay in the lap of nature.

Thobias searched his pocket and collected the coins and a few notes and stretched it towards the one who was still lying tilted to his right, "This can help you to avoid a kick some time in your life." The beggar took the money and grasped it in his hand forcefully and held it for some time without releasing. His hands were trembling and he was crying. Thobias washed his hands in the stream down the mountain to avoid any infection. He also looked at his pocket and confirmed that a few notes were still available there to take care of the return journey.

Thobias could not understand why such a thing was happening under the nose of such a powerful saint who could remove almost all his warts at one go.

Thobias was not sure that he would climb Kurishumala again. Still, he promised Amma that he would visit it. He always kept his word and the car took him to the base of the rocky uphill path the very next day. He was not aware of what was in store for him later that day.

Thobias found that the tarred road had made deep inroads into the mountain, reaching almost half way.

Thobias enjoyed the scenic beauty from midway, though it could have been a better view from the top rock. He watched the lush greenery and tried to locate places. He scanned the river that made hairpin bends here and there, the mansions that had come up on both sides of the river in different colours, the vehicles moving down below like tiny beads disappearing into the woods and, in between, he observed those happy believers who were climbing the mountain prayerfully. Beggars were absent this time as it was off-season. Thobias tried to move a few meters up, but it laboured his breathing and caused some pain in his chest.

Thobias got a little relief when he closed his eyes for some time and tried to believe that there was somebody to take care of his problems. But, it was short-lived as he could not continue in that belief for more time as earthly problems started resurfacing again.

Thobias decided to return home after a few hours. He also bought a picture of the Saint as proof of having visited the place. He prayed to the Saint to bring a smile on his face and make him cheerful when he met Amma.

While reversing the car, Thobias found another car stopping behind and waiting for the parking space that would be vacated by Thobias.

The man in the car waved his hand, requesting him to stop. Thobias could not recognise him immediately through the glasses of the car, though he stopped his car a few yards away.

It was the great Pannaverse. His teeth were still outside, making the lips insignificant, but he was not bending forward as earlier and instead stood straight, with a cool and calm face. His eyes were radiating a natural sparkle. He came forward, looked at Thobias for a second and to his utter surprise, embraced him, with his hands gently patting his back.

"Oh, Thobias. What a great surprise! I am happy to see you, and see you here. I think the Saint has forgiven my sins." Thobias was not sure about the conclusion he had arrived at, but got alarmed about the change that had taken place in him. At least, he knows now that he has done iniquities.

"What are you thinking?" Pannaverse asked, on getting no verbal response from Thobias. "I was a fool in those days and committed so many wrongs that God turned against me. Now I realise what all I did as secretary of the Revolutionary Association. I am doing penance now by visiting holy places. I used to come here every month, driving more than four hundred miles.

"This is my son Akil," he introduced a young man who was watching the action.

"You go ahead," he told his son. "I will come afterwards."

"Come, I have something to talk to you. We will sit on that rock," he led Thobias to a nearby rock.

"You are silent and not talking as earlier," he recognised the first change in Thobias. "I know you are angry with me. You should be. I acted so much against you, like I did to many. Life teaches us all lessons. I too learned my lessons. It made me understand my sins. I repented over it. Now my mind is clear and I'm a happy man," Pannaverse was continuing his monologue and Thobias thought it best not to interrupt, till it stopped automatically.

"You have retired?" Thobias stepped in when Pannaverse stopped.

"No. Resigned."

"Resigned? I cannot believe it. You were such a powerful man without any work and responsibility. You had rewritten the fate of many by overwriting that written by God."

Pannaverse kept his face still smiling and calm. There was a special warmth in his smile, different from the teeth exposure process as Secretary of the Revolutionary Association. This time, certain internal organs knew that he was smiling.

"You should know it in detail. I joined the efforts of the bank to pin you in that case. That was the only way out to save many innocent officers and managers. Otherwise, more than a dozen of them would have been behind bars now, including those who processed them, verified the credentials, recommended them, inspected them and audited them. I knew I was doing wrong, but that was for a good cause. Also, that was a minor one compared to the things I have done jointly with Smile Bank over others." Pannaverse avoided direct eye contact with Thobias. Instead, he looked at the top rock and the people climbing the mountain carrying their sins.

"Something happened in my life which was destined to teach me a lesson. I do not have any hesitation in telling you that. I have confessed it to my friends, foes and even to my wife."

"You will be happy to know about my great fall from power," Pannaverse looked at Thobias and tried to smile, but it was something between smiling and chuckling. Thobias returned the smile as if there was no harm in hearing a story on a day when nothing better was available to do.

Pannaverse looked at the greenery downwards and at the people who were going back satisfied after visiting the wonder rock. There were expressions in his face as if he was selecting the sentences to talk and rearranging the events in his mind but unable to do it easily.

"A few months after you left Smile Bank, the general transfer came. I got a very able and hardworking assistant in my department. She was more than that. It was a gift from Mehman, to relieve me from work so that I could concentrate on the management games. She was transferred from one of the Cohiana branchs. On the day of her joining itself, I could not concentrate on my work.

"Instead, I enjoyed watching the cut of her nose, her beautiful chin and innocent eyes. Her sleeveless top exposed more of her fair skin and presented her like a young girl though she was married with two children.

"She seldom talked and her full energy was used in work, keeping the relations at official level. I was a very big man for her and she used to stand up in respect whenever

I visited her seat. Probably, that respect made her come closer to me as days passed. She used to come and discuss official matters, however small they were. She was happy with my comments and innocently laughed at it, unmindful of others.

"As days went by, she became more than an assistant. She used to remind me of things which I forgot. She used to advise me on presenting gifts to my wife on wedding anniversaries, buying sweets for Akil on birthdays and wishing close friends on festivals. She enjoyed coming near the power centre.

"One day, she told me about herself; how she got bored with her husband who was an alcoholic and also a workaholic, employed in an IT company, having no time for his wife; how he discharged his frustrations over her, and why she had requested for this transfer to make herself dearer through depravity. She would return only if he apologised to her and assured her of living like husband and wife.

"Thereafter, the talks became more and private. The office became too open a space for us and we talked while walking down the stairs of the eighteen storey building or at the Marcardian Coffee House overlooking the city park. It was fun going with her to Trivania vegetable market, selecting vegetables for her and assisting in carrying them to her flat. I never did it for my wife in my lifetime.

"She faced a number of issues. Her father was bedridden and she looked after him. Her husband too had his aged parent to look after. Both were seriously engaged in their roles and it led to a big communication gap and ego clashes. She wanted love and affection, maybe in tune with her beauty, and it did not come forth. Anyhow, I got a space there to dream. I became young. I dyed my grey hair, shaved off my moustache where grey hairs were sprouting up against my wish, purchased brightly coloured shirts using my credit cards, polished my shoes daily, bleached my face, all to became contemporary to my new age. I even started searching souvenir shops to purchase unforgettable gifts for my new darling.

"'Can I trust you?' she asked me once and I got elevated to a place far higher than earth. I found my heaven.

"'Two hundred percentage. No, no, infinity.' I said from my heart.

"She smiled and the smile merged with blushing. 'You are very pretty,' the young man in me took courage to tell her.

"'Thank you,' she too agreed and she was sure about it, like me.

"It gave me courage to open up my heart further.

"'I love you,' I whispered in her ears, while walking down the staircase together.

"'Mmmm,' she made a sound only, which did not reveal whether she liked it from a grey haired uncle. I was not familiar dealing with ladies. I could not measure the meaning of her expressions. I wanted to believe that it was not a one-way traffic because I did not wish to come out of my dream. One has to understand Marcardian ladies from the expressions they make.

"I became a mariner's compass and my revolving chair was always pointing towards her movements in the office. My interest in playing the Smile Bank games came down. Better human emotions started exhibiting themselves in me. I started smiling innocently and even started telling the truth to some of my friends. Mehman observed the changes in me but never interfered.

"Things went well till some officers spotted us at the far corner of the Museum Park, holding hands together. Some saw us regularly in Marcardian Coffee House. A few observed the changes in me in the office.

"It started rumours. It was she who first heard it among us. But she did not divulge anything to me. She let things go on as they were, at the same time doing her work meticulously.

"I could not understand her when she placed the handbag between us when we went for an office tour in a bus.

"I could not understand her when she kept me waiting downstairs for her, or when she walked past me without bothering about my waiting near the leftside corner of the staircase, away from the peeping eyes of the Smile Bank men.

"I could not understand her when she said her husband had apologised to her, or when she said she was busy with work.

"I could not understand her when she showed her family album to show her attachments.

"I could not understand her when she said, 'Don't plan things' or when she said, 'We will talk at a later time.'

"She was wise enough not to antagonise the tall leader of the Revolutionary Association and she was sure that I could be easily managed by her. She allowed the rumours to continue and they *became* true stories.

"But she brought the things to a climax faster than expected. She understood my downward journey and the disenchantment with Mehman. She met the Vice Principal Manager and spoke one sentence only, 'Pannaverse is immature.' She never told him about the meetings in Vettiyoor lake or the calls she had made when she was alone. Her immediate concern was to address the rumours floating around her, like any other married lady.

"I got the transfer orders signed by Mehman a week later and took charge of Tholiyur branch which was twenty kilometers away. Mr. Bhavaskar occupied my seat and he was sent to branches to study about the effect of interest variation on deposits, and like me, he too won the next election, defeating me.

"Sushu, it was her name, replaced my number with the number of Bhavaskar in her mobile. She was his faithful assistant till she was transferred back to Cohiana after five years."

"You never met her after your transfer?" Thobias sympathised with him.

"Yeah, at our old office. She was busy in work or pretended that she was busy. I waited near that espresso coffee outlet for her. She delayed her departure from office by more than two hours, as she was sure that I would be waiting downstairs.

"Don't try to meet me again. Please, this is a request," her eyes were wet and tears started rolling down like a stream overflowing in heavy rain. I stood there appreciating the capacity of the lady to produce pure water at short notice.

"'I respected your age; that is why I did not beat you with my sandals when you said, *I love you*. You should know that I am a married Marcardian lady.' I looked downwards and I could see her thick sandals there, moving too fast carrying her to the parked car. I also regained my lost age immediately.

"It was a journey back home for me. Unable to cope with branch work, I resigned. I started living with my family for whom I had never cared earlier. I concentrated on the studies of my son. He is now earning many times more than I did. Ours is a happy family now, thanks to Sushu."

Thobias found him laughing again happily, getting relieved from the tensions that he had been carrying, carried over from a job of giving tension to others at the diktat of Mehman and company.

Thobias could see his hatred melting down within him. It gave him a far better feeling than he got from seeing the footprint of the Saint.

He was all smiles when he entered the room of Amma. The Saint must have heard his prayers. Amma was very happy with the picture of the Saint.

Thobias went upstairs and kept a small piece of paper in the red file. It was the address of Velevendran, given by Pannaverse. Velevendran had resigned and now he was residing at Chinnakanal, a hill station of the rich and famous. It was not too far off.

31

CHINNAKANAL WAS just a dozen kilometres from Muzhiyoor, the famous tourist spot. After crossing the Muzhiyoor River and a few small hillocks covered with tea gardens, the road took a straight uphill turn to reach the misty top of a mountain, crossing over to the neighbouring state. Chinnakanal was famous for its panoramic view, cool climate, unpolluted air and water, and above all, it was largely uninhabited by humans for long except for a few tourist resorts offering vacations in heaven for those who were tired of the heat and dust downhill.

It was not too hard to locate the house of Velevendran. The guard at the gate of Tapovan Resorts could identify the new house that had come up near the top of Chinnakanal Mountain two years ago. From a distance, it looked like an ordinary house, with a green slanting roof and unplastered walls made of black garden rocks, standing in the midst of a tea garden, surrounded by polyalthia trees.

The view up close was far more elegant. There was a beautiful lawn which was decorated with reddish low-lying plants on the borders. The verandah was finished in deep black granite with art work along the border. The house stretched backwards covering a substantial area.

The man who opened the door invited Thobias to sit inside, without asking for any introduction. Thobias made himself comfortable in the slanting wooden chair. The floor was panelled with rosewood and the window, with the view of the hillocks and the unending tea gardens, looked like a wall picture.

Velevendran came in another few minutes. But there wasn't any surprise in his face in meeting an old pal, that too at his residence. He made himself comfortable and looked at Thobias as if he was asking, 'What made you come?' He was very easy and casual, but neatly dressed. He had removed his moustache. Probably white hairs disturbed him. He had become fully bald. There was an element of self confidence in his casual approach.

"I chose this place for its climate. It is cool throughout the year. I love to lie on the lounge and watch the hillocks covered with tea bushes, misty clouds, sparkling but cool rays of the sun, and above all, the majestic view from here when the sun rises from the mountain."

"Nice place. Nice house." Such words rarely came from Thobias.

"I always search for new thrills, maybe because I can afford it. I like asymmetry. And, I believe in nature," Velevendran liked the comments of Thobias.

"What made you come?" Finally the question came out. He knew that for every action there is a reason.

"Nothing special. Pannaverse gave your address."

"Oh, you met him? Poor fool. That lady spoiled his life."

"It was his fault too. He should have kept a distance."

"How is it possible for a normal man? She took an interest to come closer because he was an influential man and she sensed the public opinion and simply ditched him. She was then close to the new secretary Bhavaskar for long. I knew it. She took advantage of him instead of he taking advantage of her. Poor fellow. Leave it." Velevendran simplified a story in a few words.

"Your kids?"

"Both married off while I was in service. The designation has got a weight in marriage market. So, I did it a bit early and later resigned." He was always calculative.

"There is a case against me with the MSIB," Thobias led him to his subject.

"I too heard it. Somebody told me about it. Who was it . . . ?" Velevendran raked all his cranial cells without success.

"In this case, I am very much innocent. I only prevented furthur frauds, but now I am held as the culprit."

"Yeah, I remember it now. Your boss was Kusagran, right?"

"Yeah."

"He did it in his earlier branch too. He always gave big loans which were sanctioned from the Controlling Office. He knew that if found out as frauds, the sanctioning authority would also become party to it and that would create a lot of trouble for those at the top. Smile Bank avoids full scale enquiries in such cases and instead confines the investigation to selected individuals. Anyhow your stars were bad. You believe in stars?"

"No. No belief in them but I have counted them many times in my life." The reply made Velevendran laugh.

"Yours is not the question of stars alone. You joined a business organisation and stood up for your principles. The bank has got its own rhythm. What is the use of your principles when they do not do you any good? Don't others have principles? They have instead made more sacrifices by surrendering their principles." Velevendran was slowly coming to his mood.

"Stars do count in one's life. You know how Mehman came back to the limelight after he was unceremoniously shunted out from the staff department? Everyone thought that he had reached his own level of incompetence. Still, he came back. It was the ill luck of Tilak Kumar, the Vice Principal Manager. Tilak Kumar was entrusted with the task of entertaining the parliamentary team of Marcardia which came to look into official language implementation. After visiting a few branches, the team members got bored and asked to arrange a sightseeing trip to Sarcana Dam. Tilak Kumar arranged it and took the entry passes too. But unfortunately, the passes were left behind in the office and he had to go back to get them. The VIPs got angry and they cancelled their visit to the dam. The Principal Manager did not talk to him for days together and later it became an open war. Finally, Tilak Kumar was removed from the Staff Department and Mehman came back. Mehman later became Principal Manager while Tilak Kumar retired as Vice Principal Manager."

"Excuse me, I will be back. I have to feed the dogs. I have got a pair of Alsatians and a Pomeranian. I want to get a cross of them. It should be intelligent like an Alsatian and active like a Pomeranian. But, you don't try that. You will get a cross, active like Alsatian and intelligent like Pomeranian. Because, your stars are like that!" Velevendran cracked a joke and stepped out.

He took his own lavish time to feed the dogs, unmindful of the waiting guest, calling them by name and caressing them. Thobias sat watching the blank wall in front of him and the plants arranged in the corridor. Thobias understood that the distance between him and Velevendran was not that short as earlier and decided to move out at the earliest.

"While feeding, I was thinking a point." Velevendran said, on coming back and occupying the chair vacated by him. "We humans have got many traits that are seen in animals. Some are like dogs, always licking the boss and preventing others from coming near him, some are like cats who come stealthily and occupy the lap of the boss. Some are like foxes, they never labour but enjoy the fruits of others' labour and some are like hyenas who form a team to pull down the horses and even the lions, and some, I am not saying you, are like donkeys who just like to work and die. Man-management is to find out the inherent animal nature in human beings and utilise it for the organisation."

Thobias liked the illustration and looked at Velevendran with admiration. He always deserved it.

"My wife has gone for the engagement of a relative. I am alone with my dogs. I suggest we move out. We will go for a ride and there is a place to sit. Come." It was like an order.

"This is a beautiful place. I like driving through these hairpin bends." Velevendran said while driving.

Velevendran stopped his car in front of a bungalow surrounded by an expansive lawn at the top of the third mountain from his residence. The gatekeeper of Voltas Club came running, apparently recognising the visitor and opened the gate in a hurry. Built by the white rulers, it housed their estate manager during their stay here. The high-roofed central hall was vacant, except for a table tennis board. Two side rooms were packed with middle-aged and old people playing cards, keeping filled and half-filled glasses in front of them.

"This is my pastime now. You like a try?" he pointed towards the cards table.

"Oh, no. That age is gone for me."

"Okay, leave it. There is a bar on the back side. We can sit there. You like *kada* fry?"

Velevendran approached a big almirah close to the wall. While opening its door, Thobias could see a lot of small box-like demarcations and with a small key, Velevendran opened his locker. It had a few bottles of liquor kept by him. He took out a Royal Stag and called the waiter to serve it.

Both enjoyed the *kada* fry and whisky.

"Fast learners get time to relax like this. For others, the balance time available after learning is very little," Velevendran became philosophical.

"I got the advantage of learning the game faster than you. It is better to be an obedient worker, instead of posturing like a principled useless. You cannot change the world. And why should we change it after all? Close your eyes whenever required, like your bosses do. All this came to me due to that. Now I am enjoying those fruits. I also took care that I did not harm anybody in that process."

"Admirable," Thobias limited his reply to a single word.

"You know Somi, who was in the secretariat of the Vice Principal Manager? She must be in a very high position now in Smile Bank. I lost touch with her after I resigned and left Trivania."

Thobias shrugged his shoulders.

"She asked me to locate a plot for constructing her house at Trivania. There was one vacant plot near my house and I settled it for her. I helped her in drawing the plan, getting it approved from the Trivania Corporation, distributing the bribes in all concerned departments according to hierarchy, selecting the contractor, tackling the headload workers and finally even arranging the house-warming function. She told me that her husband was abroad and he would be coming after two years. She kept a respectable distance from me and I too was forced to keep it, after seeing her aristocratic way of dealing and matter of fact sentences."

"She got promotion in the first chance but continued in the same place, secretariat of the Vice Principal Manager. It was criticised by many in the Head Office. One fine day, there came an order transferring her to the Public Relations Department. I thought she went from there. But, to my utter surprise, she was there in the same seat and only the name of the department had got changed. The researcher in me started focusing on her boss management tricks. You know, no lion tolerates a second leader in the jungle."

"I could learn that she was nearly divorced and was suffering from a disease called boss mania. She would be close to the most powerful man in the administration. I started watching visitors to her house with added curiosity. There were no visible signs. In a flash, I recollected one point she said while constructing the house. She had told me to make the car porch sufficiently inside the house, so that the people can step in with privacy. I observed that no one could see her visitors when they get down from the car and enter the house."

"If there is a will, there is a way. I found that if I climb on the water tank on the roof of my house, I could see the people entering her house. On one New Year's day, I found a maroon car entering the gate of her house which was kept open for the visitor. I was not familiar with that car, but I was sure that I had seen it somewhere. I occupied the top of the water tank, reading a book, keeping watch on the porch."

"After an hour, she came out along with the Vice Principal Manager, and the maroon car moved out, carrying him. While turning back, she saw me sitting on the top of the water tank, my mouth wide open."

"'Everything happens in Smile Bank,' she passed a remark when I crossed her seat the next day in office. I smiled and agreed. I have seen that maroon car many times thereafter. Once, I saw a black car too. I was not sure as to who was inside it because she had put a plastic curtain to prevent my view from the water tank. But, our relationship went on well. I knew that she would be there near the power centre as long as her productive age lasted, and after that she herself would be that power centre.

"When the list of managers for foreign posting was under preparation, she came to my cabin and enquired whether I would like to have a foreign posting. I could not believe my luck.

"'Yes, Madam,' I stood up and said, 'I want it desperately.'

"'Okay, I will try. The problem is that there are more performers this time,' she said and went away. Later, I knew that you too were among the probables." Velevendran stopped for a second and Thobias did not say anything.

"The Principal Manager also visited her house in the office car twice. Thereafter, I could not count the visitors because I went abroad. She got promotion in another two years, still continued at Trivania but got shifted to the eighth floor from the seventh floor. She became secretary to the Principal Manager."

"You know why I was given the lucrative foreign posting?"

"Because you kept the secret intact," Thobias said innocently.

"No. That is the difference between you and me in understanding things. I was given the posting abroad because I should not peep too much into the life of the powerful from my house. I should go happily, otherwise, I might talk things out."

"Foreign posting was the turning point of in my life. Salary alone was sufficient to pull me on for the rest of the life because Lian was very weak in those days. All the big bosses visit the foreign branches at regular intervals because they all are attractive destinations than those busy, dusty branches in Marcardia. I could get very valuable contacts there. As time passed, I found another lucrative source of income."

"We are purchasing foreign currency there, right? To send it in Lians."

"Yeah."

"At what rate are you purchasing? Who is there to audit it?"

"I do not know," Thobias said.

"Yeah, there is a rate and it varies from party to party and in tune with the other exchange companies. We all are in touch with each other on an hourly basis. We give the Lian draft and the poor customer runs with it to mail it to his waiting wife, without any arguments. We sell the currencies the next day to the highest bidder. Since the quantity is higher, we get a substantially better rate. Where does the difference go? Need I tell you?

"All are happy here. The customer is happy because he got things fast. I am happy because I got the differential. Smile Bank is always happy and ever smiling and you can see it in the emblem. The currency purchaser is happy. Now you are happy because I am going to foot the bill out of that money. I made Somi also happy by presenting a necklace during my next visit."

"Only you might have gone unhappy at that time because you did not get a good posting in spite of good performance. But see, when five are happy and one is unhappy it does not matter much to an organisation. Twenty percent dissatisfaction is very much a tolerable level."

"Somi became very close to me after I gave the gift. She invited me to her house when I came the second time. It was a less expensive oven that I gave her that time. But, I found one thing there. Her standard of life had gone up considerably. A lot of improvements were made to her house."

"Somi visited my house when I came back after the foreign posting. She even went inside all the rooms and suggested further possible alterations, as if she were an architect. Her close proximity enthused and confused me simultaneously. While departing, she whispered something to me. I did not get it first."

"'We are posting you to the disciplinary section,' she repeated. I could not understand the meaning of *we* there.

"I was to report to the Vice Principal Manager in the new department. I took charge on a Thursday after praying to God. It was customary for the disciplinary section head to report to the VPM before taking charge and I did it.

"'No one should be spared,' he exhorted with a serious face. 'I want you to clean Smile Bank of the corrupt, disobedient and lazy bugs. All should be made to obey the orders of their boss and work for the benefit of Smile Bank. You have to frame chargesheets in such a way that it should not leave any loopholes for them to escape, even if the case is fought by their best advocates. At the same time, we should have a human touch. Human touch in the sense, the innocent should not be harassed. Cases against individuals who take risk for the benefit of the Bank should be viewed lightly, even if other agencies may not agree with us. Yeah, this is a very complicated department. Don't finalise the reports without consulting me. Wish you all the best." He shook my hand strongly and I exited.

"As soon as I sat on my chair, I got a call through the intercom. It was the sweet voice of Somi. 'Did you study file No. 44?'

"'No.'

"'Study it, Sir. We will discuss it further.' She addressed me as *Sir* for the first time.

"It was an interesting file. An anonymous person had filed a complaint with the Marcardian Vigilance Department accusing a Senior Manager of Smile Bank of amassing wealth disproportionate to his known sources of income. It also pinpointed two incidents. One was that the Senior Manager had availed leave fare concession amounting to 175,000 Lians without undertaking any travelling. Again, the same Senior Manager was given medical reimbursements twice amounting to 100,000 Lians each without any hospitalisation. The bills had been permitted by the VPM."

"Why was she interested in that file?" Thobias asked.

"Guess," Velevendran kept the climax boiling by keeping silent for a few seconds.

"Somebody close to her or somebody she wanted to teach a lesson," Thobias made a guess.

"No. The accused was Somi!"

"Oh, God!" The mention of God was automatic. Otherwise, Thobias did not have any intention to call God's attention to a trivial issue, when very big problems were hanging over him.

"The VPM solved the issue from the Smile Bank's angle and I solved it from the angle of Marcardian Vigilance Department. I could get *proof* for the journeys and hospitalisation. Don't ask me how."

"Was the complaint true?" Thobias was inquisitive.

"If it was not true, do you think such a big bank needs the services of a faithful man?"

"'You have saved an innocent,' the VPM congratulated me. Actually, I thought of hitting his nose out of shape.

"'It was my duty, Sir.' What came out from me, however, was different and that is the difference between you and me, or let me call *failure* and *success*.

"'Good,' the VPM reciprocated. I tried to guess the feelings inside him at that moment. It must have been terrible. He was saying something exactly opposite to the truth and that too knowing that both were aware of it. It requires tremendous mental strength. There, I decided not to go further up the ladder.

"I was rewarded for the favour after two years. The new VPM gave me the plum posting at the Stock Trading Department in Doncity. I could understand that he too made a journey to the house of Somi within a week of his joining.

"I reported at Doncity office a week later.

"'How did you come here?' the in-charge asked me with a curious face.

"'By auto rickshaw.' It was an innocent answer from me, like you used to make sometimes.

"'No, not that. I mean, through whom?' Then only I could understand the greatness of the department and the need for a godfather to get a posting there.

"'How is the new posting?' Somi telephoned me one day. 'Don't think that you got it on your own. There is my sweat behind it.' I didn't know her body metabolism.

"I was in the outer shell in the new office and nobody was permitting me to go near the actual business function. I was made in-charge of the premises matters, back room operations and data storage. Naturally, I developed the curiosity to know what was going inside.

"'How is the new department?' Somi asked me casually when I went home for the first leave.

"'Dealing with everything except stocks,' I told my grievance.

"I found my new seat inside the dealing room when I returned to the office after ten days. There were seven managers in that room. They do the active part of trading. They are the people who conduct a study on the health and ill-health of companies and recommend them for selling and buying to the executives at the next level. After travelling a few more tables, the file goes to sleep for some time. Then suddenly it comes back with a note, 'permitted as recommended'.

"I sat in the dealing room as an outsider for a few days. Then I decided to do a bit of research on the reasons for treating me as a stranger at home. I tried to communicate with a fellow who gave a half-smile at me one day.

"'The boss is very angry with you. You seem to have complained to the Head Office about the section allocations here.' I could easily understand the role played by my well-wisher.

"I made up with the boss over a period, and he developed confidence in me that things would be as confidential as earlier."

"Can you guess a money-making opportunity here?" Velevendran tested the IQ of Thobias.

"You buy or sell the stock in advance," Thobias was right this time.

"Exactly. That is why the file sleeps for some time in between. Those who prepare the report know what is going to happen. They will do it first, followed by others."

"It was fun all the way. The fun of making money. During that process, I got a great insight into stock trading. I met a lot of bulls and bears. I understood that it was my future."

"There was disbelief all around when I chose to keep away from the promotion process. There was not much charm in going up as society started giving weightage to money, rather than the height of the chair. A career also creates a lot of disturbances in the family life."

"When you decide to stay back from the mad rush of promotion you will be labelled as negative. I got that label and they assigned me the job of a *crab*. I did not complain to Somi because I liked my new pastime."

"You know *crabs* only from outside. Working as a *crab* is not that easy. But you are aware of my manipulative skills. The first duty assigned to me was to conduct the Branch Managers' Review Meeting. I was told about the purpose of the meeting, what were the points the big boss was going to speak of and who were the persons they were bringing before the firing squad.

"The boss will be asking some questions in between and that should get very positive responses from the Managers. We had to plan for it. I seated a very positive man near the expected negativists.

"'Can you all achieve thirty percent growth this year?' the DPM Vesham Kumar took the task of target allocation among the unwilling colleagues.

"Nobody said 'yes'. The man planted by me in between also kept silent because all knew that such a growth was not possible. Vesham Kumar looked at me, as if I had not done my homework properly.

"'We will achieve it, Sir,' I stood up and said. There was no other way.

"'You are in the administration. How can you say that?' Vesham Kumar ridiculed his own teammate, just to get the applause of the audience.

"'I know, our Managers are self motivated and they will contribute their full might for a genuine corporate call,' I showed my emotional bonding with Smile Bank.

"'You all agree to that?' Vesham exhibited immense common sense there.

"'Yes, Sir.' This time the planted man gave his support but the majority still kept silent, though words like *self motivation* and *corporate call* were effectively used. Vesham also made a mistake. He should have told the gathering that our beloved Principal Manager wants thirty percent growth. Such a reference would have added to his credentials and the call would have got wider acceptability.

"'I am happy now.' Vesham was surely unhappy. 'That should be the spirit of all Smile Bank men and women. When a corporate call is given, all will rise to the occasion and will support our beloved Principal Manager.' This time he improved himself.

"Vesham changed his tone and became serious. I understood the signal. I stood up and distributed the revised targets to all. I also asked them to sign on the reverse side of the paper where the detailed sector-wise targets were given for credit cards, insurance policies, recovery of bad loans, kids' deposits, tax collections, pension payments and all.

"'I am happy now,' Vesham repeated while collecting back the signed papers. 'Send a copy to each branch today itself, so that it must be the first letter they should see in their offices tomorrow,' he ordered. I did that too, meticulously. But, after the meeting he asked me to report to his cabin.

"'You did not do your homework properly,' he was upset as if something serious had happened. 'This is the first time they were not responding enthusiastically about a revised business target. How many persons did you call over the phone?'

"'Pardon,' I did not get the meaning.

"'You have not arranged sufficient people to say '*yes*.' That spoiled the mood of the gathering.'

"'The target was very high, Sir. Maybe due to that,' I spoke innocently like you do.

"'It is not the question of achieving the target. In a meeting, we want *yes* only. You could have told those fellows that whoever says '*yes*' would be given a smaller target.'

"'Sorry, Sir,' I confessed. But, it did not prevent my transfer to Chillana. I chose to resign."

Velevendran stopped his Smile Bank story and started watching the setting sun which was dipping the mountains in reddish paint. The crowd in the club became larger and larger. Many people started wishing Velevendran and he was forced to introduce his guest too. Thobias was lukewarm to introductions as he was sure that he would not be meeting them again in his life.

"We will move out," Velevendran did not like the lukewarm response to his introductions.

"You want to get rich?" Velevendran asked when they were driving back to his house. He knew that such a proposition lures everybody like magnet attracts steel. "I can introduce you to a team of stock brokers. We do things jointly. Both buying and selling."

"I am not that keen," Thobias said.

"Why?" The answer surprised Velevendran.

"What I want is time, not money." Thobias did not reveal the importance of time for him.

"This won't take much of your time. Or you can even appoint a secretary to do things as I direct."

"We will discuss that during my next visit." Thobias was sure that it wouldn't happen.

"You are hiding something." Velevendran could detect the pain written large on the face of Thobias even under the dim light inside the car.

"I'm a cancer patient and my days are numbered." Two teardrops ran down his eyes without permission.

Velevendran did not enquire further, nor did he show any emotion. He just concentrated on his driving and upon reaching the house, parked the car.

"Thanks for coming. Good night." Velevendran was not ready to waste his time with somebody who was of no use to him in his business and, under high intoxication, could not prevent hiding the real Velevendran.

While driving back, Thobias was brooding over what Pappu said about the purpose of friendships.

32

"THERE WAS A CALL from the MSIB yesterday evening. One Mr. Tejaram asked you to call back. He has given his cell number," Teena extended a small piece of paper as soon as Thobias reached home.

Thobias was in no mood to take a journey immediately and decided not to call him back that day. But Tejaram seemed to be in a hurry and the call came again which was attended by Teena as usual.

"What am I to say?" she asked Thobias through gestures and lip movements.

"Tell him I am not well," Thobias used the same language and she said it over the phone.

"How is his health? Can he attend this phone?" The voice from the other end was surprisingly mild and affectionate. She extended the phone to Thobias, signalling there was nothing to worry.

"How is your health?" he asked.

"Getting worse," Thobias took an anticipatory bail against immediate travel. "I called you to inform some developments and to suggest a way out. We made a search at the house of Kusagran as per the information given by you. We could locate the hidden cupboard behind the modern art picture. But it was empty except for a few boxes containing not-so-valuables, pass books, cheque books and a photo album pertaining to their family."

"Sorry for that. I saw the photo of Kusagran with a lady called Abinita with my own eyes. He might have removed it suspecting I might tell MSIB," Thobias repeated the charge.

"May be or may not be. But we have got certain other clues and we are working on them."

"Like?" Thobias was anxious.

"That is not your lookout. You are still under investigation and are a culprit until proved otherwise," Tejaram reiterated that he was still a policeman.

"I am not sure I will be there to know the end," Thobias revealed his real concern. "That's why I asked."

Tejaram took a few moments to make the next sentence. Probably he was thinking about the pros and cons of telling a police secret.

"There was one more hidden cupboard in his flat. We could easily locate it. We got a few land documents which revealed certain things. They are under scrutiny now," Tejaram said, albeit very hesitantly. Thobias could not understand the connection between the land documents and the frauds in the Milky Station branch. He was afraid to ask about it further.

Tejaram also understood the hesitancy of Thobias.

"All plots were purchased in a gap of six months; all from a single person, twenty-three years ago. The seller is known to us. He is a charge-sheeted criminal. Kusagran was unable to explain the source of funds. He simply broke down and is in hospital now. Meanwhile, I thought, in case you want the passport back, you can move a petition in court and I will tell our advocate not to oppose it vehemently. You can get it back and go for treatment to USA."

"Thank you." There were tears in the eyes of Thobias Mathai.

"Thank you very much," Thobias repeated in gratitude. "But, frankly, I may not need it. The other passport will reach me any time. I am just counting the seconds." Tejaram understood the meaning and hung the phone.

33

THERE WAS SEVERE PAIN in his lungs. Some of the parts must have been eaten by the disease on its way to conquering the entire organ. The usual pain killer was not enough to control the pain. He went to bed early. Tinges of blood came out twice through the nose, dotting the white pillow cover red. Thobias could not sleep and was writhing in pain, but still decided against calling Teena or Amma.

He opened the red suitcase and took out a neatly packed box. It contained certain medicines that were to be used only when the pain did not subside even after the regular dosage of pain killers. It contained morphine which could take the mind away from the world of pain, even though characters like body and pain would still be playing their roles actively.

He was asked to use it only in extreme cases of pain as it was the start of the countdown too; the countdown for the passage from this beautiful world to an unknown world. Thobias was aware of it. So, he refrained from taking it for some time and sat watching the neatly packed box.

There was an element of hope too that the pain would recede after some time and there would still be time for him in this world. He swallowed a few more pain killer tablets and waited for the response. He was enjoying the hope; the hope of living for a few more days. He tried to stand up just to make sure that he was still fit to live. Hope was giving him a pleasure, and there was nothing else left out. He still hoped that the oozing of blood would stop and his body would recoup the lost cells which went to soak the pillows. But he could not stand for very long. He collapsed on the bed and the white pillow got a few more red spots.

Thobias tore off the neatly packed cover and swallowed a small black pill. As expected, it gave him fast relief from the pain and gave Thobias time to have a second look at the pillow. It was wet and most of the area was red. He removed the pillow cover and replaced it with another one. The rest of the night was under his control.

In the morning, Thobias signed the cheque which was given to him by Sahaloshan and moved to Rajan's house. Early morning visits are usually with a purpose and that was exactly why Rajan raised his eyebrows when he saw Thobias. He moved the newspaper aside and looked straight into the eyes of Thobias.

"Just thought of seeing you," Thobias lowered the importance of his visit.

"You cannot deceive an honest friend who knows you from childhood. There's something serious about you. I wanted to ask about it many times but thought it appropriate that you tell me on your own," Rajan guessed it right.

Thobias did not reply.

"I observed a calm in you, like the frightening calm of a river, ready to join the sea, leaving everything behind, after galloping through the hills, gushing through the valleys, collecting everything possible," Rajan stopped.

"A bit serious," Thobias decided to open up.

"Something I can help?" Rajan offered his assistance.

Thobias shrugged his shoulders and tried to smile. However, the chest pain did not allow him a perfect smile suited to the occasion.

"Nobody can do anything about it. My days are numbered and the pace of counting is getting faster than expected. Thobias narrated the background and predicted the future too. Rajan sat back on his armchair, covering his face with both his hands.

"Give this to Sivan," Thobias extended the cover Sahaloshan gave him. "Now it does not have much value for me. For me, they are just paper pieces which can be collected from the Bank of Paradise. But it will be useful for Sivan. He has got time to spend it."

Rajan took a few minutes to respond. The response was on unexpected lines.

"I do not want it for Sivan. Let him chase it and get it. Chasing is more fun than getting things free. Otherwise, he may get bored in life or go wayward." The value of the cover went down further and Thobias took time to make his next sentence.

"That's okay. But I want a help; a small help to reach the tomb of Pappu. I have already made all arrangements and even paid the demanded donation to the church. You have to supervise it. Actually, it is fate that I have to manage everything for me from childhood." He tried to control his emotions, but tears rolled down from his eyes and fell on the white cotton shirt.

"Take this for those expenses," Thobias stretched the signed cheque towards Rajan.

Rajan did not say anything. He stood up for a moment, trying to adjust to the news he got in the morning. He came closer to Thobias and put his hands over his shoulders. He attempted to say something but refrained. The hand was there for some time till he took it off for accepting the cheque. Thobias exited immediately as there were many things to do.

Back in his room, Thobias decided to call Theresa. He was not sure whether to tell her about the imminent departure, as it could be a botheration especially if the departure was delayed further. The cancer was due to his excessive smoking and nobody enjoyed being with him at that time. He only enjoyed it alone, during his donkey days, as an escape route from the drudgery in a milling stone called Smile Bank.

"What made you remember me at this time?" Theresa expressed her surprise on receiving his call at that odd hour. She liked it even though it was past midnight in USA.

Thobias took time to answer, though he had planned the sentences well in advance.

"I love hearing your voice," he replied in a choking voice.

"Oh, my God! You are becoming romantic again at this old age." She laughed and Thobias enjoyed it, listening to it full length. "Cheer up. You seem to be feeling lonely. Do you want me to come there?" she detected the choking of the voice.

"I think you will have to come. Plan for it," Thobias said.

"Okay, dear. I have to get up early and want to sleep now. Bye." Theresa did not show interest in continuing the conversation at that moment. Her reasons were very genuine. Thobias did not dial again, as he thought it was not necessary to connect her to something to which she was not a party. He believed that death is a solitary experience and it cannot be shared at all, whatever be the intimacy.

Thobias did not disturb the other members of his nuclear family at that late hour and waited for the US to wake up in the morning.

It was Annie who came on the line.

"Hi, Papa. How are you? How is your second childhood?" she teased.

"Going fine dear. And it will end soon,"

"Are you growing up that fast?" she asked. "I want to go early today. I have to take a session for the new batch and I ain't prepared anything so far. I fear driving when I can't concentrate. Have to pick up a taxi. See you, Papa. I'll call you back." Thobias understood her hectic schedule.

"Okay, carry on. Sweet kisses to you." His full-night waiting ended in planting a kiss through the phone.

Thobias did not get any response to the calls he made to his home number in USA thereafter. Abi must be still sleeping or he may have already left for office. The same must be the case with Ashi. Thobias recorded a voice message, '*Hello, how are you?*' to their mobile numbers and withdrew to bed early, to compensate for the lost sleep of the previous night.

He woke up to the deep hooting of an owl. The childhood story flashed in his mind and his face paled like the white pillow cover. Something is going to happen here tonight. Pappu is not around to go out with his country gun in search of the owl and shoot it down to save the family. Thobias concentrated on the origin of the hooting. It was from the top of the tall jackfruit tree which stood a few yards away from the building. The tree was easily visible through the window, thanks to the light from the big neon bulbs placed on the pillars of the front gate.

Thobias calculated the distance of the owl from each member of the family. Amma is downstairs and he upstairs, closer to the tall jackfruit tree. Teena is an outsider and must be unknown to the owl that lives in the forest far away. Thobias listened to the increased frequency of the hooting.

Fear started growing inside the heart of the brave modern man. Thobias sat on the bed, hoping the hooting owls would go away on their own after some time. But, they did not and the fear inside him grew. He could also feel the pain developing in his lung region and decided to go downstairs, further away from the owl.

"Amma . . ." Thobias knocked at the door of Amma's room very gently. It was Teena who opened the door. She went out as soon as Thobias entered the room.

"There are two owls on that jackfruit tree," Thobias told her softly while sitting on the bed where Amma was lying.

"So what?" Amma was more modern than Thobias. "It has to sit somewhere and hoot. There are no big trees nearby, so they must have come near to our house."

"But you had told me that an owl brings bad luck to the family."

"That was fifty years ago. You still remember those things? And still believe in those silly things? You have not grown up." Thobias could not believe Amma this time unlike in his childhood days.

"Can I sleep here for a day?" Thobias was shy to seek that favour.

"Are you crazy?" the response was on expected lines. "Teena has to sleep in this room to attend me. What shall I tell her? That you fear owls even at this age?"

"Okay, Amma. Good night." Thobias exited from the room and Teena re-entered.

While climbing the staircase, Thobias found that he was not getting sufficient oxygen. He stood on each step and expanded his lungs to the maximum to breathe. On touching the nose, his fingers got wet and he could immediately make out that it was blood. He could taste blood inside his mouth too. Thobias hurriedly entered his room and swallowed a few pills without looking at the labels and fell on the bed closing his eyes like a cornered monkey does before the guns of the hunters, to get shot by the luckiest hunter.

The owls were hooting throughout and one of them came closer to the window where it had got no business other than frightening the half-dead Thobias. Thobias tried to get out of bed, but his body would not obey his instructions. He tried to call out, but the sound would not come out fully, as in a bad dream. The pain was lingering. The brain was still working and he made an intelligent move to make some sound by tapping on the side of the wooden cot with full force. Although his hands were weak, the pain inside him gave him sufficient strength to beat it louder and louder.

Finally, the door opened from outside and the visitor switched on the lights. He could see Teena standing there pale, like the already pale Thobias, after seeing the blood which soaked the white pillow cover and part of the bed-sheet.

"My God! What is this?" she screamed.

Thobias pointed his fingers towards the red suitcase. She ignored it and tried to lift him up to a sitting position without success as Thobias was too heavy for her and he was flopping like a fish out of water, gasping for breath.

Teena was forced to look at the red suitcase as Thobias was repeatedly pointing his fingers towards it. She opened it and the neatly typed medical report was visible at the top. Though she started reading the report slowly the pace increased immediately and ended the reading with a loud call, "My God!"

There were a few moments of silence after the exit of Teena running downstairs as if she was going to witness something terrible shortly. The owls seemed to be tired of hooting or they might have left the place. Thobias was happy that somebody other than those owls was also nearby for his send-off. He kept his hopes alive till the owls started repeating the hooting from very close to the window. But the siren of the ambulance overtook its sound after some time. Teena must have had the phone number of the hospital handy with her, in anticipation of something happening to Amma.

Two persons helped Thobias to sit on the bed and they carried him downstairs. They laid him on a stretcher and rushed him to the ambulance.

"One minute," Teena stopped the duo when they reached near the door of Amma's room. "Let Amma see him," she commanded.

"It's okay," Amma said from her bed. "If he is not well, let him go to the hospital fast. I can see him after he comes back. Tell Theresa also that he is not well," she directed her assistant.

"I have informed them already," Teena said.

"Why so fast? Is it something serious?" Amma had a doubt this time. She tried to stand up and immediately looked towards the direction where the owls were sitting and hooting. She did not stand up, but gently pressed her face on the pillow. She did not lift it till the ambulance left.

Thobias saw nothing else except the grey ambulance top. He also started enjoying the gentle jerks the vehicle was occasionally giving, as it was a welcome distraction from the severe pain.

"Oh, God. Why me?" he asked himself.

"Because you smoked," he found the answer too.

Things were fading slowly. Another set of events started appearing; little Thobias walking near Amma unable to catch her apron strings, Pappu extending toddy in a spoon to little Thobias but spilling it before it reached his mouth, the half-fallen coconut tree in the farm getting straightened, the old gooseberry tree devoid of leaves standing over the dried up paddy fields, little Thobias unable to peel off the thin layer of rubber from his soft palm, the chair at Smile Bank revolving like an electric fan and the officer Thobias gasping for breath, handsome Thobias unable to tie the knot on Theresa's neck during their wedding, Pappu coming rolling down from the hillock at Asinus land, a child waking up after an operation and trying to run back to where it had come from, Thobias trying to hold him close to his chest but unable to stretch his hands, a white Mehman smiling with his dark teeth, Velevendran trying to drink Bacardy rum that would not come out of the bottle, Kusagran trying to hold on to a red box but the box moving away to an unknown lady, the crowded train at Doncity moving backwards, a phone jumping out and dancing before his face, the ice cubes falling down at Wellmart like a black cascade, a dark doctor researching the half-broken reddish lungs, an old Thobias trying to kiss Theresa but unable to reach her face, Tejaram giving a soothing sleep, the pillow getting darker after the clotting of the blood, the owls flying away to the west . . . . Thobias understood that the history of lonely death was going to repeat itself.

"Bye, dear planet. You were good to me; you gave me air and water, days and nights. I enjoyed your colourful seasons, walked over your beautiful green mountains and danced in your windy valleys. You gave me to eat, allowed me to grow, permitted me to procreate and to leave imprints, and now you are calling me back. Errors, if any, were just mine."

Suddenly, the pain stopped. It was a great relief. Thobias could also feel the sudden weightlessness. All the feelings in him just vanished into thin air instantly.

"He is dead." It was a loud announcement from the man who placed two fingers near the nose of Thobias.

"The instruction is to take him to the hospital," the man sitting in the front near the driver said.

It was complete darkness for Thobias for some time, though the hospital corridor was fully illuminated. But, as time passed, things became slightly visible, as if he were looking through a thick glass. He could also hear the voices around him. Thobias could also feel a great pull from an unknown centre. The soul was unwilling to depart the home it had resided in for sixty long years.

"Why are you all crowding here?" the nurse at casuality was not happy with those who came in to have a look at the newly arrived dead man. She was tired after a full day's duty and of continuing into the night shift as her substitute had not arrived. The soul did not find any fault with her temperament.

"You can take him. He is dead," the young doctor in charge of casualty diagnosed very fast.

It was complete dark inside the mortuary except for the occasional rays that entered while opening the door for the new entrants or for the exit of the old ones for the funeral.

34

IT WAS THE FOURTH OPENING of the mortuary door. Four was always the luckiest number for Thobias. He was born on the fourth day of an August. It was his turn to move into a seven foot long mobile mortuary which was taken inside a big ambulance. He was surrounded by unknowns. Still, one face was familiar though he could not recollect his identity.

"Theresa and the children have already started," the familiar man told the group. In that case, we can have the funeral on Thursday."

"That means one more day for the mobile mortuary." They were discussing the expenses.

"Don't worry. You can charge it in the final bill," the familiar face was confident about proper bill settling.

While alighting from the ambulance, Thobias could see a black flag hanging on a short pole tied to the gate as a black patch in the air.

The Soul could also see a sticker pasted on the pillar of the gate as a yellowish patch with a few words written on it in red. There were only three lines.

He has gone but nobody cried.
He held our Legal Heir Insurance policy.
Contact Great Escape Insurance Company.

There was a large crowd in the courtyard, but only a few were identifiable. Some were wearing black badges on their white shirts and their faces were in a sober mood to suit the occasion. There was a banner tied to the tall jackfruit tree which showed the picture of a wedding ceremony and a single line *'Make your functions great—Express Event Managers. Phone 284484434.'* The Soul understood that the organising of his funeral had been given over to an event manager.

Amma was in a wheel chair in the porch, attended by two ladies supporing her, one on either side. She seemed to be in some difficulty, unable to raise her head to look at the body of her son. Her younger sister Celina was there at the extreme end of the long porch, watching the goings on.

Two candles were burning near the head-end and a joss stick was smoking the area. The Soul was getting a pull to go somewhere, but was still unable to go as it wished to watch its last ceremony.

"How was the end?" a neighbour asked one of the neatly dressed men wearing a black badge. It was a customary question equivalent to expressing condolences, but he could not answer anything and he simply pointed his fingers at another man who must have been his boss. The fellow did not take the pain of enquiring further as the answer was highly immaterial for him.

Thobias could see patches of different colours—red, yellow, pink, and white—in the porch, and guessed the types of flowers that would possibly decorate his lifeless body.

One man in uniform came forward, removed the glass top of the mobile mortuary and implanted a rosary into the hand of the stiff body and tried to keep the palms crossed. But the hand went back to its original position without any respect to the rosary.

There was heard a deep cry and Thobias' soul could detect the voice of his mother who was trying to control her cry from coming out but was unable to succeed. She must be unable to adjust to the reality of sending off her fourth offspring to the mercy of Satan and God so early.

The music started. It was the same old song sung at the time Thobias planted the last kiss on the stiff body of Pappu. It was so touching and beautiful that no one could improve upon it.

Everything is perishable,
This world and its bodily desires.
Everything fades and,
Ends like bubbles in water.

This time Thobias could not enjoy the lines, as his feelings had already departed.

The Soul could see a white taxi entering the courtyard. It must be somebody very much connected to him, as no car was permitted to enter the courtyard where the body was kept. Four persons got off.

"They have come," the Soul said to itself. So today must be Thursday. The Soul wondered at the pace of time. It was more or less the same when he was working in Smile Bank.

Theresa touched the mobile mortuary and stood silent for some time. The silence did not last long. It went out of control and burst into a cry spreading to Annie, Ashi and Abi within a few seconds.

The event manager was quick to act. A man in a tie came forward and took them inside the house.

"We can go ahead. Decorate first. Andrew, you go and fetch the Father," he ordered his assistant.

The body got transferred to a neatly decorated coffin. It had jasmine flowers arranged on its sides in a zig zag manner using a long string.

"Oh!" The Soul could see an old man moving towards the coffin. It was Rajan. Where was he till now? He must have been sitting behind the event managers unnoticed, without coming into the limelight. He came closer to the coffin and Thobias could see a folded cheque in his hand in a nearly crushed condition. He stood there for some time, watching the face of his childhood pal. The Soul could not guess what he was praying for. A good rebirth for Thobias Mathai? Or a possible entry on the right side of God? Rajan put the crushed cheque to the coffin unnoticed and covered it with flowers.

He too does not want it.

Things were moving in a hurry. Theresa and the kids were called for a photo session.

"She wants to be alone with him for some time," a female voice whispered to the event manager.

"How can it be? We have got one more funeral to be arranged today," the event manager knew that this was not the time for exhibiting silly emotions.

"Stand in the order of height," the photographer was concerned about the quality of his photo.

"She is touching those flowers. It can spoil the photo."

"Oh! No, no," the event manager jumped in and prevented Theresa from touching the body.

The Soul tried to have a clearer picture of his one time soul mate. It could not succeed entirely.

"You can sit near him during the ceremony," another soothed her and invited the next set of relations to be photographed. It followed an order, in tune with the extent of blood relations.

"A commotion there?" The Soul concentrated on the direction of a few protesting voices. Theresa and Abi were trying to come back again and the event manager was trying to dissuade them. Poor fellows; they did not know that their claim on Thobias had ended after his death and that the body was now owned by the soil, from where it was said to have come.

Everyone was standing now. The priest had arrived for the last rites. He did not waste time and went to the same songs which were playing there earlier through the microphone. He was going very fast, turning the pages of his small prayer book rapidly. He seemed to be bothered about the next funeral, a few kilometres away.

The Soul watched the facial expressions of the event manager and his frequent glancing at his watch to ensure that things were moving as per schedule. The ceremony was interrupted twice due to shrill cries from the porch. But it was complete silence when Father started his funeral speech.

"Thobias Mathai came up in life amid abject poverty, studied well and got a good job. He brought up the other members and made them fly away to better horizons. He was a good son to his parents, a good brother to his siblings, a good husband to Theresa, a good father to his children, a sincere worker at his work place and a good citizen of society. He was a man who performed his roles well. Now the roles are over and God has called him to His side. It is a solitary journey and let the soul rest in peace. All live to fulfil the role assigned to them by God and one has to go when the role is over." The Soul discovered the reason for his lung cancer.

"Now you can give the farewell kiss," the parish boy announced.

It was Theresa to kiss first. She planted a warm kiss on the right side of the cheek. It was warm for the body but must be chilling for the kisser. Abi did not press the lips much and the same pattern was followed by Annie and Ashi. Amma kissed on the forehead sitting from the wheel chair and her lips remained there for some time.

"We can lift the body. Where is Andrews?" the event manager searched for his assistant.

"He will come just now," another staff member answered. The function stopped for him for a few minutes. Andrews came back and stood near the head of the body. The Soul could recognise the familiar smell of alcohol from him instantly and understood where Andrews had gone in the middle of the function.

"Good bye to the home,
Which gave me shelter,
And sent off, in this short life . . ."

The song went on, unmindful of the fact that it was not his home.

The procession ended at Parakad church. The coffin was kept on a table covered by a black cloth. Theresa got one more chance to kiss her life partner.

The Soul could hear rain drops splashing on the asbestos roof of the church. The sudden summer rain took away the heat and dust. It took away the electricity too. The prayers became inaudible, and the accompanying song stopped. A few from the crowd standing outside entered the church and a few escaped to the nearby shops. All prayed to God fervently for the rain to end.

The journey to the tomb took place immediately after the intensity of the rain came down. Only a few accompanied the body, to avoid getting drenched in the rain. Moreover, it was no fun to walk through the muddy water inside the cemetery for one more glimpse of the coffin top.

Abi covered the face of the body with a white cloth. The Soul could not watch his facial expressions, as it was preoccupied with the general view of the last scene above the soil. Soon, the lid came over the coffin and it got lowered to the tomb over the bones of Pappu and Chinnu, with the last prayer,

Dust indeed you are,
And it is to dust
You shall return.

The Soul could feel the falling of a few drops of frankincense on the lid of the coffin as a parting gift, followed by shovels of sand one after another, sufficient to cover half the tomb. The Soul could also hear the sound of the dragging of the concrete slabs to cover the tomb.

For the world, Thobias Mathai S/o Pappu was gone forever. But the Soul was still there, adjusting to the complete darkness inside the tomb, without knowing the surprise that was in store.

35

THINGS WERE CHANGING inside the tomb on unexpected lines. The initial darkness was replaced by twilight and nearby things became clearer. The Soul exited from the coffin and the entire tomb became its command area. It could see the bones of Pappu as a small heap in the middle. Surely they belonged to Pappu because the biggest one was broken and part of the steel rod was visible outside.

The Soul spent its time watching the body it had resided in for sixty years and the changes that were happening to it minute by minute. It could also hear some sounds, which were becoming clearer and clearer.

"The soul is about to go," Thobias heard a whisper from near the body.

"This seems to be a contented soul. Maybe he had a good life on earth," the same voice continued. "I think I know this person."

"But how?" It was a different voice, which was softer. There was an element of wonder and admiration in those words.

"Don't you know the history of this tomb?" The Soul concentrated its entire energy towards the source of the voice, as it found the topic very interesting. In the twilight, the soul could see two worms. They were quite big in size and the larger one was about a foot long, with a flat head and two big, bright eyes. There were two big sensors at the top of the head like antennae, with a bulge at the end of each. The mouth was almost round, located just below two prominent spots which must be its nostrils. The body was black, with bands of white rings at intervals of half an inch. Thobias had never seen such a worm in his lifetime, though he had spent a lot of years working in the farm with Pappu, ploughing and digging.

"How do you know the story of this tomb?" the smaller one, having a soft voice, asked.

"It was my grandfather who told me about it when I was young. He told me about a soul who came here along with a bunch of bones and lived here for seven long years. It was unable to go from here because it was not detached from the earthly feelings it was carrying. It was in anger most of the time, sometimes too sad, sometimes revengeful, sometimes trying to express love and at times longing for love. Grandpa detected a lot of emotions in it, some of which only humans can understand. It could not go from here till the emotions ended and it was always wandering here and there murmuring and whispering. Grandpa learned a lot of things about human life from that soul."

"It was in love with the world, it was in love with its wife, it was in love with its children and it was even in love with all those who made its life difficult on earth. It was so immersed in fetching food that it did not get time to show its love. It departed from the earth before expressing those emotions."

"This must be his son."

"They too live in families like us. The father works and fetches food as I do," the leader started lessons for his better half. "But human life is different from ours. They are always progressing in life and the rate of progress is measured in terms of the bills one has to pay at intervals called months. It is not an easy task. One has to labour well for that and the intensity of work can drive one mad. This fellow lying before us was running around to pay his bills. He did not get time to love back, and never took time to understand the inner urge of a loving father. It made his father a rebel and in that process, he got alienated from the dear ones further and further."

"This fellow, whom the father loved most, did not do his role."

"Don't say that this fellow is bad. See the cross in his hand. He must be a God-fearing pious man," the wife gave the benefit of doubt.

"It is put by others only. In their world, it is others who thrust sainthood. Nobody claims it because they know that they are not saints." The leader was a real scholar on human life.

"I heard that humans are a saintly lot. You are bluffing."

There was no discussion between the worms for quite some time. The Soul was getting a pull towards an unknown destination and he understood that his time was coming for departure to the next world. The worms were whispering about their family matters and about their erring son who was yet to join them for the grand dinner on the body of Thobias Mathai. There was an air of festivity among them.

"This soul is about to depart," the leader could foretell. "Unlike its father, it has admitted life as it was and was capable of losing things gracefully."

"The father must have cursed him?" The wife believed in curses.

"May not be. Those who love never curse. They suffer and still continue to love them. One cannot say that this fellow was bad. In human life, the pressures of the job and the roles to be performed are so high that it can convert even saints to villains."

"I have not seen a live human yet." She was not happy with the role of her husband.

"I will take you to the top soil some time," he assured her. "But it is a risky place. We can get killed anytime; we can get ploughed in with their big machines, or can be spotted by big flying animals. Nobody, who has gone to the top soil, has ever returned." Her desire to go up ended immediately and the husband solved a big complaint in seconds.

"In their world, all are chasing a thing called money."

"What is that?"

"It is a piece of paper, a small one, with a lot of pictures on it. If you get more of them you can make a big house, buy big cars, purchase love from beautiful girls, make grand holidays and achieve what they call the enjoyment of life. Others have to spend their whoe lives chasing it. The people with money rule over others, to make more money."

"Who makes that paper?"

"The ruler. Others are not allowed to print it. It takes a lot of time to reach those people who do not have it."

"Where did the soul of the father go?"

"No idea. Even human beings do not know it. Some say it will go to heaven or hell. Some say it will take rebirth and come back. Some say that only human beings have a soul while some others say that all have a soul. When humans are unable to find a sure answer to this vital question, you can imagine our plight."

"They take birth like us, eat like us, grow like us, procreate like us and die like us. Still, they consider themselves superior to all. In fact, we are superior to them:

We are magnanimous to admit that all have got a soul,
We do not tell lies,
We are not confused like them,
We never feed on our own people,
We never say something and do just the opposite,"
he was to continue with the list, but got interrupted.

"They eat their own people?" his wife expressed a doubt.

"Not exactly; they live on the weakness of others."

"It is essential to get a human life to reach heaven," he continued. "But living a human life is not that easy. They have systems to teach us about God, to teach cooking, to teach others to make machines, to teach them to fly planes and cure diseases. But there is no one to teach them how to live."

"They cannot live without meaning. To find meaning, they make a hypothesis. Some believe in that hypothesis and develop habits, behaviours and beliefs based on it. They dedicate their lives to believing in that hypothesis and making others believe in it. Some hypotheses die down along with those who believed in them, but some outlive them as they are unable to be disproved."

"These are all big subjects for us worms," the wife showed her disinterest. "We have to make our son live better. He is now on the wrong path; he never tries to make burrows and search for food. He is flirting with the neighbour's daughter and his friends are so bad. How can we depend on him in our old age?"

"You call him now. I will advise."

"Talk to him but don't quarrel. He is still young and he can rebel easily," she cautioned.

The mother made a sound like '*mew*' but there was no response for it. She absented herself from the scene for a few minutes and when she reappeared, there was another worm with her. It was equal to her size, but its body was shining more. The sensors were stretched full length, as if it doubted something.

"Where were you until now?" the father geared himself into authority mode for which Mew did not reply.

"We were discussing an interesting topic; about human life. I thought you too should hear it," the leader came down from the authority mode.

"You know about human life?"

"No," Mew replied.

"The top soil is full of humans. They live in big houses, not in burrows like us. They need not creep like us; they move in big machines. They can fly in the air. They can see the full universe. They cure their diseases."

"It is a garden, washed off its dirt by the rains, covered by the spotless blue sky. You can see sunrays peeping all around with the morning freshness, evaporating the suffocating dews from the foliage and finally exiting, making long shadows that merge to form the night. Seasons take away your monotony and the gentle breeze kisses you in your loneliness. You can play in the grass, skate on the ice, walk in the rain and swim in the lagoons."

Mew was silent.

"You do not believe in it?" Father did not like the non-response. "Come with me to the top soil, I will show you big houses. I can show you moving machines in which humans travel."

"It is true, Mew. Your father never tells lies," the better half lied.

"Okay. It may be there," Mew came around, though half heartedly.

"Many of us do not know that we can become humans if we want," he was determined to make Mew show interest in the deliberations. Mew turned his head and looked at his father in disbelief. Father did not explain further about it and returned to the main topic.

"Life is great from the moment you take birth as a human kid. You get toys to play with. They put you in a cradle and later give you a walker, then to kindergarten to sing songs and to pools to learn swimming, then to . . . ." he was interrupted by Mew.

"Who will do all these things for me?" Mew still doubted things.

"That is not a big deal there. There are a lot of people dealing with what I called earlier, money. They will take care of all your needs. They finance everything starting from your diaper, feeding bottles, walkers, toys, milk powder, school fee, tuition fee, ink bottle, pencil box, eraser, notebook, school guide, and what not?" Mew never had an exposure to the vast knowledge his father was having.

"To know about human life, you should become a human," father continued.

"To become a human? Can I become a human?" Mew was not sure yet about the mysteries after death.

"Sure."

"In the human world there are lots more," father continued. "They have got,
Seedless fruit for people without teeth,
Sugar-free sugar for the obese,
Tobacco-free cigarettes for non-smokers,
Bone-free chicken for gluttons,
God-free religion for atheists,
Blood-free wars for politicians,
Pain-free delivery for mothers,
Love-free sex for non-lovers,
Tax-free bribes for the people in power, and . . . ."
the leader stopped and smiled for a moment.

"What a great life these humans are living?" Mew started moving its antenna, as if it had detected a great secret of life.

"You will wonder at the list of people waiting to serve you there. Serving the people is the biggest and noblest profession in their world. There are people who dedicate their entire lives to serve others without expecting anything in return. They form herds called political parties to protect the society and to serve you better. At times, these herds become very powerful and annihilate others, again to protect society and to serve you better. You will be safe, always wooed by one or the other herd, till you can go to the polling booth or till you apply your brain.

"There will be people to educate you about the right and the wrong. They teach you the best practice code to reach heaven, absolutely free. They are capable of emptying your sin box, so that you can fill it again. They too live for you and devote their entire life for your welfare."

"I want to become a human," Mew was getting impatient. The father understood that it was time to talk about the risk factors.

"The road ahead will be tiring, if you aim at a good rebirth," the leader gave the first warning.

"No problem," Mew was ready to face anything for a human life.

"Okay, I will tell you the way," his father looked at his better half and smiled. "Always do good things only."

"Yeah, that is the only way," the wife supported her husband.

"Good worms work hard and make big burrows. It will be so big that it can accommodate all of us," the father gave an idea about good deeds.

"Good worms share their food with everybody," the mother was concerned about food.

"Good worms never go to the top soil and try to see the world outside," the father was concerned about his security.

"Good worms never talk to their neighbour's daughter till they marry her." Her husband's morality came to her mind.

"Good worms never ask '*why*'. They always obey," the father was concerned about future protocol.

"Good worms love without expectations," he was sure that he won't be able to give anything back. "You go through the great teachings of our God," the father has no more points worth elucidating.

"I can try that," Mew was ready to try another life.

"Are you sure?"

"Very sure."

"But it has its drawbacks too. "Humans are a confused lot. There are people who even live on making confusion. They are always confused,

Whether the government is good or the opposition is good?

Whether the thief is good or the police are good?

Whether corruption is good or honesty is good?

Whether war is good or peace is good?

Whether death is better or living is better?

Whether capitalism is good or communism is good?

Whether management is good or the labour union is good?

Whether the egg came first or the hen came first?"

"These are minor factors," she kept the spirit up. "When there is somebody to take care of all the needs for free, why should we worry about it?"

"For free? Who said?" the father retorted.

"You spoke about toys, walkers and school fees, all free, from people who deal with money," Mew remembered all the points.

"Not free exactly. Your employer will pay it back," the father stopped, wishing that Mew wouldnot pose any more questions.

"Why will they do all this for me?" Mew enquired.

"Companies want you. That is why they do all this."

"What should I give in return to them?" Mew was a fast learner and he was aware that nothing happens without a purpose.

"You need not give anything."

"Absolutely free?" Mew could not hide his surprise.

"You need not give; they take. They take your thinking, they take your time, they define your living, they define your behaviour, and to put in short, . . ." father paused for a moment as if he were thinking deeply.

"They take your life," he concluded hesitantly.

"Life?" Mew did not like the price of living.

"Otherwise too, what is its use?" the wife intervened.

The Soul understood that confusion was universal.

It did not get time to listen further. The pull from an unknown centre was too much and it departed. The Soul looked back and watched the would-be human again and again. A smile came to it at the thought of Mew taking birth as a human being.

The Soul developed its feelings and started laughing. It laughed all the way.

Those who depart laughing are the luckiest.